Spiralling out of the shadow

MICHELLE DENNIS EVANS

A catalogue record for this
book is available from the
National Library of Australia

For every girl who is a friend to someone...

Your unconditional love and grace
mean everything.

Spiralling out of the shadow

MICHELLE DENNIS EVANS

Contents

Chapter One

I MISSED HER LIKE I'D MISS my arms if they were removed. I tried to study at the library, in the park, in front of the TV—anywhere but in my room. My room was where Stephanie and I always studied.

We'd get to hang out again soon. Mum said I could go visit for the holidays. If I could just get this stupid assignment to make sense. I pushed my tongue to the roof of my mouth, hoping to block the tears from forming.

My best friend had only moved twelve hours north—it wasn't like she'd died. *What's wrong with me?*

By the time the sun dipped behind the mountains, nothing I'd written was good enough. I shuffled around the house looking for inspiration but gave up and returned to the desk in my room. An hour passed and I'd done zilch, zero. The landline interrupted my useless train of thought.

'Tabbie, Stephanie's on the phone,' Mum called.

I raced downstairs and grabbed our ancient corded phone.

'Hey, I really miss you.' I blinked to keep my eyes dry.

'Yeah? This town is a hole,' said Stephanie, the most beautiful, sophisticated and elegant fourteen-year-old I knew. *My best friend.*

'There's this English assignment I've got to do...' My voice trailed off and Stephanie's took over.

'It's worse than you could ever imagine.' Her voice was wobbly.

'Why? What happened?' I twirled the phone cord between my fingers.

'The boys whistle at me, and the girls don't talk to me.' She sniffled, then blasted my ear as she blew her nose.

'Oh, Steph ...'

Miss Popular was telling me she was miserable and would never fit in. Apparently co-ed schools were different. Well ... *derr!* Had she really thought it would be the same? Boys = Hormones. Boys + Girls = Distraction and ... well everything else that goes with boys and girls mingling their time.

'The worst is in the mornings. When I walk through the gates, the boys' hoo-haaring irritates me.'

'Why don't you just smile and say hello politely? That should shut them up.'

'I'll try tomorrow.'

'Dance rehearsals are—'

'Tabbie, I've got to go.'

The hang-up clunk echoed in my ear as a stream of tears flowed. I trudged upstairs into the bathroom to splash my face with cool water. Then I slipped on my running shoes and headed to Mum's treadmill.

The smooth whirr of the machine's belt filled the silence between my steps. A fresh set of tears threatened, but I shunted them away as I turned on Mum's iPod. Her favourite eighties playlist dried up the tears and freed a smile. After half an hour I jogged straight back to my desk and wrote.

    Spiralling Out of the Shadow

She's gone
It's sad
But great
At times
I miss her
But also
I've found delight

She's gone
It's hard
Alone, so lonely
She's sad
Me too

She's depressed
I'm not
But I'm missing her
Missing much
Here and now
Today

It wasn't exactly a response poem for the short story I'd read, but now I'd written one poem, I began to think in verse. I imagined Stephanie right beside me. I could smell her fruity shampoo and hear her bite down on a piece of chocolate. I wrote and rewrote until I had a poem worthy of at least a B.

I cried myself to sleep and awoke with wet cheeks. It was obvious. I was a mess. My ridiculously beautiful and perfect best friend had moved interstate. *Gone.*

Where would I be ranked now without Miss Fabulous Dancer Stephanie by my side? I rolled back and forth across the mattress in a sheet-tangled insomnia that went on and on.

Ouch! What's that?

I pulled the doona off my head. What had I'd crashed into? *My floor.* Stupid.

I stretched, checking for bruising from my klutzy fall. *Nothing.* Not even a red mark to laugh about at school. Tension pulled from my shoulders to my toes. I threw the sheets back on my bed and changed into my bike pants and trainers, ready to escape my room.

The house was quiet, so I tiptoed downstairs and closed the door without making a noise. Our usually quiet street whispered an eerie silence before the sun came up.

I ran without a plan, pounding my feet in autopilot. I'd be fine. It was only a couple of weeks until I'd be visiting Stephanie's new home. I stopped at a wall of trees, blocks from home. Heading back, fatigue stripped my muscles. One foot in front of the other. Keep the pace. Breathe. Anything to take my mind off her and the way she'd left me.

I still had Jaya and Suzie to hang with at school, but life would be different. The four of us had hung out since the first day of year seven, but Stephanie had been by my side long before then.

The house was quiet as I returned home for breakfast. I swirled my spoon around my cereal, unable to shut off my mind. Stephanie had been there when Fluffball, my cat, died. She was there when we surveyed the neighbours, imposing an investigation on Santa and the Tooth Fairy. I swiped at the trickle of tears and shoved another spoonful into my mouth.

'Are you okay?' Mum asked as she breezed past me in her dressing gown with a basket of laundry.

'I miss Steph.'

'You'll be fine, love.'

'Your mum's right.' Dad kissed me on the cheek and tucked a ringlet of untidy hair behind my ear. He pulled on his pinstriped suit jacket, jingled his keys. 'Chin up. Not long now until you'll see her.'

　　　　Spiralling Out of the Shadow

Chapter Two

How COULD ONE PERSON LEAVE such a hole? Suzie, Jaya, and I met at our usual table under the tree overlooking the oval for morning tea. Now there were three instead of four.

'I can't seem to get the steps right now.' Suzie seemed to shrink into her own skin with each word. 'I've always followed Stephanie.'

'We're meant to be blocking soon.' Jaya pulled a file from her pocket and began shaping her nails. 'Everyone else might get a chance to dance lead now, hey?'

That'd be right. Jaya was probably happy about Stephanie leaving. 'I guess so.' I swallowed the thickness in my throat.

Stephanie had been our lead dancer. She was the star of every show. Everything revolved around dance. If I had a choice, I'd rather hang out with my friends. Most of the time, I preferred to go for a run. Dancing was just something I'd followed my friends into.

After school finished for the day, I trekked across the school grounds to dance class. It had only been a couple of weeks, and Stephanie's shadow still drew me along the same path. But now I was alone. I warmed up as I waited for our teacher to arrive. Suzie and Jaya's voices preceded them, distracting me.

'I don't know why I'm here,' Jaya whined like a cat. 'I don't want to compete in front of other schools.'

'But you're such a great dancer.' I stood up and moved towards them.

'It's all changed this year. I preferred when it was just us girls,' Suzie said, glancing around the room through her lashes.

'But you know what Miss Skinner said. She wants to add partnered routines. Just think—some really hot guys might join us.' I hoped, anyway.

'Anything would be an improvement on the boys we've got now,' Jaya said in a low voice, looking towards Joey as he walked through the doorway.

I had to agree—the two boys who'd come into our after-school dance program weren't the blokiest of boys. Jaya ignored them, and Suzie blushed whenever they danced near her, especially Joey.

Miss Skinner breezed through the door. 'Right, everyone. If you could all move outside, I want to see you one by one. Treat this like an audition.'

An audition without Stephanie seemed wrong. She lived to compete. I sat on the brick wall, listening to magpies warble in the gum tree as I waited. One by one, our teacher called us in. My imagination ran off on a tangent. *What would it be like to dance lead?* It would be pretty cool to dance in the spotlight for a change. Even though I knew I wasn't the best, something inside urged me to prove them wrong.

After my name was called, I stood in front of Miss Skinner and her assistant, Miss Ray. Standing alone, I checked my centre and took a deep breath to calm my shuddering heart as I waited for the music. When the beat bounced off the walls I burst forward with a split leap, then steadied myself before spinning into a pirouette. It was an old routine, one Stephanie and I had danced over and over, one I could do without thinking. Choreographing something new hadn't crossed my mind.

Miss Skinner stopped the music after a few minutes. I heaved for breath as I skipped towards the door. Miss Ray called Jaya next. She stormed in, glaring straight ahead as we passed. If she didn't want to be here, why was she?

After everyone had auditioned, Miss Ray waved her hand at the entrance to grab our attention.

'You can all come back inside,' she said in a lyrical tone.

Miss Skinner stood in front of the mirrored wall. Every cell of her body spoke to the world, 'I'm a dancer.' My shape was all wrong to ever have that effect.

'We won't keep you in suspense any longer. Today was about finding the lead dancer for the upcoming competition.'

I rocked from my heels to toes willing her to spill the details.

'Congratulations … Tabbie.'

Oh my goodness! That was *my* name. *Me.* I couldn't believe I got it. Did I even want it? *Oh my goodness!*

I turned to my friends, wanting to share my excitement. Suzie's face mirrored the wooden floor planks. She flung her school bag over her shoulder and stormed out.

Jaya mouthed, 'Who cares,' as she flicked her hand.

Sometimes her attitude was too much. Perhaps they were both hoping to be picked. Maybe one of them should have been picked. They were better dancers than me. My heart raced as I hurried towards home with extra bounce. I had to speak to Stephanie and tell her. I pushed the front door open and went to pick up the phone, but it rang before I reached it. It was Stephanie.

'I have to tell you—'

'Are you packed?' she cut me off.

'Nearly.' Maybe I could wait and surprise her when I got there. 'I can't believe it's only a few days away!'

'I know. I've got to warn you, this place is abysmal.'

'I can't wait to see you.'

My thoughts flicked back to Suzie and Jaya and their plans to go to The Royal Easter Show. It would be the first I'd ever missed. Steph and I always went, but this year I was giving it up to visit her.

'Yeah,' Steph said in a whisper. 'You coming will be the only good thing that's happened since I left Sydney.'

'What if you could come and stay here and finish school at Hill Top Private?' I'd suggested it before I realised what was coming out of my mouth.

'Tabbie, you're a genius.' Her voice was high-pitched. 'See you soon.' She was gasping, like she was jumping up and down.

It was time to pull on my excited face. Stephanie sounded homesick and depressed. I was about to embark on a new mission of 'Cheer up Stephanie'.

Chapter Three

I BOARDED MY FLIGHT TO QUEENSLAND, checking the rows as I shuffled down the aisle, and *oh my goodness!* The hottest guy was sitting in the seat next to mine. I breathed in his citrusy scent and a shiver ran through my body. Not that I was interested. I didn't want a boy distracting me from school. Right now, all I wanted was to have fun with my friends.

I glanced at him again as he turned the page of his *Business Review Weekly* magazine. He smiled, pushing together his crow's feet. Hmm, at least ten years older than me. This man was the ultimate in gorgeousness.

My tongue died in my mouth. I couldn't think of a thing to say. He clipped his seatbelt nudging me with his bulging bicep. I sat in silence letting my imagination run rampant, turning him into the perfect man. A gentleman who always opened the door. A man who was strong enough to fight off a lion, yet soft and sincere inside. A man who was polite and caring. A man who could focus and chase his dreams.

Touchdown. Bounce, bump, bounce.

Our less-than-smooth landing brought me smash-bang back as to why I was on the plane and why I was landing in Brisbane. This week was all about best-friend-visiting-duties. I thought about the last conversation I'd had with Stephanie. In hindsight, I'd been swept away in the moment. My suggestion for her to come live with us was probably one of the craziest, most hare-brained ideas I'd ever had. I mentioned the idea to Mum before I flew out and she seemed as thrilled as Stephanie. 'Well, of course she could stay with us,' she'd said. 'We can offer her Peter's room now he's planning to go to Melbourne.'

My brother's room had been pretty much empty since he met Phoebe, his new squeeze.

I exited the plane and left Mr Biceps behind, expecting to see Stephanie waiting for me. I'd imagined we'd scream, 'Hello!' then wave our arms and do a couple of leg kicks, something Stephanie liked to do in public to let everyone know we were dancers. *But no.* No one was waiting. I followed the signs to the baggage carousel, drifting along with the other travellers. *Alone.*

Where are they? I hit Diane's number and wedged the phone between my shoulder and ear. I looked up when he came near. The phone slipped off my shoulder and I only just caught it before it crashed to the floor. Standing beside me was the perfect Mr Biceps.

'Tabbie, are you in?' Stephanie's voice snapped me back to reality.

'Yes! The plane just landed. I'm so excited. Are you here?'

'We're caught in traffic. I'll ring again when we're closer.'

'Who else is with you?'

'Just Mum. April's at a friend's house and Dad's working.'

I threw the phone back into my handbag and swung around to watch Mr Biceps walk away. Content that I'd now burnt his image into my memory, I dragged my bag off the conveyor belt, then bumped my way through the crowd and out into the sunshine.

My mobile buzzed. 'Hi Tabbie. We're just driving in.'

'I'm outside.' I waved to a sea of cars lined up, searching for their bomb of a family car. 'I can see you.'

They pulled up in front of me. Stephanie jumped out and opened the back door of the car and we embraced. Her body trembled against my arms but when she pulled away her face gave no clues. Diane opened the boot, dumped my bag, and said a quick hello before she jumped back into the driver's seat. She was like that.

'What have we got planned?' I slid into the back seat and Stephanie followed.

'Nothing really. Maybe a day of exploring tomorrow.' She leaned back against the seat and swiped away a tear.

'Steph ...'

'Stop.' She held a hand up to my face. 'I'm fine,' she whispered, flashing warning eyes towards her mother. Steph and her mother weren't close.

I stared through the window, mourning the schedule of socialising on the agenda back home. I had to let it go and cheer up Stephanie. 'So I've been dancing, but it—' She cut me off before I could finish saying, *it isn't the same without you.*

'Suzie and Jaya still irritating?'

'You've never called them irritating before.'

'Well, they are.' Stephanie pulled at her fingernails.

I bit the inside of my mouth and turned away. She used to only be like this when she was super stressed about something. Maybe it was more than just the move and the kids at her new school.

'Is it better having your dad around more?'

'We don't see him any more than when we lived in Sydney and he travelled up here a couple of days each week.'

'Oh, bummer.' Maybe that was adding to her problems.

Stephanie shrugged.

'Co-ed is more different than you thought it would be?'

'Yeah.'

I expected her to go on but she looked out the window.

'What's Peter up to?' Stephanie asked.

'I haven't seen him since you left. He spends all his time with his girlfriend or working at the servo. Mum and Dad are happy now he's planning to go to university next year, even though he wants to go to Melbourne.'

'What about his girlfriend?'

'Phoebe? Yeah, I don't know. His course doesn't start until next year. They mightn't even be together then.'

Silence echoed off the internal car walls, doing my head in until my mobile chirped. I seized the moment to entertain myself texting back and forth to Jaya. Stephanie forced a sigh. I put my phone away. Conversation had never been stilted between us like this. We always talked without stopping, like we survived on each other's breath. I broke the silence and whispered, 'Have you talked to your parents about the possibility of moving back to Sydney?'

'Kind of ... No, not really. Just ... I'll tell you about it when we get home.'

The road wound its way up the Great Dividing Range to Toowoomba. We got caught behind a slow, fumy truck. Their old Ford gurgled and surged forward, only just picking up enough speed to pass the truck by the time we drove out into openness again at the top of the range. We kept going another fifteen minutes to pick up Stephanie's little sister. The snaking road mixed with inconsistent speed meant my stomach was churning by the time we arrived at their house.

Steph led me to her room where I collapsed onto her bed and hoped the motion sickness would settle.

'Keep out!' she told her little sister, then closed the door with a slap.

'Has there been any change at school?' I asked.

'What do you mean?' Stephanie sat beside me.

'Have you ignored their comments and smiled at the guys harassing you?'

'I tried. But no, they're still the same.'

'Give it time. Now tell me, why aren't you dancing?' I rolled over onto my elbow, thankful my stomach had stopped churning.

'Tabbie!'

'Come on, Steph. You love dancing and you're so good at it.'

'I guess I was angry with Mum and Dad and everything, so I told them I didn't want to dance. Like, ever again. Now I've said it, I guess it's true.'

'Just because you said it to your parents doesn't mean you can't ever dance again. Let me show you part of the new routine we've just started.' I was willing to try anything to get her out of her mood. I found the song on my iPod, plugged it into Steph's dock and started to dance. 'Make you want to join in?'

'No.'

'Just a little?' I pulled a cute and cheesy smile to lighten her mood.

'No. I've made my decision.'

'There's more to it than the fact you told your parents you didn't want to, hey?'

'The girls who dance here hate me.'

'All of them?' *Oh dear. Tears.* I found a box of tissues and passed her some. 'They just don't know you yet.'

'They don't want to know me, Tabbie. They hate me. They're mean. They're rude. And they're different to us.'

I was lost for words. Now was definitely not a good time to tell her I was dancing lead. *Should I console her? Should I encourage her to be stronger? What am I meant to do to help her?*

'Dinner's ready,' April said through the door.

I sat back and observed the Stronges. Their amusing antics made them interesting to watch. Sweet April wanted to be a superstar. Mr Stronge worked long hours and didn't seem to care too much about home life. Mrs Stronge and Mum had been friends when we were in primary school, but for some reason they stopped shopping and going out for coffee together. I never understood why. I did ask Mum once, but she brushed off the question with a comment about Diane not caring about anything deeper than shopping.

After dinner, we retreated to Stephanie's room. I needed to lift her out of her tank of misery.

'I need to get back to Sydney.' Stephanie smoothed out the creases on her doona.

'So let's work it out. How can we get you there?' I had to admit, life would be better with Stephanie around again.

'Mum and Dad are anti boarding school.' Stephanie shrugged. 'I don't think Dad has good memories of going himself. Plus I don't think their budget would extend that far.'

'What if you come and live with us?' *I won't regret this, will I?*

'Have you said anything to your parents?'

'I asked if you could come for the next holidays and maybe stay for a while next year.'

'What did they say?'

'They said that it should be fine. And if Peter does move to Melbourne next year, we'd have a spare room.'

'Really?'

I nodded. *Like, would I be telling you all of this if it wasn't the case?*

'I just have to talk Mum and Dad round.'

'Imagine that! Living together. It'd be so much fun.' Life could return to how it was before she left.

Stephanie dragged me around the streets of Toowoomba. Boring, outdated clothes lined the shop windows. I'd had enough. 'The shopping here is abysmal!'

'I did warn you. Help me get away from here.' Steph clung to my arm, scuffing her shoes on the concrete path, making a scene. Always the centre of attention.

We walked to a huge, leafy park a block away.

'This park is gorgeous.'

I ran from Stephanie into the lush green lawn that seemed to flow forever. I was in love. With the park, that is. I wanted to run over the rolling grassy plain and dance through the tulips—well, if there were tulips. Guess it was the wrong time of year. Stephanie didn't seem to be in a running mood. She dawdled behind me.

'I guess it's nice.' Stephanie looked from left to right. 'First time I've been here.'

'Let's sit in the shade under that giant tree.' I led the way. 'You should come here whenever you get sick of living in this town. It's just delicious!'

'Yeah?'

'Doesn't it lift your spirit? Being here in such beautiful gardens under these giant trees?'

'I suppose it does.'

Had Stephanie taken time to open her eyes to anything nice that surrounded her since she'd moved?

'Yeah.' She gazed from one end of the park to the other. 'It is pretty.'

We sat on the grass and chatted for hours. The silences had stopped and I was sure our friendship had survived the move. The shade slid forward with the arc of the sun. Diane returned to pick us up as I was getting drowsy from the warm rays.

For the rest of the week, ferocious winds and downpours hid the sun and kept us indoors playing cards, watching movies, and laughing until our sides split. I had accomplished my mission. My best friend looked much happier than when I'd arrived. My job here was complete. It was time to go back to the real world and get out of this country city. 'You know I'm going to miss you hugely.' I wrapped my arms around her, not wanting to let go. 'Now, will you please keep smiling? The world can be a happy place here, just like it was in Sydney.'

'Thanks, Tabbie. You're the best.'

'I know. Send money, cards, flowers.' Okay, so I was trying to be funny. Stephanie didn't laugh, but at least she didn't look like she was about to burst into tears. I hadn't mentioned dancing again or told her how much I actually loved taking a walk in the spotlight.

I boarded the plane, homeward bound, ready to find my minute of fame.

Chapter Four

'SERIOUSLY, MUM, WHAT PARENT in their right mind would want to throw their daughter a princess party for their fifteenth birthday? You just don't want me to grow up. You have to face it sometime. I'm taller than you, which means I'm no longer your little girl.'

'I know, honey. But you're still so sweet. I thought having a few girls over for a tea party would be fun,' she said, and then laughed.

'You're joking, aren't you?'

Mum was now doubled over, cracking herself up.

'Maybe a high tea, but not a princess tea party.' I bit my lip.

'Gotcha!' She pointed a finger at me.

'High tea?' I snubbed her joke, swallowing a giggle. I was so glad she wasn't serious.

'Devonshire Tea?' she asked with her head slightly tilted towards her shoulder.

'Mu-um.' A gravelly voice vibrated through my throat.

'Leave it with me. Shame your birthday falls on a dance rehearsal day.'

'I could skip dance.'

'But love, your friends are there. Perhaps we could celebrate on Friday afternoon.'

'Okay. Friday sounds good. And Mum, an everyday afternoon tea will be fine.'

When Mum wasn't watching, I checked the pantry to make sure she hadn't bought any princess cupcake papers to use.

My birthday arrived. *Fifteen*. I woke up expecting the world to be different. It wasn't. It was still the same. My ridiculously beautiful and almost perfect best friend still lived half a continent away. There would be school classes and dance rehearsals as usual. My day looked ho-hum.

I couldn't concentrate. Everyone should be given a personal holiday on their birthday. Staying focused in class was virtually impossible. I wondered what Steph was doing. At least when I had her in class with me on birthdays, we'd write notes to each other and sing the *Happy Birthday* song all day.

A little tingle ran through my body when the final afternoon bell clanged. Maybe dancing on my birthday would be fun. Jaya and Suzie weren't at their lockers, so I traipsed across the school grounds by myself to practice for our upcoming eisteddfod. Why was I pursuing something I only enjoyed fifty percent of the time? Dancers didn't even get paid well. I'd heard some of the girls whispering about the extra dollars available for dancing virtually naked. There was no way, absolutely no way, that would ever happen. I mean *never. Never. Ever.* I'm completely modest. Give me the change room with a door every time. None of that 'we're all girls' garbage. I like my privacy.

I knew I had nothing on Stephanie when it came to dancing, yet I had the lead. If she could move back here, she would surely be back to her usual self, and I might even start enjoying dancing again.

Nah—probably not.

If she did move back, I'd have to step back into her shadow. Which would be fine. Dreamily reminiscing of past years of dancing with Stephanie, I walked through the door of the dance studio to ...

'Surprise!'

Balloons.

Streamers.

Party poppers.

The whole dance class and some other girls were there, celebrating me.

Squee!

Extravagantly decorated tables with tiered platters peeked through the crowd. *Bliss.*

'Thank you, thank you, thank you!' I cheered after they sang the ever-popular birthday song.

'There, honey, you have your high tea.' Mum pushed through the crowd and squeezed me. 'Now, shall I go and bring out the princess cupcakes?'

'You're so funny, Mum.' I laughed. I did love the way she attempted to have fun with us. 'I can't believe you kept this from me!'

Mum waved a finger at me. 'I baked your favourite caramel mud cake. And I couldn't help myself—I baked a double batch and put the second in cupcake papers.'

I moved through the crowd to suss out if there were any more surprises. She'd outdone herself. Mum had brought in great-grandmother Annie's sweet hand-painted floral tea set, which she usually kept on the top shelf of the display cabinet, a gold-embossed set, and my all-time favourite, the set with delicate bluebirds. Petite caramel cupcakes decorated the tiered centrepieces. Sandwiches filled with smoked salmon and cucumber cut into small squares covered silver platters. Mum had planned well. My heart overflowed with gratitude.

I nearly let my head run away with an 'I'm so popular' moment, until I remembered Stephanie. How I wished she was here to join in. But if she was, I'd be in her shadow. Even on my birthday, she would have been the centre of attention. My phone vibrated, pulling me from my thoughts.

'Happy birthday.' Stephanie's on-the-verge-of-tears voice echoed through the phone.

'Thanks. It's the first one since we met that we haven't spent together.'

Oops. Wrong thing to say. Now she wasn't talking. Sniffles crackled through the line. 'But, I'm sure things will start getting better for you at school soon.'

'Urgh.' Stephanie snorted.

'Would you like to come here next holidays?' I asked, hoping to cheer her up.

'Yes.' Sniffle, snort, sniffle. 'I'll ask Mum.'

'Your birthday is just around the corner. Have you got any plans?'

'No one to do anything with.'

'Why don't you and your mum set up a high tea?'

'She's too busy making friends for herself.'

'Oh.' *Why's Stephanie finding it so tough in Toowoomba?*

A few minutes later I said goodbye and reached for a cupcake. The hum of the crowd filled my ears, bringing Mr Biceps to mind. *Such a fine sight.* The image without essence gave me some distraction after chatting to my depressed best friend.

I did wonder, like way too often, what it would be like to have a boyfriend. Was it strange that no one in my immediate circle of friends had had a boyfriend? Not Stephanie or Suzie or Jaya. We talked about boys all the time. We even checked out the boys from our brother school, Hill End Boys Grammar, at our combined social events. Mum tells me, 'Don't be so boy crazy.' But it's not like I go chasing them or anything. They're just a little eye candy. *There isn't anything wrong with a little eye candy, is there?*

Most boys target one thing. And I wasn't into that. Stephanie and I used to talk all the time about staying celibate until we got married. We would dream about our wedding day and how we would save ourselves for that one special person.

I know it's not the coolest thing in the world. Thankfully being popular at our school didn't revolve around having the right boyfriend or wearing the right clothes. That made our school pretty cool.

'What are you doing over there, love?' Mum's voice made me jump. 'Come over here for some photos.'

I needed to stop thinking and start enjoying. It was my party after all.

By dinner I'd made a decision. I'd enjoyed the afternoon off rehearsals so much I wanted every afternoon off. 'Mum, I want to quit dancing.'

'But love, you're doing so well this year.'

'It was Stephanie's thing, not mine. I want to get into running, or maybe even swimming.'

'How about you see this year out with the school dance studio, then decide over Christmas?'

'Why?'

'Because we've paid for your classes for the entire year.'

'So it's about money?'

'Attitude,' she warned, raising her eyebrows at me.

'And money?'

'Yes.'

Great, so I was going to be spinning and twisting my pear-shaped body, trying to get it to move the way Stephanie could get her body to move, for the rest of the year. Stephanie moved like a swan. I moved like a baby elephant. I could see it now, 'Watch out, everybody. The pear-shaped elephant is about to dance a solo.' And the crowd would roll with laughter. Maybe I was being too hard on myself. I must have been doing something right. I did get the lead.

Later that week, Jaya bowled me over on the way to school. 'Party is on. This weekend at my house. Mum and Dad are away. We can have the party we've always dreamed of.'

'Sounds fantastic.' *I hope.*

'Who would you invite?' Suzie bit a fingernail.

'Everyone,' Jaya said.

But Suzie was thinking straight. *Who would we invite?* It may as well be a pyjama party if we didn't invite any boys. We had to balance it out. Good-looking boys, of course. Younger versions of Mr Biceps would be perfect. Just for a little eye candy.

'Tabbie.' Jaya snapped my attention back to here and now. 'Are you daydreaming about something?'

'Just Mr Biceps.' A warm flush tickled my neck.

'Mr Who?' Suzie and Jaya chimed in, laughing together.

I giggled. 'On the way to see Steph, I sat beside this dreamy guy.'

'Why haven't you told us?' Suzie asked.

'Did you talk to him?' Jaya's eyes widened. 'Did you hook up?'

'Be real. As if. He was like thirty or something.' And as if I'd hook up with a random guy on a plane.

'So, why were you just thinking ...' Suzie's voice trailed off.

'We'd need to include some boys—for balance.' I shook my head to remove the biceps image from my eyes.

'Like who?' Suzie asked.

'I don't know. Jaya, can you think of who we can invite?'

'Hmm. Perhaps the whole Hill End football team?' Jaya smiled, nodding.

'That's crazy. We'd need a bouncer if we invited the whole team.' I gathered my books and attempted to leave for class. 'Actually, I think a bouncer would be a good idea anyway.'

'What about the guys from dance?' Suzie suggested as she grabbed my arm.

'Sounds like a plan.' I walked away but this time Jaya pulled me back.

'They're a bit ... ahem. But I guess if we asked them to bring their friends, you never know who they might bring.' Jaya stared into the distance. The bell vibrated through the walls. 'Great. I'll send the boys a text and tell them to bring a couple of mates.' Jaya tapped her phone as we trudged off to class.

    Spiralling Out of the Shadow

Chapter Five

Jaya ripped the plastic wrap off the six-packs of Cruisers her father had purchased and wedged them into ice-filled eskies already laden with beer. I wanted to offer soft drinks to everyone, but my friend had manipulated me into other plans.

Thankfully, Jaya's parents grew money on trees. When she asked if we could hire security for the party, they jumped at the idea. Having bouncers at the front door would keep their daughter and home safe, or so they thought.

Jaya handed a copy of the guest list to the bouncers when they arrived. She bustled them to their post on the porch and returned, grabbing a drink from the top of the esky. 'Cheers!' Jaya opened a Cruiser, drained it, and grabbed another before our first guests arrived.

I'd spent the afternoon making sure we'd have loads of great tunes to groove to and soon the house was bumping to the beat. My geography buddy Sarah arrived with her cousin Peta, who'd played netball with Lily. The three of them grabbed a Corona each. 'Hey, Jaya, do you have any lime wedges?' Lily asked.

'No, sorry. I didn't think of lime for the beer.' She opened a drawer loaded with stubby holders and passed one to each of them.

Mum and Dad had drilled my brother and me from birth, 'You only know if you're an alcoholic after your first drink. We don't want you ending up an alcoholic like your Uncle James. Once you take that first drink ...'

Over the years I'd become more and more fearful that I might have the addictive gene and become the family alco, the black sheep, the troublemaker. I took another sip of lemonade. The sweet drink gave me a sufficient sugar buzz.

I passed Suzie a can of soft drink, knowing her parents would probably ship her off to some super-strict boarding school if she even smelled an alcoholic drink. The guests flooded through the door and soon Suzie and I were the only ones without alcohol running through our veins. Everyone else indulged in Jaya's supplies.

Just before nine, Joey waltzed in. Seriously, he looked like he was doing a Fred Astaire impersonation. He was the definition of a dancing dork. I had hoped some hot boys would join our dance school, but so far, Joey was as good as it got.

Stop.

Get out of here.

Who just followed Joey in?

'Suzie, Suzie,' I whispered, grabbing her shoulder. 'Mr Universe has just entered the house.'

'Calm down, Tabbie.' Her voice was smooth and molten, until she faced the door. She turned back to me, a blotchy pink trail down her neck. 'Joey.'

The boy, lurking in the doorway beside Joey, was unmistakably a younger version of Mr Biceps. 'Have you ever seen that other boy in your life?'

Jaya had returned for another drink and rolled her eyes. 'In my whole fifteen years? No, I can't say that I have. Anyway, I thought you weren't interested in boys.'

'Nothing wrong with a little eye candy. Have you got his name on the list?'

'I'll check.' Jaya ran her finger down the guest list. 'Hmm, let me see. Possibly Danny.'

'Check ya. I'm off to catch me a boy.' Goosebumps tingled through my arms. I'd never seen anyone so gorgeous.

'Catch? What happened to eye candy? You're hilarious, Tabbie.' Suzie giggled.

'Jokes!' I laughed and headed straight for him. *Well, life's about fun.* If Steph was here, she'd probably rush over to chat to the new boy. But she wasn't here. Project Check-Out-Young-Mr-Biceps was about to begin.

'Hi Joey,' I said in a way-too-sweet voice before turning my attention to young Mr Biceps. 'Hi, ahh ... did you come with Joey?'

'Yeah, Tabbie.' Joey sighed. 'This is Danny.'

'So where do you go to school?'

'Urgh.'

'Is that far from here?' *Did he just grunt at me? Would he have grunted at Steph?*

'Yeah.' He looked to the floor.

'Can I get you a drink?' Maybe he was a one-word one-syllable Mr (young) Biceps.

'Coke.'

I turned and spoke out loud to myself. 'You really like to talk then, hey?' Maybe his supreme looks were his only drawcard. I fished a Coke from the esky and handed it to him, then left Joey and Danny to grunt at each other.

'Maybe he's just shy,' said Miss Always-Looking-For-The-Best Suzie.

'Or purely eye candy.' Either he was shy, tongue-tied, in awe of my not-beauty or he was a total dweeb.

The party continued while Suzie and I collected bottles. The guests drank like fish, spilling plenty on all the slip-n-slide zones.

The party got ugly.

'Tabbie.' Jaya squinted to see me. 'Grrreat pardy, hey?'

'It's getting a little messy.'

'The cleaner can fix it t'morrow. 'll be fine.'

'Should we start sending everyone—'

'Argh! I think I'm gonna be ...' Jaya stumbled into her parents' ensuite. I followed, catching her hair just in time as she projectile-vomited, getting most of it into the toilet. At least I'd saved her hair.

I searched the drawers for facecloths to clean her up and found some towels to mop up the mess. She puked until nothing was left but bile. Her face had morphed into a pasty shade of green, and her eyelids drooped and fluttered. I tucked her into her parents' bed, leaving a bucket beside her, and asked the bouncers to round everyone up and out.

Suzie locked the door after everyone had left and busied herself wiping down benches and searching for sneaky bottles under cushions or behind curtains. I was worried Jaya might choke on her own spew, so I sat with her until the voice of an older woman ranted outside. I rushed to the front door. Suzie's mum.

'You mean to tell me this is the sort of party you came to?' Mrs Peters pointed towards Sarah and Peta, who were both clinging to a tree for support.

Suzie hung her head.

'Get in the car now!' Mrs Peters looked towards me. 'And that will be the last time Suzie ever comes to one of Jaya's parties. I can see there are no adults here. I'll be on the phone to both of your parents in the morning!'

I rushed down the stairs to apologise, but Mrs Peters had ushered Suzie into the car and rushed off too quickly.

The kerfuffle had left my heart racing. I rang home. 'Mum, is it okay if I stay the night?'

'Sure, love. Everything okay?'

'Yeah, I just don't want to leave Jaya here on her own. She's had too much to drink.'

'You mean too much alcohol?' Mum's voice was strained.

'Yes.' I balanced on one foot, waiting to see if she was about to freak out.

'Have you had anything to drink?' She sounded calm. *Phew.*

'No, Mum. I didn't realise Jaya was going to get alcohol until the last minute.'

'Do you want us to come over?'

'No, I'll be fine. I'll stay here with her.' I hung up and nudged Jaya until she rolled over a little, leaving room for me to sit on the side of the bed.

'Jaya.' I bounced the bed to revive her. 'Jaya, what's your mum's number?'

'Left her phone here. Can't call her.' Jaya turned away, pulling the doona over her head.

'Your dad's?'

'Same. His phone's over there.'

There, sitting on the dresser, were two phones.

At midnight, I used my mobile phone flashlight to find my way to the other side of the bed. I turned it off, staring until the ceiling came into view as my eyes adjusted to the darkness. Jaya's continued steady breathing kept my fear of her vomiting in her sleep at bay. I listened, breath after breath, and only succumbed to sleep as the birds began to tweet.

Jaya woke with a throbbing head. I dragged myself out of bed, exhausted. I rang Mum to rescue me from Jaya, who insisted she hadn't been drunk and had started to plan her next party. She'd be fine now the sun had risen, but I had to get some sleep.

Chapter Six

On Monday morning, my eyelids hung heavy and my mind wandered. Jaya bragged to everyone within earshot that she'd hosted the most fabulous party of the century. Suzie was absent. Her mum had blasted my mum over the phone on Sunday. *Major overreaction.*

I reminisced about the times spent with my best friend, my ridiculously beautiful and not-quite-perfect best friend, who I missed today more than I had in a long time. I needed to talk to Stephanie, but every time I rang, she was either in the shower or not home. When I tried again at the end of the week, her mother told me she was out on a date. A second date with the same boy.

'Tabbie, you won't believe what just happened!' Stephanie finally returned my call.

'You saw Jason again?'

'How did you know?'

'Why else would you be this excited?' *Ha. She doesn't know how I know.*

'But—?'

'I rang while you were out. Second date, hey?' *This was it!* No more 'only interested in eye candy' garbage. If Stephanie had started dating, I wanted to date boys too.

Steady breathing was her response.

'Your mum told me. So do you think he's into you?' I wondered if this guy was as good-looking as Mr Biceps.

'I don't know. How would I know?'

'I don't know either.' I chuckled a fake laugh. *How would I know?* I was inexperienced, clueless. But why would he want to hang out with her if he wasn't into her? 'How did you meet?'

'At school. He said he'd been watching me. Is that creepy? Should I be worried about that?'

'Not if he was watching as in checking you out.'

'Mm, I guess. He invited me to one of the senior's birthday parties. He was such a gentleman.'

'Is he a senior?'

'Uh-huh.'

'What gentlemanly things did he do?' If there were gentlemanly types out there, I wanted to find one too.

'He was really kind about Dad's curfew. And his eyes, his hair, his muscles. Wow.'

'Well, guys do have eyes, hair, and muscles.' I laughed. Looks don't define a gentleman. The image of Mr Biceps flashed in my mind again.

'Monica, the class cow, told me he's dating me for a dare to get me to sleep with him.'

'Maybe Jason's into you and Monica's jealous.'

'But what if Jason is planning on using me to win a dare or a bet or something?'

'No sex.' Because if she did, she'd be a numbat. Seriously, she just met the guy. Plus we'd agreed we'd both wait until we were married. I hoped she'd remember those details herself.

'I wasn't planning on it.'

'You need to make it clear to him.' I swallowed the extra saliva pooling in my mouth.

'You don't think that's being a bit presumptuous?'

'Steph, you weren't planning on having sex with him, so just be up front about it.'

'It's not really third date conversation material, is it?'

'Do you want to know whether he's dating you for a dare or not? I reckon, if he's playing some sort of game, he won't hang around when he knows where you stand.'

Stephanie mumbled into the phone. I said goodbye and clutched the phone until the repetitive beep irritated me. I could tell she was really into the boy, but she'd kick herself if she gave in and he was a fraud just wanting to get into her pants. One thing I did know—I wouldn't have the guts to talk about sex on the third date.

The conversation with Stephanie led me to think about Danny. Sure, he was a bit of a freak with his lack of words, but he did resemble Mr Biceps. I wondered how well Joey knew him.

I rounded up Joey at our next dance rehearsal and apparently Danny hadn't stopped talking about me. *Did that even make sense? Um, no.* What was it with boys? He'd barely spoken to me then talked nonstop about me. *Gah!* I should just forget about him.

Stephanie rang with all the gory details of her third date. She went through with it. I couldn't believe she actually brought up sex. It sounded like she scared him off. The little bit of nasty in me, the bit that hoped they wouldn't last, grinned. I hated to admit it, but I had been turning green with envy.

'Did he say it was over?'

'No, but I'm sure it is. He seemed ... really nice.' She blew her nose and hiccupped into the phone.

'You're thinking Monica was right, aren't you?'

'Maybe.'

'Try not to think about it anymore. See what happens next week. Hey—'

'Mum needs the phone, gotta go.' Stephanie cut me off. Her mother's yelling echoed through the phone before it cut out. Silence.

I was meant to be the super-caring best friend. But something in me sang with joy that she'd scared him off. *Could I be any shallower?* My heart flooded with remorse. I had to call her again the next day.

'Hi, is Stephanie there?'

'No, I'll get her to call you.' Mrs Stronge wasn't in a chatty mood—she rarely was.

It was hard focusing on homework while I was expecting a call from Stephanie. But her call never came.

Suzie returned to school after a week, telling us she was pretty much grounded for life, and her parents were this close—she showed us millimetres pinched between her fingers—to home-schooling her. The sweetness that had radiated from Suzie since I met her disintegrated before my eyes.

'Are you girls up for a big one tomorrow night?' Jaya ambled into school on Friday with her chest puffed out.

I laughed. Since when would Suzie, who was grounded for life, or I, who cleaned up her vomit at the last party, be keen for a 'big one'?

'Look what I've got.' She held her phone up. A text message with our three names at the top. 'Come on girls, you could at least look a little excited.'

You're invited to a BOOZE-UP! The text was from Macie, one of the girls from dance who we rarely spoke to.

'Straight to the point, isn't she?' Oh, to go back to the way hang-outs used to be—music, soft drinks, and lots of laughter with the girls.

'There's no way I'll be allowed to go.' Suzie pulled her lip between her teeth.

'Come on, Tabbie. We'll have a ball,' Jaya said.

Tears pooled in Suzie's eyes. My heart ached to see her so sad. 'Why don't you go to this one on your own?' I handed the phone back.

'I won't know anyone there. It'll be boring without you.'

'I'll check with Mum and Dad. Can you forward the invite so I can show them?

'Why?'

'Because that's what I do.'

'You haven't told them I drink or anything have you?'

'I told Mum you'd had too much at your party.'

'Why?'

'Because I stayed at your house that night to make sure you were okay.'

'Can you like ...' Jaya stepped closer, towering her anger over me and hissing. 'Mind your own business. Your parents don't need to know what I do.'

'I'm sorry, but ...' I shuffled backwards. 'I'm not going to lie about this party.'

Jaya did have a point. It was one thing to tell Mum and Dad about me, but perhaps I had broken the confidential friend code.

Mum looked at me with a long gaze after she read the invitation. 'I'll have to double-check with your father.'

I kind of hoped Mum and Dad would say no, but Dad only reminded me of my uncle and made me promise not to drink. If I didn't go, I'd feel guilty all weekend knowing Jaya had gone on her own.

'I'll be back to pick you up at midnight,' Mrs Range said.

'Please, Mum,' Jaya whined. 'Can you come back at three?'

Mrs Range shook her head. 'I'll come in and get you if you aren't waiting here by the kerb at midnight. And take it easy. I don't want another earful from anybody's mother in the morning.'

We waited as the Audi's amber indicator blinked and the tyres scattered small stones along the gutter, before it headed down the street.

'Seriously.' Jaya shook her head. 'I can't believe Suzie's mum.'

'She rang my parents as well.'

'She's such a cow, adding fuel to my mother's foul mood of late.'

'Your mum didn't seem that bad just then.' I replayed the car conversation in my mind. 'Midnight isn't early.'

'It's not just that ...' her voice trailed off as she walked. I followed her towards a two-storey brick house. 'Can you watch the time?' she asked me. 'I'd hate her to embarrass us and come in.'

We followed the funky music to the backyard. Macie's smart parents had kicked the party outside in the cold. They'd lit a couple of fire warmers to prevent everyone from freezing.

Jaya pulled a bottle of bubbly from her bag.

'Where did you get that from?'

'The fridge,' she replied.

'Your parents?'

She nodded.

'Did you ask?'

'They wouldn't care.' Jaya shook her head.

'But didn't your mother just say—'

'Take it easy.' Jaya finished my sentence. 'She didn't say I couldn't have a few.'

'Well, can you take it a little slower this time?'

The bottle was empty within half an hour, and Jaya flirted with every boy she came face to face with. I found Macie and began to follow her around picking up bottles. Thankfully, she was being a responsible hostess and not consuming copious amounts of alcohol. Macie was a year older than us.

'What do you like to do other than dance?' Macie twisted a dark ringlet of hair around her finger.

I told her the usual—running, hanging out, and the odd bit of swimming. I wanted to ask her why she still danced, but I was worried I might be put my foot in my mouth. She looked more like a donkey than a dancer.

'Hey, I'm in the running club. Why don't you join us?'

'Maybe,' I said, but I wasn't ready to commit.

I ran to escape what was happening in life. If I joined a club, I might have to interact while running and that wouldn't allow for mind-blowing peace and quiet. Macie was refreshing. I liked her. She was different to the person I thought she'd be. I'd expected her to get drunk like Jaya. But she didn't.

Out of the corner of my eye, Jaya was smacking a kiss on one of the objects of her flirting. As I went to interrupt her, she pulled away and rushed to the bathroom. For the next two hours, I played nurse Tabbie while she purged everything possible out of her body.

Sensible me was kicking myself for coming.

'This is the last time you drag me to a party. Do you realise how vulnerable you are when you're drunk? It's dangerous. Someone could take advantage of you. You mightn't …' I stopped, knowing she wouldn't remember anything I'd said. My speech went in one ear and out the other. But part of me was glad to be there. She needed someone to watch out for her.

Chapter Seven

T‌HE FULL IMPACT OF S‌TEPHANIE GOING continued to leave me stranded like I was on a deserted island. Empty and alone. I wanted my best friend back. She never used to be too busy to talk to me, but time now stretched like an eternity before she returned my phone calls.

'Tabbie, I think Monica was telling the truth,' Stephanie blurted through the phone.

'About Jason?'

'Yeah. And the dare.'

'So forget him.' *Move on. Get a life that doesn't involve a boyfriend. Live like the rest of us.*

'But I don't want her to be right.'

'If she was right, then Jason isn't worth it.' *Sorry,* I said to myself after hanging up. *She's hurting.* My best friend, the ridiculously beautiful and nearly perfect one, seemed to be slipping into depression.

The mornings began to get the shiver factor with midyear school break just around the corner. Every time Steph and I spoke on the phone, a nervous sweat clung to my armpits. I was the worst best friend. Sure, I missed her. Every time attention came my way, a niggling whisper reminded me that I was not Stephanie. *If she was here, the attention would land on her.*

'So, Tabbie, got anything on this Friday night?' Joey cartwheeled in front of me in his black full-length tights.

'Why? What were you thinking?' Perhaps a date with Joey wouldn't be so bad. It would be pretty bad, but not the-end-of-the-world kind of bad. Then at least I could say I'd been on a date. No, I couldn't do that to Suzie. I couldn't help noticing the way she glanced at Joey.

'Danny and I are going to hang out at a youth group thing.'

My ears alerted at the sound of Danny. 'What? Like at a church?'

'Yeah. Why don't you join us?'

'Who else is going?'

'Don't know. I haven't been before, but Danny goes all the time. Says it's heaps of fun.' He pulled his left leg up to his face, proving his ridiculous flexibility.

'Can I bring Suzie or Jaya?'

'Guess so.'

So maybe it wasn't a date. But at least I had somewhere to go on a Friday night instead of sitting at home. Mum would be pleased to see me going to a church thing. She'd given up trying to get the family to go to the old church around the corner. Dad wasn't interested, and Peter and I sided with him.

'Hey.' Jaya rang Friday afternoon. 'Don't think I'll get there tonight.'

'But it'll be fun.'

'Yeah, well, I hope you and Suze have a good time. I'm not up to it. See you on Monday.'

'But Jaya—' She'd already hung up. Thankfully Suzie was still coming. Her mum had let her out because it was a church youth group.

A nervous tingle ran down my back as we entered the church building. It was strange, but in a good way. Great music bounced off the walls and the party-style lights were dim. We had to weave our way through the kids already there. Hot boys were everywhere, distracting me as we wandered around trying to find Joey and Danny.

'Joey!' Suzie saw him pulling a Coke from a vending machine.

'Hi. Glad you made it. Kind of boring, isn't it? Think I'll head off soon.'

'Why? Where's Danny?' I asked as I looked over Joey's shoulder.

'It's his gig. He's playing in the band when they start.'

'What band?' Suzie beamed.

Yep, she definitely has a crush on Joey.

'I got here early, and heard them warm up,' Joey scoffed. 'You'll see what kind of band, if you hang around. Danny would like that.'

I looked back at Joey. He winked at me. I looked the other way, heat rising in my cheeks.

What do I have to lose? Suzie and I made our way to a table where a bunch of girls were painting their nails. They slid around and invited us to join in. It'd been a while since I'd done my nails. I picked out a metallic purple, then found some transfers and stuck glitter to each nail. Super-impressed with myself, I helped Suzie with hers. Her fingers trembled in mine as I painted her nails.

'Do you think Joey left?' A small crease formed between Suzie's eyes.

I looked up. 'I can't see him, but he might still be here somewhere.'

Suzie lifted her hand to chew on her fingernails. I grabbed her wrist, pointing to the new pale pink polish, then slapped her hand back down on the table to add a top coat.

'You should stop biting your nails. They'll grow, if you give them a chance.'

The crowd moved like high tide, so we rode the wave and found some seats in the hall.

'Thought I'd lost you.' Joey slipped into the seat beside me.

'Yeah, we wondered if you'd already gone.' I turned to Suzie and again swiped her hand away from her mouth. 'Don't wreck the artwork!'

Suzie blushed. I clenched my teeth. I'd embarrassed her in front of her crush. *Stupid me.*

The band started to play. Loud grunge-rock music drew a mass of kids to mosh in the front. The lights feathering down on Danny plucking his bass guitar made him look mega-cute. For a guy who supposedly couldn't stop talking about me, he didn't lock eyes with mine, nor did he serenade me. I suppose the spotlights in his eyes would have left him looking out towards a black sea. After they'd played a few songs, Danny left the stage and I lost him. Not that I was looking for him. *Really.* Joey waved a quick goodbye before he slipped away as the crowd began to sit.

A guy dressed in jeans and a black T-shirt spoke into a microphone about life having a plan and purpose and that God loved everyone—no matter what we'd done or who we were. It kind of made me feel all warm and fuzzy, but it mustn't have had the same effect on Suzie. 'I've got to get out of here.' She pulled her phone out of her bag and thumbed the keypad.

'Why?'

'Mum sent a text,' she whispered.

'Can we stay 'til this guy finishes?'

'No, that guy is speaking crap. Mum will be waiting.' She stood up and dragged me outside. Mrs Peters was already at the kerb when we got there.

'I was about to come in to find you.'

'Have you been waiting long?' I climbed into the back of the car.

Suzie hung her head and slipped a fingernail between her teeth. *What didn't she like about what the guy was saying?* I'd have to remember to ask her later.

'Long enough to hear that wretched music,' Mrs Peters said. 'And they call this a church?'

'But Suzie only just ...' I stopped speaking when I realised Mrs Peters had been there long before she'd texted.

'That'll be the last time you come here, Suzie.'

Suzie's jaw tensed.

     Spiralling Out of the Shadow

I had always assumed they were a religious family. Both Suzie and her mother's reaction confused me. Neither of them spoke as I said goodbye when we reached my house.

I wasn't as close to Suzie as I was to Stephanie. If that had been Steph, I would have asked what was going on. But I left it and waved as they drove away.

Alone. Lonely. And missing Stephanie. Even though I was second-best when she was involved. Even though I couldn't make a decision without involving her. Even though I went along with whatever she wanted to do. I missed her. My new freedom was lonely.

I rang Stephanie to make sure she'd booked her tickets to visit. The school holidays were just a few weeks away.

'Mum and Dad don't have the money, so I can't come.'

'But I thought you said it would be fine.' She had to visit. It'd been way too long.

'I don't have the money. Do you?'

'Maybe. I'll call you back.'

I ran into the kitchen and blurted out Stephanie's predicament to Mum.

'Hey, don't panic. They paid for you to go and visit in Toowoomba. We can pay for her flight down.'

'Really?'

Mum nodded.

I called Stephanie back. 'Steph, you can still come!'

'How? Did you raid your piggy bank?'

'Ha ha, no. Mum's happy to pay for your flight.'

'You mean I can get out of this freak-town for a couple of weeks?'

I was thinking one week, but ... 'Yeah, for sure.'

If she was to accept the offer to come and live with us next year, now would be a good time to start getting used to being around her twenty-four seven.

Out of nowhere, my thoughts went back to the black T-shirt guy at youth group. I would love to hear more of what he had to say.

And hear Danny play again. I hated to admit I wanted to watch him play his bass guitar again. Not that I was interested in him.

'So I guess you don't want to come with me to Joey's youth group this week?' I asked Suzie on the way to class.

'Don't even mention it again.'

'Okay. But I liked it.'

Suzie squinted, shook her head, and headed for the library. While Suzie was preoccupied with researching an assignment, I talked Jaya into coming with me next time. The mention of hot boys swayed her.

Later that week, as we walked into the youth group, it was like I was putting on my favourite pair of jeans. I just felt comfortable. I smiled when the music began. Everyone around us started jumping to the beat. I couldn't help but join in. Jaya yawned as soon as the music stopped.

'Humour me, would you?' I turned to her, raising my eyebrows. 'Suzie dragged me out early last week. Can we just stay 'til the end?'

'I don't get it.'

The room quietened as everyone sat.

'What is there not to get?' I whispered.

'I don't know what all the hype is about.' Jaya didn't lower her voice and leaned forward in her chair with a hand on her hip. 'The—'

'Okay, let's go then.' It was time to get her out of there before she became overtly rude. I ducked my head and tried to leave discreetly. Standing at the back of the room, I scanned one more time, hoping to grab one last glimpse of Danny for a little eye candy. *But no.*

'Hey, are you off?' A friendly voice grabbed my attention.

'Yeah, Jaya here is about to turn into sleeping beauty. I'd better get her home.'

'No worries. We'd love you to come again next week. There's a band coming in two weeks. It'll be kind of like a party.' The girl smiled as she straightened her oversized T-shirt then tucked her thick curls behind her ear.

'Sounds great, I'd love to come.'

'Fantastic. See you next week.' The girl appeared a couple of years older than us. 'Oh, I'm Shelly.'

'My name is Tabbie. I'd love to come. I might have another friend with me. Is that okay?'

'Sure, bring anyone you like.' Shelly sauntered back inside.

'I'm not coming back,' Jaya said in a monotone don't-mess-with-me-voice as she stomped down the stairs.

'Really? You're sure?'

'Uh-huh.'

'Next week might be different. And Steph will be down.'

'Whatever. I'm not coming.'

It bothered me a little. Well, it bothered me a lot. I'd have to work on not letting it get to me so much. My two school friends wanted nothing to do with this new interest in my life. Perhaps I was only interested to check out the cute boys like Danny, or maybe there was more that attracted me. I hoped Stephanie would enjoy the youth group as much as I did so I could stay to the end next week.

Chapter Eight

'I'M SICK,' JAYA RANG ME on the way to school.

'What do you mean?'

'Gastro.'

'Are you seriously faking a sickie on the last day of the term?'

'No. I've gotta go. Argh! Sick again.'

'But what about our performance—' Jaya hung up in my ear when I was about to ask about the eisteddfod performance next week. And rehearsals that afternoon.

She really was sick. And this time, it wasn't from drinking too much.

Stephanie arrived that afternoon with a fake smile. She looked kind of happy, but I could see she still mourned the split-up with Jason. What if Steph could stand in for Jaya, just for rehearsals? *Maybe crazy. But maybe it'd cheer her up.* It was worth a try. 'Come on, Steph. You'll pick up the steps,' I said to her as soon as I could bring it up.

'I don't dance any more,' she said.

'You *are* a dancer.'

'I was a dancer.' Steph's jaw tensed. 'Past life.'

'And now you're back, living in your past life for the holidays. We need someone to fill in for Jaya. Just this once.'

'You didn't tell me this was on.'

'Please?'

'You didn't tell me you had a performance coming up!'

'Please, please, pretty please with sparkles and pink sugar on top. Just for rehearsal. Jaya will be fine by next week.' I had tried to tell her over the phone, several times.

'Okay. Just this once.' Stephanie moaned.

I almost regretted asking her to stand in. She slid straight back into the limelight and even though I was lead, it was like I'd been pushed to the side. Stephanie soaked up the attention. Everyone loved having her back.

'Why didn't you tell me you were dancing lead? And what's going on with Suzie? She barely said hello.'

'Long story. I'll fill you in later.' There was a definite glimmer in Stephanie's eyes. 'You loved it, didn't you? Come on, admit it.'

'Yeah, it was fun.'

'You *are* a dancer. You have to get back into it.'

'Yeah, maybe one day.' Her eyes continued to sparkle. 'Just not while I'm in Toowoomba.'

'So are you moving back to Sydney?'

'I haven't asked yet.'

'Seriously? Why not?'

'Um …' Stephanie bit her lip. 'Not sure.'

'Jason?' I knew before I asked.

'But I guess that won't matter if he goes to uni. I'll ask Mum and Dad when I get back.'

'You've had a whole term to ask.'

'I promise I'll ask when I get back.'

I had to let it go. 'I went to a youth group last week. I thought it could be fun to take you tonight.'

'Can we catch a movie instead?' Stephanie scrunched her nose up.

'We can see a movie next week.'

'But won't it be full of religious mumbo-jumbo?'

'No, it's heaps of fun. You'll love it.'

'I really don't want to.' Stephanie looked through her eyelashes.

'Please? I'll never ask you to come again, if you don't like it.'

'You don't accept no for an answer, do you? Will it be on again next week? Can we go then?'

'Sure.' The return of Steph's spunk stopped me pushing her.

I raced upstairs to shower, change, and cool off after dance rehearsals. I'd been looking forward to taking Stephanie to youth group. A twinge of regret hit me.

'Sorry.' Stephanie blinked wide cow-like eyes at me when I returned downstairs. 'I really didn't feel like going out tonight.'

'That's okay. I could do with an early night.'

We set up a mattress on my floor, ate chocolate, and giggled until my stomach churned from too much sugar. The next day I took Steph to the mall, and she gushed over all the new season clothes she'd been missing out on. On Sunday, we met Jaya for lunch. I'd never noticed any spite between Steph and Jaya before Stephanie moved away, but now they were at each other the whole time.

'Got a boyfriend, huh?' Jaya clattered her fingernails on the table.

'Not any more. You got one?'

'No.'

'Didn't get the lead, huh?' Stephanie smirked.

I glared at Steph. I couldn't believe how nasty she was being.

'I don't care about dance.' Jaya turned away.

'Me neither,' Steph mumbled.

'That's garbage. You live to dance.'

'Girls!' Their sharp tone and the way they cut each other off had me edging to leave the café.

'What?' they said at the same time.

'Okay, now I have your attention. Would you like to go to the movies this week?'

Steph nodded.

'Mum and Dad are shipping me off to Granny's again. Today.' Jaya curled her lip.

'What about the eisteddfod?' I asked.

'I'll be there.' Jaya stood. 'I've got to go. Mum and Dad are waiting for me.'

'That went well,' Steph said as she watched Jaya walk away.

'Were you two always like that?'

'Yeah, like peas in a pod.'

'Why didn't I notice 'til now?'

Stephanie laughed and shook her head.

I rang Suzie as we walked out of the cafe. Her mum said she was too busy to come to the phone. 'Stephanie's down for the holidays. Can we pop over to visit?' I asked Mrs Peters.

'No. It's best you stay away.' Mrs Peters hung up before I could speak again.

'Have her parents gone over-the-top strict or what?' Stephanie said while I was still looking at the phone.

'I just don't get them. How can pulling her away from all her friends help?'

Stephanie shrugged.

On Friday, Stephanie caught up with some girls I didn't know well. Happy to have a day to myself, I dusted off my trainers and took off on a long well-overdue run. I found myself under the dense canopy of the nature reserve. The earthy plant scent and the damp crisp air on my face filled my soul. I slowed down to walk across the uneven ground, letting the bulging roots massage the soles of my shoes.

On the way back, I took another path that led me to a playground. A weathered bench-seat gave my legs rest. Laughter, squabbles and giggles of children in the playground made me smile. When the dampness of dusk began to fall, I pulled my fleecy jumper on and slowly jogged home. Stephanie was sure to be finished visiting her other friends by now.

Peter's laughter caught my attention before I reached the house. I'd hardly seen him since he'd hooked up with Phoebe. Mum and Dad had pressed him on the rule of no girlfriends in his room. Conveniently, Phoebe was flatting with friends and he enjoyed the freedom of her place. I'd missed his deep rumbling laugh.

'Pete!' I gave him a sweaty hug. As I stepped back, a web of tension strung across the room caught me. 'Did I interrupt something?'

'No, of course not.' Stephanie pouted as she twirled a sliver of hair in her fingers.

'Love to stay, but I have to get going.' Pete's neck tensed.

'But … I haven't seen you for ages.'

'Sorry, sis, I've been busy. Let's book in a time to hang out. Maybe next week.'

'How about Sunday week?' I wasn't keen to share him with Stephanie.

'It's a date. See you then.' He planted a kiss on my cheek, rubbed Stephanie's shoulder and left.

'Why did you get weird on us?' Stephanie asked.

'I don't know. It just felt funny when I walked in. Were you flirting with my brother?'

'No. As if! Should we start getting ready for youth group?' Stephanie ran upstairs, but not before I saw a slight blush rush to her cheeks.

Chapter Nine

'Who are you trying to impress?' Stephanie eyed me up and down.

'Just want to look nice.' My black A-line party dress sat just right, covering my tights, sure to stand out in the crowd. *I hope.*

'You look fantastic in a pair of jeans. What's with the frock?'

She made me laugh with her 'frock' talk. But perhaps she was right. Perhaps I had overdone it. 'Do you want me to get changed?'

'No, just tell me why you're wearing a dress.'

'It's not their basic youth group tonight. They're having a band, and I guess it'll be more like a concert.'

Stephanie's shoulders tensed, her hand flung out to her side. 'A concert? At church?'

'It's not like the churches you know.' I opened my wardrobe. 'It's more modern.'

'Okay, but it sounds strange to me. Jeans would be fine for a concert.'

'You're right, jeans would be fine.' She had me there. *What was I thinking? Who am I really trying to impress?* I separated my clothes hanger by hanger, looking for something else to wear. 'And if you're happy in jeans, go for it.'

'Whatever.' She glared at me. 'But I didn't bring anything nicer than jeans.'

'Try this.' I passed her a knee-length teal dress.

'I love the colour. You know, I haven't bought a dress since I moved. I live in jeans in Toowoomba.'

'The colour is you. Try it on.'

Her eyes sparkled. The dress reflected in her blue irises, making them appear teal. Stephanie checked herself from every angle in the full-length mirror. Seriously, all her curves and bumps were in perfect proportion. I decided to give her the dress—there was no way I wanted to wear it again. She really was picture-perfect.

'Perfect!'

'The length is a little odd.' She kicked out one leg.

'It looks great.' It wasn't a mini or a maxi, but it was gorgeous on her.

'You don't think it's too tight?'

'You look stunning.' I found a loose beige cardigan similar in length to the dress and handed it to her. 'You can keep the dress, if you like.'

If I dared wear it again after seeing her in it, I'd feel like a balloon. Stephanie pulled on some black tights and short boots and looked like a model.

'I still can't believe you're getting so dressed up for youth group.'

I didn't want to tell her that it was the first time I'd dressed up to go there. Nor did I want to tell her I was looking forward to checking Danny out again. Not that I was interested in him.

We walked into something that looked like party central. Wow! 'This music is pumping! Isn't it great?' I yelled into Steph's ear.

She screwed up her nose. Shrugged. I scanned the crowd and saw some younger girls from school and a couple of familiar faces from the previous Friday nights I'd been there.

'Glad you made it, Tabbie.' Shelly appeared out of the crowd, her mass of curls piled into a knob on the top of her head.

'Hi, Shelly. This is Steph.'

Steph smiled then looked to the floor, her fingers clinging to the sides of her dress. It was strange to see her act so awkward. My ridiculously beautiful and perfect friend acting like she wasn't beautiful or perfect. It was bizarre.

Unlike Suzie and Jaya, Stephanie didn't ask to leave early. She stayed by my side until the band finished. 'Well, that was all a bit weird,' she said after we'd climbed into bed.

'I enjoyed it.'

'Humph. Goodnight.'

'Night.' I missed my old best friend. The girl lying on the mattress beside me was not the same girl I'd known for half my life.

On Saturday afternoon, we had to be at the eisteddfod an hour before our performance. Jaya hadn't arrived.

'Suzie! I've missed you.' I ran to hug her when she trudged in.

Suzie's lip quivered. She turned away and warmed up by herself.

'Suzie?' I followed her.

'Don't want to talk.' A tear tumbled off her eyelashes.

'Can't believe how lame my parents are.' Jaya bustled in, ten minutes before our performance time.

'What happened this time?' I asked.

'Mum said Dad would pick me up and Dad said Mum would pick me up—neither showed, so Granny had to drive me down. She never drives in the city. We sat on forty kilometres an hour the whole way.'

'You'd better warm up now you're here,' Miss Skinner interrupted, pointing to her watch.

We performed first. Jaya's timing was out during the entire routine. I danced with precision but all I could think about was the fact that Jaya's parents hadn't shown up, Suzie made it but ignored me, and Stephanie was shrinking into a shell of who she'd been.

Jaya turned the wrong way, and her foot clipped my ankle. I stumbled with clenched teeth. A moment passed and I knew I had to concentrate on the beat to get back in time with everyone. When the music stopped, I couldn't look Steph in the eye. It was our worst performance ever.

We didn't win the competition. We didn't even place in the top four, and there were only five other studios. 'You'll do much better next time,' Miss Skinner said, but I could see disappointment etched in her face and body language.

For most of the week that followed, Stephanie and I were like kittens that playfully enjoyed each other's company—but there were times when we pecked at each other like chooks. Her spunky confidence was no longer a standout attribute, and I didn't know how to help her find it again. It was like our roles had reversed. She used to be the major decision-maker, and now I was calling the shots. *Me*, the one who was a little frumpy and not so pretty.

I turned the computer on while Steph took a shower. An email from Jaya flashed into my inbox—a forwarded party invitation for Friday. Mum called us for dinner before I could read the finer details. 'Peta's having a party tomorrow night.'

'Who's Peta?' Stephanie's face had a pink tinge. I couldn't tell if it was from hot water or if she'd been crying.

'Sara Clay's cousin. I met her at a party Jaya threw a couple of months ago.'

'Sounds good. Are …' She hesitated. 'Are we going?'

'I'd rather go to youth group.'

'We went last week. Once is enough.'

She had a point—we'd made a deal. I had agreed not to ask her again. And I liked it when she stood up to me.

There weren't any parents or hired security in sight at Peta's. Everyone held alcoholic drinks and a vodka bottle was being passed around. Each person took a swig before handing it on. I dry-retched, imagining how much backwash was swirling around in the bottle. The speakers pumped out B-grade songs distorted in a muddle of decibels. I checked each new arrival for hot boys, but no one caught my attention.

'When did everyone start drinking?' Stephanie asked.

'Probably when they got here,' I said.

'I mean ...' She gave me the over-the-top-rolling-of-eyes look. 'No one drank before I left town. Now it looks like everyone's getting drunk.'

'We're not. Guess they'll have a headache tomorrow and we won't.'

'Can we go now?' Stephanie tugged on a stray hair. 'Being here feels weird.'

'Steph, relax. They're just having a bit of fun.' Youth group was weird. Parties were weird. What did she do for fun these days?

'Tabbie, they're being stupid.'

'Hey, you're the one who wanted to come.'

'But—'

'It's not like you to be so easily offended.'

A bottle crashed on the pavement. Stephanie jumped. Several more bottles smashed as they played throw-the-bottle-closest-to-the-broken-bottle.

'Everyone was drinking when I hung out with Jason's friends, but no one was being stupid like this.' Stephanie stood with her back against the wall. Her eyes darted back and forth.

'Okay, okay. I'll call Mum.'

She looked the other way. I glared into her back, burning holes with my angry eyes. Next minute, Stephanie turned around and dragged me out to wait for Mum. Sure, I didn't want to look after anyone getting drunk, but being at a party was better than sitting at home. Stephanie seemed to want the opposite—the dull and quiet, mundane and boring.

'Everything alright?' Mum asked as I climbed into the front seat.

'Stephanie's stressed out.'

'It wasn't fun.' Stephanie slammed the back door closed. 'Why hang around when it's not worth it?'

'You didn't even give it a chance, Steph.' I faced the windscreen. 'We could have gone inside. It might have been quieter in there.'

'Tabbie,' Mum said with a husky voice.

'Well ... she wanted to leave as soon as we arrived.'

'How about I make you both a hot chocolate when we get home?' Mum said.

'No thanks. I'm going straight to bed.' I was thankful to get out of the thick tension in the car and into fresh air as soon as Mum pulled up.

Stephanie must have accepted the hot chocolate offer because she didn't follow me upstairs. She was still my best friend. My best friend who'd be going home tomorrow. I was sorry I'd been crabby with her.

In the morning, I found her outside sitting on our garden seat. She must have woken early to escape any more of my unpleasantries. If iron sharpened iron within friendships, I needed to stop cutting her down. 'I can't believe you're going home already.' I was ready for her to go, but sad she was leaving again.

'I know,' she said.

'I still want you to move back here.' I tried to convince myself as well as her.

'Me too.' A tear ballooned in her eye.

'Make sure you talk to your parents, okay?'

'Okay.' She nodded.

'What do you think will happen with Jason?'

'I think it's over.' She shook her head. 'He hasn't called. I haven't spoken to him for over three weeks.'

Soon after our conversation, Mum drove us to the airport. A trickle of tears escaped down my cheek as Stephanie walked into the tunnel to catch the plane. The little bit of nasty in me was glad to see her go. But seeing her misery turned something in my stomach that gave me a yearning to help her.

　　　Spiralling Out of the Shadow

Chapter Ten

'Was it good seeing your best friend again?' Peter pulled into a car park outside our local café.

'Yes and no. She's changed. She might come stay with us next year when you go to uni.'

'Can't wait to get rid of me, hey?'

'I'd rather have you around more. But ...' We ordered our drinks and found a seat. 'Pete, why do you spend so much time at Phoebe's?'

'Is this going to be one of those conversations? Perhaps you need to talk to Mum and Dad about the birds and the bees.'

'Ha ha.' I slid into a bench seat in the corner of the coffee shop. 'But Mum and Dad aren't okay with Phoebe going into your room, so why are they okay with you sleeping over at hers?'

'I'm eighteen, an adult.' He nodded to the waitress as she delivered our drinks. 'You'll get to make your own choices soon enough.'

'Do you think you'll marry her?' I sipped my hot chocolate.

'I'm way too young to make any decisions like that.'

'But you're not too young to sleep together?'

'Tabbie ...' Peter stirred three sugar sachets into his cappuccino.

'Why don't you bring her over more? I've only met her once.'

'Don't tell anyone I told you ... but she's scared of Mum and Dad.'

'Really?' A giggle escaped my lips.

'I know. Who'd be scared of our parents?'

I wondered if Mum and Dad were okay with Peter sleeping at Phoebe's, or if they'd backed off because of his age.

During the next week, Stephanie rang. Apparently, she'd had lava running through her blood and stars in her eyes. Jason had turned up and it was back on. It had barely been a week since she'd left. She had it bad. 'You're falling in love,' I told her. 'Careful, or you might break your rule.'

'Remind me about the rule.'

'Are you saying you want to?'

'I just felt this crazy urge to wrap myself around him and ...'

I held the phone loose against my ear as she raved. The way she was talking, I expected the next call to be, 'Guess what, Tabbie? ... We did it.'

'We both said we'd wait.'

'Do you think I should wait?'

'You know, Steph, I think it's what God wants us to do.' *Whoa, where did that come from?*

'What?' She laughed. 'How do you really know that?'

'I just know. Anyway, we both agreed to wait.'

'You don't think I should?'

'You have to make that decision yourself.'

'Whatever. Things change. Gotta go.'

'Bye,' I said as she hung up.

I sat on my princess doona, thinking about it for a long time after I'd hung up. It was her decision to make. I closed my eyes and focused on God. *Is staying celibate the way you really want us to be? God, if you are hearing me, could you watch out for Steph? She's changed since she moved away, and I don't know what to do about it. Thanks.*

I sat still and quiet, tracing Cinderella's hair with my finger. The strangest sense of peace spread over me, like a freshly washed

     Spiralling Out of the Shadow

white sheet. I'd never felt anything like it before. I took my calmness downstairs to the lounge room.

'Mum, can you tell me more about God?'

'Sure, love, what would you like to know?' Mum's words came out with enthusiasm.

'Guess I'll go somewhere else,' Dad mumbled as he eased his way out of his recliner.

'No, love, no need to leave the room. Tabbie and I can talk about it another time.' She nodded to me and smiled.

Dad returned to his comfy chair, ending the conversation.

Since I had to stick with dancing for the rest of the year, I decided to enjoy it, even if it wasn't my thing. 'Hey, do you still hang out with Danny?' I asked Joey at rehearsals.

'No. He's too busy with that church thing he goes to.'

'Youth group?'

'Yeah. Are you auditioning for the lead at the end of year concert?' Joey looked me in the eye and then took two steps into a split leap. His compact physique enhanced his dancing.

'Maybe.'

'You'll get it for sure.' He moved towards me, leaning in a little too close.

I looked at him out of the corner of my eye. *No way. Stop flirting, short dork!* It was the funniest attempt at flirting I've seen. Where was Jaya when I wanted to share the hilarity with her? Then I remembered Suzie's crush. Making fun of Joey would be wrong, so wrong.

Jaya stormed in while we were warming up, in an over-the-top bad mood. 'What's up your nose?' I asked.

She stretched her left leg. 'Dad just walked out.'

'What? Left your mum?'

'Yeah.'

'For good?'

'I don't know.' She changed legs and stretched again. 'It's not the first time. He's come back in the past. I just wish they'd decide. I'm so sick of their fighting.'

Now definitely wasn't the best time to be laughing about Joey.

After rehearsals, Miss Skinner called out, 'I nearly forgot. Auditions for the end-of-year concert will be held this time next week. Be on time if you want to have a go at it—including you, Jaya.'

'Whatever,' Jaya mouthed with more attitude than a kid on TV.

'You aren't going to have a go at lead?' I asked her.

'No, you can have it. I couldn't be bothered. Don't think I'll even come in next week.' Jaya paused for a moment. 'But, hey, you're dancing really well. Go for it.'

I was dancing really well. Better than ever before. Perhaps it was a blessing to have Stephanie leave when she did. By the time I reached home I was ready to take on the world and ask Mum to take me to youth group.

'I don't like leaving you here by yourself,' Mum said as she parked out the front. 'Are you sure you don't want me to come in?'

'I'll be fine. I'm sure I'll find Shelly as soon as I walk in.'

There was no way I was about to let Mum chaperone me into the building. I waved goodbye as I bumped the car door closed with my elbow. A slight tremor rolled down my spine, but I walked in anyway. My breath lodged itself on saliva in my throat, choking me. I searched each group to find Shelly, Danny, anyone. But all I saw was a fuzzy blur. I clenched my teeth, willing myself not to faint.

'Hi, is this your first time here?' A sweet voice grounded my feet and kept me upright.

My breath resumed normality, floating up and out. 'No, I've been here before.' The fuzzy blur stopped. I pushed my shoulders back, super cool once again.

'I'm Priscilla.'

'Tabbie.' I put my hand out to shake hers, but she didn't see it, so I slipped it into my pocket.

'So lovely to meet you.' Priscilla twisted her long blond waves around her fingers as she looked up to me. She was tiny.

I pulled the sweetest smile I could muster.

'Come with me. Let me introduce you to some people.'

She took me to a circle of girls. Priscilla pointed to each girl. Name after name. By the time she finished I couldn't remember who was who.

I spoke before thinking. 'I really like it here.' *Lame.*

'Yeah, it's different, hey? Sure beats going to high school parties.'

'Yeah.' I agreed, though I did like going to parties. The conversation rolled on and the subject changed. I listened, smiling and nodding, commanding my confidence to stand strong for the rest of the night.

When I saw Mum pull up out the front, I said goodbye. My cheeks ached from smiling all night.

Thankfully, Jaya arrived on time for the end-of-year concert auditions. Unfortunately, she only came to watch. Suzie stayed away. I attempted another one of Stephanie's routines. I could never master it when she was here, but now that she'd moved, I wanted to give it a go. Nerves knocked my knees together while I waited. They called my name. I braced myself, took a deep breath and put everything into it.

As soon as I'd finished, I knew I had it. I'd done it again. I'd won the lead spot. I blissfully headed home, letting go of all the issues forever surfacing in my friends' lives. I rang Stephanie to share my excitement, but she wasn't there and didn't return my call. I tried again the next night. No return call. I rang a third time to be told she was out.

Argh! Talk about frustration.

The next day when I tried yet again, her mother copped an earful. 'I've rung every day. Why isn't she returning my calls? What makes her think everything there is more important than what happens here? Just get her to ring me back, okay?' I hung up and took a deep breath, hoping there wouldn't be ramifications for my outburst.

Chapter Eleven

'Hɪ, Tᴀʙʙɪᴇ,' Sᴛᴇᴘʜᴀɴɪᴇ'ѕ ᴠᴏɪᴄᴇ ᴅʀɪᴘᴘᴇᴅ through the phone, soft and sickening.

My voice, on the other hand, boomed. 'Hey, I've been trying to ring you all week.'

'Yeah, had a lot on,' she whispered.

'You're quiet tonight.' Something told me all was not good. I had to suck it up before I lost control. 'Everything okay?'

'How are you? How's Sydney?'

Did she just ignore my question?

'Great. That's what I've been ringing you about. I'm dancing lead in the end-of-year performance, though if you were here, of course you'd have it. But I'm so excited.'

Hmm. No response. Was she even listening?

'And then there was the pink rat ... and it was doing cartwheels.' I paused. *She really isn't listening.* 'Yep. And then the orange poodle joined in, right in the middle of rehearsals last night ...' I stopped and waited.

'Yeah,' she said. *No acknowledgement whatsoever.*

'And I'm guessing you've stopped listening because there wasn't a pink rat or an orange poodle at rehearsals.' All I'd done was humour myself to stop being angry.

'Oh, sorry, Tabbie. I'm the worst friend.'

'Forget it. I'm guessing by your quiet demeanour, that you have something to tell me.'

Her deep breaths funnelled through the phone. *Oh no.* It hit me. 'You slept with him?'

'Are you annoyed with me?' she whispered.

'Why would I be annoyed?' But I kind of was. She was meant to wait. We were both going to wait.

'Disappointed?'

'No. Are you okay?'

'Yes, oh ... who am I trying to kid?'

'When, how?' She was a mess and I was a whole state away.

'Last Sunday.'

'Was it good or bad?' *Wow, now I want to know the details.*

'I don't want to talk about what happened.'

It slammed me between the eyes—what if she was pregnant? The question of contraception was so loose in my thoughts I blurted it out. 'Did you use something?'

'Like what?'

'Like a condom?'

'He had one.'

So he was prepared. I couldn't believe she'd actually done it. She really had changed. But it didn't change the fact that she was still my best friend.

My shoulders ached after talking to Stephanie. *God, what is it that makes us do crazy things?* What made me talk to God sometimes but not other times? Her news weighed me down. I wanted to ring her back and try to sort her out, but instead I changed into jeans and a T-shirt and asked Mum to take me to youth group.

Shelly stood on the edge of a group and waved to me as soon as I walked in. She dragged me around introducing me to Linda,

Penny, Ina, Mia, and Juliet. Another barrage of names turned into vapour that flew into my brain and got lost in the grey. Shelly found another group of people and introduced more names until the band played and the general flow of people traffic took us into the hall.

More words of encouragement saturated my soul that night. I'd been chosen by a greater being. I wasn't sure what continued to lure me into the youth group, but whatever it was, I wasn't fighting it. The burden, the heavy weight Stephanie had cast onto me earlier, was now lifted.

'Why don't you come on Sunday morning?' Shelly linked her arm through mine as we left the building.

'What? Come to church?'

'Yeah, it's pretty much the same as tonight, just with families and everyone else.'

'I'll think about it.' I waved goodbye and found Mum.

When my head hit the pillow, I blanked out until I was woken at midnight with an uneasy squirming in my stomach. I shuffled downstairs to pour a glass of milk. Visions of Stephanie invaded my mind. She appeared like she was in a dream, but I was standing in the kitchen, wide awake. Visions of her taking dark paths instead of following the light wouldn't leave me. The images replayed for the rest of the night while I tossed and turned.

I lay in bed on Sunday morning as slivers of light crept across my doona. Again, I thought of my absent friend. Whether Stephanie decided to move back to Sydney or not, I couldn't see us being best friends like we had been. Our relationship had morphed into more of a sisterly phase. We were taking different paths. If I thought of her as 'sister', my frustrations decreased. Holding on to this revelation, I could love her and respect her crazy choices.

I hoped my dreamy visions would never see the light of day. Stephanie would end up in an awful mess if she behaved the way she had in my dreams during the night. My quest now strengthened—I needed to be there for her.

I stretched, remembering Shelly's invitation. The warm glow that filled my insides whenever I went to youth group spread through me at the thought. Clueless as to what time the church service started, I showered, dressed, and headed out to catch a bus.

A few cars were parked out the front and the church doors were still closed. I read the transfer stuck to the glass. The service didn't start for another hour, yet music echoed out through the crack in the doorway. The door wasn't locked so I pushed it open and meandered inside to find the band doing a sound check.

When I couldn't find any familiar faces, I sat in the back row and listened to their beautiful music. It was similar, though the volume was a little softer than on Friday nights. This could very well be my home away from home. Or had I come home?

'You're here early.' Priscilla plonked herself down beside me.

'I wasn't sure of the start time.'

'Don't sit all the way back here. Let's grab a coffee and then sit a bit closer.'

The auditorium soon filled up with an overwhelmingly large crowd. My heart thudded in my chest. Danny sat two rows in front of me. I stared at the back of his head while I listened to the preacher speak of grace and favour. I didn't see Danny as I was leaving. Not that I was looking for him.

That afternoon, Stephanie interrupted my study time when she rang. 'Everything's okay. Jason's okay with not doing it again.'

'That's great, Steph.' Everything in me wanted to say: *don't believe him.*

'Are you still annoyed with me?' Stephanie's voice was almost a whimper. 'Do you think God is angry with me?'

'Are you sorry?' I asked.

'Yeah, you bet I am.'

'He's a forgiving God.' I repeated what the pastor had said that morning.

Steph sighed.

'Hey, you know that youth group I took you to?'

'Yeah,' she said, in a flat tone.

'I went to church there this morning.'

'Why?'

'Because. I really like it.'

'Did your family go?'

'No. I've made some friends there.'

'Mum reckons it's a church for those who don't have a religion.'

Hmm, no. Not really. My tongue fell hard against my teeth. 'Can I pray for you?' I hoped my offer hadn't freaked her out.

'I'm starting to think church and God are ancient and outdated anyway. But if you think it'll help me.' Stephanie giggled. 'Gotta go. Bye.'

She was amused. Good. Amused was better than being angry. I closed my eyes and took a deep breath. *Please watch over Stephanie. Keep her safe. Amen.*

A soothing warmth relaxed me as I opened my eyes. She was in unknown territory.

Catching me off guard, my green-envious-monster rose up again, wishing I had a boyfriend and hoping she'd get dumped.

With Joey as my partner for the end-of-year performance, rehearsals weren't too bad. Joey listened to my woes about Stephanie and helped me encourage Suzie. On the odd occasion when he did cross the friendship boundary, I promised him I'd land on his toes if he kept flirting. The alluring behaviour died down, and I began to trust our friendship while his toes remained unbruised.

There was nothing quite like the thrill of running towards Joey full pelt, to do a lift. Instead of just going straight up into an aeroplane flying position, I was to go up, pause, then slink over his back like a snake, grab his waist turning my body inside out to flip, spin, twirl, and land on my feet right in front of him. After a million run-throughs, we were sure we'd perfected it. Every time I jumped my blood rushed, sending me into a natural high. From every angle in the wall mirror, we looked fantastic.

'I can't wait to tell Steph. She'll be so impressed.'

'Just concentrate, or you might land on your head.' Joey laughed.

'Ha ha.' I faked a belly laugh, grabbing for my stomach.

'Okay.' Miss Skinner clapped her hands. 'One last time through tonight and we're done.'

The music started. I knew every step so well, I could have done the dance in my sleep. Run full pelt, spring, rise, lean, grab, flip, spin and ... ouch!

Ker-thump.

'Argh!'

'What happened?' Joey turned and rushed towards me.

'Stupid! Stupid! Stupid!' I curled up on the floor, rocking, holding my leg and foot.

'What did I do?' he asked.

'Me ... stupid! I've twisted my ankle.'

It was bad. Emergency room bad. Swollen to the shape of a soccer ball bad. Gulping back tears bad.

Chapter Twelve

Dr Frank scratched his head and readjusted his glasses. He turned from the X-ray and spoke to Mum and Dad, leaving me on the examination bed like a little child. Torn ligaments and a slight fracture. I needed to keep off it as much as possible with orders not to dance until it healed.

I rested on the loungeroom couch, stuffing my face with chocolate while watching old movies with a box of tissues. Stephanie rang just before ten that night, sounding over-the-moon-happy. 'I just had dinner with Jason's family.'

'Are they nice?' I asked.

'They're a little strange. They didn't talk. We ate dinner in silence.'

'How did you cope with that?'

'Silently.' Stephanie giggled.

'Why are you so happy?' I couldn't help but laugh with her.

'Because his parents leave tomorrow.'

Oh no, warning ... warning.

'Careful.' She was entering a danger zone.

'Why?'

'He'll be home alone?'

'With his brother,' she said.

'Temptation might get the better of you.' *Oh, Lord, help her.*

'Don't be crazy. I'll be fine.'

As if. She needed help. 'I've stuffed my left ankle,' I said, rearranging the bandage.

'No way! How?'

I told her. She seemed glazed-over-distracted, disinterested. But I continued, trying to keep my mind off her relationship with Jason.

I did as I was told and kept my foot up and my head planted in school books until my hands were sore from writing and typing mid-semester assessments. I didn't have time to check up on Stephanie, and she hadn't called. Probably too focused on Jason. My focus right now was school. I looked forward to youth group. Danny and all the other good-looking boys could tempt other girls' eyes while I wore blinkers.

When I got the guilts and rang Stephanie a week later, all she could talk about was Jason this, Jason that. She told me she was keeping things cool, but it seemed pretty obvious their relationship was hot and steamy. With a crutch in one hand and the phone in the other, I paced backwards and forwards along the walkway into the kitchen. I turned on the kettle to distract myself. When the kettle whistled, I said goodbye and banged the crutches into the doorway as I moved to the kitchen. I poured the boiling water into my teacup too fast, splashing the bench and steaming my hand.

'Argh!' I flipped on the cold water tap to cool the burn. It was minor. Only pink. But when I pulled it away from the cold water it stung again.

I wanted to talk to Mum to tell her about all the crazy decisions my best friend was making. But I couldn't invade Stephanie's privacy and break the best friend code. She wasn't the only one making crazy decisions. So I prayed and kept her confidences.

I hobbled around, balancing on crutches, trying to carry my bag, trying to do everything with aching armpits. *Stupid crutches. Dumb ankle. Dumb dance. It was never my thing. Why was I even dancing lead? Was I trying to be like Stephanie? Was I trying to be Stephanie?*

No way!

Oh, boy. I hated self-realisation.

I thought I was dancing because I wanted to hang out with my ridiculously beautiful and definitely not perfect best friend. But now it smacked me between the eyeballs. I was actually trying to *be* her. *How could I? How could I have spent years trying to be just like my best friend?*

Study and crutches made the rest of the term torture. I needed to burn off some frustrated energy. Mum agreed to drop me at the aquatic centre. It was close enough to walk if I wasn't on crutches.

Leaving the crutches to the side, I hopped to the ladder and climbed in. While I pulled my arms through the water and let my legs float along, my ankle didn't hurt. There, in the water, was freedom. I could be me. No Stephanie, no Suzie, no Jaya, no Joey, and no Danny. After three sets of ten laps, the thump of my heart echoed in my ears. I clutched the pool edge and caught my breath. When I reached the ladder, Mum was holding my towel.

'Thanks. I really needed that swim.'

Apart from a couple of assignments lurking, the school holidays brought a blissful change of pace. I handed the crutches back in and walked with a slight limp. The doctor urged me to keep off my left foot as much as possible for another week. I knew as soon as it healed, I'd be expected to return to dance classes.

'Mum, I really don't want to keep dancing. I know you've paid for the year but—'

'That's a shame, love. But if that's what you want.'

'Are you annoyed with me?'

'You said a while back you weren't enjoying it. I'd rather you be honest with me. Maybe that's why you twisted your ankle.'

'No, I just made a mistake.' I flexed my foot to stretch.

'But you were doing something you weren't enjoying.'

I nodded. 'But I was enjoying that dance. I think I just got overconfident.'

'You can stop, if you like. We won't force you to finish the year.'

'Really?'

She nodded.

'Thanks, Mum.' She was such a treasure. I had great parents—which made me think of Stephanie. Hers didn't seem as nice.

'Hi, Steph, how are you going?'

'I'm dreading my report card.'

'Not going well?'

'I've been distracted.'

'Distracted? Jason, I bet.' Here goes. Another trip around the mountain.

'He's away with his mates this week. I really miss him.'

'I'm sure you do.' I sighed, pulling my hair out of an elastic. 'Have you got round to talking to your parents about coming down here next year?'

'I did bring up moving back, but Mum shrugged me off, telling me I'd eventually find friends here. As if! Mum suggested you come up and stay the week before Christmas. Can you? You can meet

Jason. He can't wait to meet you. You'll see how amazing he is. He's the perfect boy —'

'We're going to our unit on the Central Coast that week. Steph, are you going to ask them, or should I tell Mum and Dad it's not going to happen?' I cringed at my spiteful tone. But I'd had enough of her going on and on about Jason. Talk about being obsessed.

It took everything in me to stop willing them to break up. I was happy to see Stephanie no longer depressed, but I was sure he wasn't the right guy for her. Maybe I just needed to meet him.

After swimming laps again at the local pool, my energy fluttered like a butterfly. I was keen to go out for the night. I'd sat at home for long enough. 'Hey, Mum. Jaya wants me to go to a party with her tonight.'

She frowned at me. 'Your father and I are concerned after the last few parties you've been to.'

'But you also know I'm the responsible one.' She had a point. *Do I really want to clean Jaya up again?*

'As long as you stay that way.'

'Of course.' I smiled and hoped I wouldn't regret tagging along with Jaya.

The party was at a friend of a friend of a friend's house. Jaya didn't even know who they were. She'd stuffed her backpack with cheap wine coolers.

'Did you have to bring so much?'

'I'll share some with you.'

'You know I don't.' I raised my eyebrows.

She shrugged.

I'd brought a bottle of candy soft drink and was ready for my sugar high. Jaya downed her coolers in record time, turning her face a strange shade of green. I was back on duty and left the soft drink to rest in the bag. I found a facecloth in a drawer while she found the toilet. After each spew, I wiped her chin, her cheeks. *Gross!*

'Jaya, you're disgusting.' I could say anything to her. There was no way she'd remember tomorrow.

I pushed my way through the party to the kitchen. Thankfully the coffee jar was on the bench next to the jug. I scooped two heaped spoons of instant powder into a cup, filled it with boiling water and pushed the spoon through it a couple of times. Slapping her cheek gently to snap her back to life, I fed her the thick brew. She kept drifting off.

'Jaya!' My attempt to keep her awake failed. This time I was ringing her parents. 'Mr Range?'

'Yes?'

'Jaya's not feeling so good. Could you come and pick us up?'

'Not at the moment. I have my hands full.'

Mrs Range's phone was turned off.

'Jaya, what do you want me to do?'

Silence. Scary non-responsive silence. Like, if it was the first time, it wouldn't have bothered me so much, but we'd been there before. And I didn't like playing nurse.

A trickle of drool rolled onto her chin. 'Geez, Jaya! I'd rather not ring Mum and Dad. They were already concerned about me coming out tonight. But if I don't, we're stuck here.'

'Don't worry, sweetheart.' A stray Mr Macho walking by stopped and gave me a sly grin. 'I'm staying in a room upstairs. You're welcome to sleep over. I'll share my sleeping bag.'

Eww. Gross.

'Jaya, we have to get out of here.' I looked into her backpack and found her purse. A twenty dollar note peeked through the folds. *Good.* I had some cash too. Enough to get us home.

'Just try to stand for me.' I shook her and tried to pull her to her feet, but she was a dead weight. I looked to the sky, almost ready to abandon hope when she leant forward a little. I pulled again and

          Spiralling Out of the Shadow

she rocked up onto her feet leaning on my shoulder. The two of us shuffled outside where I ordered a taxi.

We arrived back at Jaya's house to hear the kind of noises I didn't want to hear coming from her parents' bedroom. *Flip!* I had to get out of there. I pulled out my phone and rang Mum.

'Are you ready to come home already? I thought you were staying the night.'

'So did I, but I don't feel comfortable, it's ... I just want to get out of here.'

'Be there in ten minutes, love.'

I tucked Jaya into bed fully clothed, making sure she was lying on her side, with a bucket nearby. Then I left.

Chapter Thirteen

I sat heavy on the couch, weighing up whether to call Jaya or not. Her father's attitude and the details of last night plagued my thoughts. What would I say? Was your mum home last night? Because, well, I heard them … If it wasn't your mum, who was it? Who wanted to hear that?

As I rubbed the dead skin peeling off my finger from the steam burn, the phone rang. *Stephanie.* Jason had gone overseas for three months. 'So did you break up?' It seemed the obvious question.

'Why would we?'

Just hoping. 'Did he ask you to pine after him while he's away? Did he tell you he would stay faithful?'

'No. Neither. Why?'

Thoughts of Jaya's parents and what I'd heard wouldn't leave me.

'Aren't you scared it won't last over the holidays?'

'No. He said we'd be okay to start where we left off when he comes back. He's hoping to get into university in Sydney. So if I move to Sydney ...'

'Didn't he say Sydney, or Melbourne? Anyway, you know how big Sydney is.' With all those uni girls swimming around him like fish, did Stephanie really think he'd still want her?

'Meh.'

I had to let it go and let her live her own life. 'Hey, you won't believe what Jaya did to me.'

'Sorry, Tabbie. I have to go. Mum's yelling something.'

Before I could finish, she'd hung up.

'Argh!' *No worries, Steph. I'll listen to everything you have going on. I'll listen to all your dramas. But hey, don't worry about me, everything's fine. Let's not bother you with anything outside your little world.*

How had my best friend become just as demanding as Jaya since she moved to another city? Where did that leave me?

Inhaling deeply three times, I held the last breath and looked to the ceiling. *Shelly.* I hadn't seen her since I'd been on crutches. It would be good to see her again. Now the crutches were gone, I'd be able to move around without tripping someone up at youth group.

I needed to get out and burn some energy. Was Stephanie really planning to follow Jason? What if he went to Melbourne? Would she follow him there? My stomach pulled to a knot. I needed to stop the ember igniting into a full-blown fire inside me. I'd give anything to run and pound the concrete for a while, then pummel my feet into the grass around the oval. But my ankle was still too weak. I grabbed my swimmers and towel, kissed Mum goodbye and caught the next bus to the indoor pool.

Changeroom lights are the worst. I knew I look like a pear, but seriously, why would they put full length mirrors with bulge-illuminating lights in changerooms? I took one quick look to make sure all the important bits were covered, dumped my bag of clothes into a locker and threw my towel over my shoulder. *Churning pit of frustration, get ready to be burned off.*

Ropes fenced off the shallow end where kids clung to kickboards with instructors correcting their style. The centre lanes were filled with seasoned swimmers lapping each other.

I dropped my towel onto an empty chair and dipped my toes into the water. The chill sent goose bumps up my thunder thighs. Wasn't this pool meant to be heated? Shivering from the cold water on my toes, I walked towards the ladder to elegantly lower myself into the water. I glanced across the pool ... *Danny?* Blinking, I looked again. He lifted his hand to give me a slight wave.

My toes caught the drainage grid on the edge of the pool, jarring my body to a halt. I reached for the handrail, grabbed it with one hand, but slipped. Stupid shiny thing hadn't helped me in any way. I face-planted into the pool, my stomach slapping across the lane ropes. Willing myself to die, I pretended I hadn't seen Danny and faced the other direction.

It would've been pointless to climb out. Everyone in the entire swimming complex had fixed their eyes on me. I ducked underwater.

When I came up for a breath, Danny stood right in front of me, dripping. He still looked ridiculously like Mr Biceps, only slightly smaller. Perhaps he hadn't seen my klutzy move? I could live in denial.

What, in the name of love, was I even thinking about Danny for? And why was I here? To burn off the aggro-at-my-best-friend energy. I needed to swim so I could be the best friend I'd always been.

With cheeks still burning I found a vacant lane and swam. Face down. Freestyle. Breathing every eighth stroke to keep my face in the water as long as possible. I punched every stroke. Angry at Steph. Angry at me. Angry at the world.

After ten laps, every stroke became more like a paddle. A paddle downstream. A paddle to dry land. A paddle to kindness. To love my best friend. To get to know more people like Shelly and Priscilla. To make an effort to go back to youth group. I hadn't been for over a month. My muscles soon tired and I took breaths every second stroke. I'd released the anger. A sense of peace and calm washed through me. I swam back to the ladder and climbed out.

He was sitting right in front of me, holding my towel in his hands. Hands attached to the ends of his arms. His arms with those biceps. *Danny.*

    Spiralling Out of the Shadow

'Hi,' he said, glancing at me then back to the pool.

'Thanks.' I ripped my towel out of his hands and quickly wrapped it around my body to hide my thighs, thankful he'd kept his eyes focused on my face. 'You waiting for something?'

'Yeah, just catching my breath after laps. I was about to head off.' He stood. Our eyes locked on a level horizontal gaze.

'Oh.' I pulled a little tighter on my security towel.

'Well, I guess I'll see you around sometime.'

'I guess.' I raised my eyebrows.

That boy was so flipping weird. Sure, he had the looks of Mr Biceps, but he was seriously nerdish to the point of being weird. I shuddered as we peeled off in opposite directions, him towards the door and me towards the changerooms. My left ankle had already ballooned again. Shades of purple streaked the sides, but I refused to resort to crutches.

I hobbled my way around for the last few weeks of the school year. My perseverance was spent. Every spare moment I had my head down and ankle up.

Jaya seemed more messed up every day. That bothered me. I had a feeling she was sneaking drinks out of her parents' alcohol fridge. She said her parents were fine and they'd sorted out their differences.

Suzie retreated, becoming quieter by the day. That bothered me as well. Her parents pulled her out of everything except school. I wracked my brain, searching for a way to help her, but came up with nothing every time.

At least my end-of-year results were the best they'd ever been. Thanks to a stuffed ankle.

Chapter Fourteen

On the first day of Christmas holidays, the sun streamed through my window, waking me up early. I swam some laps, packed, and ate breakfast before Peter even showed his face.

It was the first night he'd slept in his bed for months. He told us it was so he didn't have to wake up extra early. But I had a feeling something had happened between him and Phoebe.

'Is that all you're taking?' Mum glared at my small roller bag.

'Sure. Three swimsuits, towel, pyjamas, strapping tape, and a novel. What else do I need? I'm chillaxing this holiday.'

'Guess you deserve to relax. You did work hard this semester.'

'Tabbie.' Dad shuffled on the spot. 'Can you wake Peter up? It's a long drive. We should get going early.'

I rumble-knocked with both hands on his door as hard as I could. 'Up, up, up. Family journey starting now. Get up, get up, we're leaving town. Come on. Up, up, up!' *Dr Seuss, eat your heart out.*

'Seriously, Tabbie.' He pulled the door open, rubbing his eyes and squinting. 'Way too perky for this time of day.'

It took him another half an hour to sort his things before we piled into the family car to head to Terrigal on the Central Coast. When we entered the apartment a few hours later, I flung open the balcony doors to see the ocean. We were close enough to check out all the hot boys. The only annoying part was that—I had to share a bedroom with Peter—a serious snorer!

'Are you really going to have a sleep?' I asked as Peter fell onto the bed. 'We just got here. It's beach time.'

'Sleep,' Peter mumbled. 'More sleep.'

Leaving him on the bed, I found my cutest red bikini and slipped into the bathroom to change. Then I strapped my ankle to keep it from further damage while walking on the sand.

'Do you have a beach cover or something, love?' Dad looked up from the paper as I walked through the unit.

'Yeah, this.' I wrapped my towel around my waist. He had a point. I didn't need to show off my thighs. 'Need to get a tan. I'm so anaemically powdery white.'

'Do it gradually, love.' Mum stood in the doorway. 'How about I rub some sunscreen in before you head out?'

I had no choice but to accept the sunscreen application before leaving for the beach.

Day one: expectation of meeting Mr Dream-Boy—high.

But the beach was bare. Everyone must have stayed home, out of the wind. The sand kicked up, stinging my legs as I searched for a spot to lie. Just when I found the perfect position, my towel wouldn't stay flat until I lay on it. Within minutes, another gust came and the sting of sand pitted into my skin, gluing itself to the sunscreen. Not comfortable at all. Sand-coated Tabbie was definitely not the look I was hoping to achieve.

I stretched my ankle backward and forward a couple of times before I jumped up. My towel blew over and over, rolling down the beach until I caught it and pushed half of it under a pile of sand. I jogged towards the surf, jumping over the small curls of water until it was deep enough to swim past the wave break.

I bobbed up and down on the ocean side of the crashing waves, watching in case any interesting people arrived on the beach. No hot boys, but plenty of interesting people. A large man with an overhanging stomach stood knee-deep watching kids in full sunsuits splash in the shallows. Over-weathered women power-walked on the hard wet sand.

Perhaps tomorrow would bring some hot boys.

We ate dinner together, then Mum pulled out a trivia game. Peter, the brother of all trivial knowledge, blitzed it and won the game before I had a chance to get any questions right.

I was over it and pushed my chair out. 'I've had enough family fun. I'm off to read a book in bed.'

'Or look out the window to check out the boys,' Peter called after me.

'As if!' I called back without looking. My face glowed. *How did he know?*

But that's exactly what I'd planned to do. I took in the fantastic view from our window. With my novel open on my lap, I sat on my bed, leaning against the window, watching everything that happened on the street. Not much. And again, no hot boys.

'See, I knew you'd be perving on someone.' Peter sprung me with my forehead on the window.

'Just people-watching.'

'When are you going to get a boyfriend?'

'They're way too much trouble. I'll just dream about the "one day when" of having one for a bit longer.' I smiled. An image of Danny flashed in my mind. With a few rapid blinks, I cleared it away. 'What's happening with Phoebe anyway?'

'I don't know. We want different things.'

'Does she want to get married?'

'Yeah.' Peter shook his head.

'And you don't?'

'Nah, no way. Not yet.'

'But what if she was the one?' I closed my book.

        Spiralling Out of the Shadow

'I'm way too young to even think about it.'

'Then I guess she is, too.'

'Yeah.' Peter looked away with glassy eyes.

'You love her though, don't you?'

'Yeah, I do. It's hard to stop loving someone.'

'So what's the problem?'

'I know we shouldn't be together.' Peter lay on his bed. 'She doesn't want to go to uni, or come with me to Melbourne next year. Best we call it off now. Who knows? Maybe after a break we'll work it out again.'

'Why don't you have a long-distance relationship? Stephanie and Jason are staying together while he's overseas and then—'

'Long distance relationships don't work.'

'Why not?'

'You'll understand in a few years.' He shrugged and pulled out his phone.

Maybe he was right. But why was Jason okay with distance instead of taking a break and Peter wasn't? Relationships were way too confusing. Staying single was best for me.

Day two: after breakfast, the beach called me again. The wind had calmed. From the balcony, the sun reflected off the sand, showing sure signs of the day being a scorcher. I slipped out the door before Mum could plaster me with sunscreen. This time I decided a jog before a swim would be more fun. That way I could check out the surfer boys further up the beach.

I took my time to jog a fair distance, concentrating on keeping my ankle from rolling. My heart began to pound and sweat dripped down my back, so I entered the water to cool off. There were some fine-looking boys out on boards. Possibly a little old for me, but nonetheless, they were enough to get me dreaming about one day when I'd meet Mr Wonderful.

I lay on my towel and pulled out my novel. The sun warmed my brain into a groggy haze, urging me to close my eyes. I gave in, dropped my book and drifted off, dreaming about my 'one day when' Mr Wonderful, who looked a lot like Mr Biceps but even more like Danny. He swept me off my feet and took me off into the sunset to live an incredibly wonderful, expansive, and luxurious life.

'Tabbie!' Peter's voice woke me. 'Tabbie, you've been down here for hours.'

'Oh ... must have fallen asleep.'

'Your back.' He gasped.

'Is it bad?' I didn't need to ask. It stung as I rolled over.

'You'll need some aloe vera on that tonight.'

'Ice, I think I need some ice right now.' Major pain shot through my body every time I moved.

Mum and Dad told me off as I walked into our apartment. That night, I tossed and turned, pulling the sheet up then throwing it off again. It had to be third degree burns. My clothes clung to all the sorest spots.

Day three: I asked Peter to turn the air conditioning on. I didn't want to get out of bed. I had no intention to leave the apartment until my sunburn had calmed down.

After lunch, I was bored out of my brain and rang Stephanie. She still hadn't told me whether or not she was going to move back to Sydney. I was sick of waiting.

'Steph, do you want to move back or not?' I probably could have at least spent some time on the niceties.

'I thought you were going away this week?'

'We are. I'm on the balcony overlooking the beach ...' A group of boys distracted me. 'Just checking out the hot boys.'

'Tabbie!' She laughed like I'd said something completely hilarious.

'Tell me. Have you spoken to your parents yet?' I gritted my teeth as the sun hit my burns, and I retreated back into the air-conditioning.

'I did ask, but my timing was lousy—again!' Stephanie said. 'I'll ask again this week—promise.'

Whatever, Steph. My brain heated up like it was sunburnt too. Maybe she didn't want to move back. I'd just have to get over it. I'd built a fantasy in my mind with Stephanie back in Sydney and I'd grown to expect it to happen.

For the rest of the week, the unit became my hideaway. My back came up in blisters that stung when they burst, leaving patchy red and white skin. Not attractive. Definitely not what I'd choose to take into public.

My mood was as fiery as my burns. I yearned for three things. A best friend I could rely on. Like the one I'd had for years, before the Stronges left town. A hot 'one day when' boyfriend. And a fit, healthy, toned, to-die-for body. Was that too much to ask for?

Peter bought me some magazines to flick through while my burns were settling down. They were filled with who was dating who in the land of Hollywood, where all the beautiful people lived. Yes, that's where everyone starts beautiful and ends beautiful.

I closed my eyes, resting the magazine on my chest. Hollywood became my home. I had the hottest boyfriend, the hottest body, and I was adored by all. I awoke with a vile acidic taste swirling in my mouth and reached for my water bottle.

I had to shake off the dream. Those pictures don't portray the truth. We only see what the stars willingly reveal and what the media wants us to see. We don't see them with third-degree burns because they hide away just like I was hiding away. If I had a personal trainer, chef, and a glamour entourage, I'd look that good.

Why was I attracted to good looks? My 'one day when' boyfriend had to have more going for him than just looks. Danny ... now, he had Mr Biceps' looks but was such a dork. Jason, Stephanie's amazing boyfriend, was good-looking—so she'd told me—yet she seemed to be a mess most of the time.

Where was the balance?

My sunburn had calmed by the end of our holiday and my mood had cooled as well. I rang Stephanie. 'Hey, sorry I was kinda cranky the other day.'

'You don't say.'

'I got really sunburnt. Dumb, hey?'

'Yeah.'

'I really want you to move back to Sydney. This year has been pretty crappy without you around.'

Silence. She didn't even breathe.

'Steph?'

'Nothing. Well, I haven't heard from Jason or anything, and I guess I should move on, but I just don't want to.' Her voice wavered. 'I'm such a mess.'

'Please talk to your parents about coming to live with us. See what they say.'

'Okay,' she whispered.

'I hope you have a nice Christmas if I don't speak to you before then.'

'Sure.'

I returned to youth group. It was fresh and new and even more exciting than what I'd remembered.

The friends I had made through the youth group weren't replacing Steph. They just filled a void. I still hoped she'd return.

Chapter Fifteen

'I'M COMING.' STEPHANIE'S VOICE boomed through the phone.

'What? Where?' I asked. She hadn't even said hello.

'To Sydney, next week, if it's still okay.'

'Of course it is.' My Christmas wish was about to come true. I hung up and tried to gather my spinning head. I hoped Mum and Dad would still be okay with Stephanie staying with us. It hadn't come up in conversation for a while.

Thankfully, they were.

'Do you think we could use your old doona cover for Steph? Would that be okay?' Mum asked.

'I don't think Strawberry Shortcake would be right for her. She screws her face up when she comes into my room. She hates little girl things. Remember, Steph is sophisticated and elegant. Can we buy some new things?'

'Why not?' Mum smiled, waving her hands in the air.

I could have jumped over the moon at Mum's enthusiasm. She even seemed a little more relaxed. Steph arriving was something to distract her from the fact that Peter was about to move interstate.

The next day, Mum and I stood in the driveway and waved them off. Dad drove Peter's rusty hatchback, loaded with clothes and sports memorabilia that looked like junk but was precious to Peter. The plan was for Dad to stay in Melbourne until Peter was unpacked, then check out some cricket and whatever other sport they could find and then fly back next week.

Mum and I jumped head first into playing interior decorators. We searched the internet for ideas then traipsed from one home decor shop to another. We came up with a fresh, sleek look using shabby chic furniture with clean lines. Our approach was to create a minimalist yet warm room, so Stephanie would get nothing but excellent school results.

After we sorted out the room, I spent a few hours getting crafty. Using my primary school creative talent, I found old paint, glitter, and some streamers in the cupboard. The result was an eye-catching welcome home poster. I knew Steph would be more than embarrassed if I made a dodgy one, so she got the best. It looked almost professional. So much so, I wondered why I hadn't taken art as a subject.

Mum and I stood a couple of metres back from the doorway in the arrivals lounge. People streamed past us. Mum held one side of the poster as we flapped it in the air. We laughed at the serious people who shook their heads at us.

Stephanie walked down the tunnel like she was on a cloud.

She cried.

I cheered.

The poster fell to the floor.

I wrapped my arms around her and we happy-danced while Mum picked up the poster. 'I can't believe you're really here!'

'I know, I know,' Stephanie said as she kissed Mum on the cheek.

'We've fixed up your room already. You're going to love it!' I said.

Stephanie's smile wilted. Maybe she didn't trust my decorating skills. Little did she know.

I climbed into the backseat with her and whispered, 'Have you heard from Jason? Is he back?'

'No.' She stared through the front windscreen.

'Maybe it's for the best.' I knew it was a lame comment. I wished I hadn't said it.

Stephanie's chin jutted forward, her focus unwavering.

I wanted to say, *come on Steph, you're here with your old friends now. You'll be fine.* 'You didn't really think it would last forever, did you?' spilled from my mouth instead.

'Guess that's what I was hoping.'

I had to help her move on. *Quickly.* And control the words jumping out of my mouth. 'Everyone is going to be so happy you're back! School just hasn't been the same.'

She mumbled something I couldn't quite make out.

'Did you get your classes sorted?' I asked.

'Yeah. I couldn't get into all the subjects I wanted. Some were full. Are you going to get a part-time job this year?'

A job? I was talking about school. 'Mum and Dad aren't pushing me to get one. I'll see how I go.'

'I worked over the holidays. I loved it. I'd rather work,' she said.

'No way, Steph. You've got to finish school and go to uni.'

'What if I don't want to go?' Stephanie said. 'I can't think of anything I want to do that needs a degree.'

'At least finish school so you get some qualifications. You used to want to dance and perform and get your Bachelor of Fine Arts.'

'I've changed. I told you I don't want to dance anymore.'

'I thought that was just because you were in Toowoomba.'

'No. No more dancing.'

She had said it several times to me over the last year, but surely that would change now she was back. I looked her up and down. It was like she was trying to be someone else. I knew all too well what chasing someone else's dream looked like. I glanced at her. Had she become someone else?

'I'm going to look for a job,' Stephanie said in a low voice.

We drove the rest of the way in silence.

When we arrived home, I grabbed Stephanie by the hand and pulled her upstairs to see her new room. She walked through slowly, looking over every detail before she pulled open the curtains. She turned, running her hand along the fresh doona and cushions, then sat in the new chair at her desk.

'Thank you, Tabbie.' Stephanie pushed herself out of the chair and hugged me with a little tremble. When we parted, tears were swelling in her eyes.

'You're welcome, but I didn't do it by myself. I kind of pointed Mum in the right direction and helped put it together.'

Once we'd brought all her luggage inside, Stephanie demanded we go for a walk to our local shops. She found a dodgy shop-slash-café that was hiring part-time juniors. Her eagerness to jump at the opportunity to work a trial shift that night tripped me up. I'd assumed she'd want to get settled into school before she went off searching for work. But I was wrong.

'Hey Mum, what's for dinner?' I was starving by the time we arrived home.

Mum smiled, pointing to the chicken in the oven.

'Mm.' Saliva gushed into my mouth. I could've eaten the whole roast chicken, but it wasn't quite ready.

'Where did you girls disappear to?'

'Steph wants to work at some dodgy place down on Mainland Road.'

'I've got a trial. Tonight.' Stephanie glared at me. 'And it's not dodgy.'

'Are you sure you want to get a job straight away?' Mum lifted the saucepan lid and stirred the veggies. 'You don't have to. We're happy to help with any costs the government youth allowance doesn't cover. Why don't you settle into school and see how you go?'

'I just want to see what it's like. I won't take the job if it's horrible.'

'Let me drive you, then. I don't like the idea of you walking around on your own at night.'

I spent the night in my room, sorting through my desk to start the year fresh. I dreamed of having a job and all the new clothes I could buy. Maybe Stephanie had the right idea, and I was wasting time.

The next day, the owner of the shop rang Stephanie. I waited nearby for her to finish the call. 'Did you get the job?'

'Yep.' She began to walk away.

'Did you get the hours you wanted?' I asked.

'More.'

'More? Like?' I asked.

'Like ... twice what I hoped for.'

'How are you going to manage school working that many hours?' I dipped my eyebrows until my vision blurred.

'I told you I hate school. I'd rather work.'

'Since when do you hate school? Didn't you just hate the school in Toowoomba? Now you're back at Hill Top, that'll all change. You'll see.'

Her sarcastic smile could have cracked cement.

'Hey, I'm going to youth group this Friday night. Want to come with me?'

'No, thanks. I'll be working.' Stephanie walked into the kitchen and turned the kettle on.

I followed. 'Can't you take the night off?'

'I can't ask for time off in my first week. Tea?'

'Love one.' I knew she was trying to distract me, but I continued anyway. 'What if you give them some notice? Can you come with me next week or the week after?'

'They'd probably tell me to get another job if I try to take a Friday night off.'

'That sounds like a great idea. There are heaps of other jobs available.'

'Okay, okay. I'll look for another job in a couple of weeks.'

I hoped she would. I was beginning to see that I couldn't force her to do anything she didn't want to do. It was good to see a smidgen of her confidence return.

     Spiralling Out of the Shadow

Chapter Sixteen

SCHOOL RETURNED WITH A BANG. Well, as much of a bang as you'd expect in a private all-girls school. On the first day, we were shown no grace. It was straight into assessments with due dates.

'Don't expect a free ride this year. If you want to get into uni, you'll have to work your tails off,' was the message from our welcome-back assembly. I had assignments for three subjects due way too close to ignore. More work than I wanted to do, but I couldn't get out of it.

During the first few weeks, I couldn't fathom how Steph kept up. She worked late nearly every night. I was already in bed when she got home, yet somehow, she managed to get to school and be organised.

Just as I was finishing my homework, Steph ran in. 'Tabbie, Tabbie, he's back. Mum called. Jason's back.'

No way! He was meant to be out of her life. 'I thought you were moving on. He can't neglect to call you for nearly three months and expect you to hang around for him.'

'He dropped by Mum and Dad's yesterday and asked for my number.' Stephanie bounced on my bed like a pre-schooler.

'Steph, careful.'

'Why?'

'Just be careful. I don't want to see you getting hurt.' Like in the major tears and dark depression kind of way.

'Jason would never hurt me. He's just really bad at keeping in touch when he's away. But now he's back—'

'Steph, he's in Toowoomba, and you're here in Sydney. Remember? Your hometown.'

'I guess.'

Her face glazed over. I'd burst her bubble. My comment had cut her deep. I wondered how I could smooth over the blow.

But that little piece of nasty in me almost delighted in seeing her miserable. *Where on Earth does it come from?* I detested it. I did want her to be happy. Yet in all of her elegant and sophisticated beauty, she was a mess when it came to Jason. I left for youth group appalled at my own behaviour. I was nasty. Stephanie was hurting. It wasn't something to delight over.

While engaged in reading my Biology textbook, our ringing landline snapped me out of a trance.

'Hello.'

'Hi, is Stephanie there?' A male voice. *Oh no, I hope it isn't Jason.*

'She's sleeping. Can I take a message?' I smiled, trying to keep my voice pleasant but I knew a narky tone had already slipped in.

'It's Jason. Can you get her to ring me?'

'Umm ...' I could hear water running upstairs. Steph was up, but I didn't want to let him know. The nasty Tabbie monster reared its face again.

'Don't worry about it. I'll call her back later.'

     Spiralling Out of the Shadow

No rush, I wanted to tell him. But all I said was, 'Okay.'

'Jason just rang,' I told Stephanie when she came downstairs.

'Why didn't you come and get me?'

'I thought you were still asleep. He can ring back. You've got to make him chase you after what he's put you through.'

'Did he say he'd ring back?' Stephanie checked her fingernails.

'He said he'd call back later. Don't worry about him. Let's go see a movie.' I was ready to take the night off schoolwork. 'Mum and Dad have gone out to some work dinner.'

'Is there something we can watch on TV?'

'Nothing's on.' I'd already checked. 'And you know we don't have streaming.'

'What about a video?'

'Sure, but we don't have much here. Mum cleaned them out.'

Steph started shuffling through the DVDs piled under the TV and asked if we could watch an oldie.

'You're hoping he'll ring back right now, aren't you?'

She grinned.

We watched old movies with Stephanie glancing at the phone every few minutes. Jason didn't call. It seemed Jason had edged his way back into Stephanie's life before we were able to restore our best-friendness.

I woke up the next day still stewing over Steph and Jason and how my best friend had changed. I had to get used to it. After climbing out of bed and turning on the shower, I let the hot water wake me up until I was interrupted by someone knocking.

'Are you going to be long?' Stephanie stumbled over her words as she spoke quickly. 'I've got to get to work.'

'Be out in a minute.'

With my hair still full of shampoo, I turned the tap on a little harder and tussled my fingers through until the suds dissipated. Then I rubbed through some conditioner, shutting off the water before rinsing. *A treatment, perhaps?*

'Shower is free,' I called before I was ready to leave the bathroom—only to find my rushing had been wasted. 'Oh. You're already dressed.'

'Yeah. Why were you in the shower so early?'

'Church. You're off to work?'

'Yep, bye. Got to go.' Steph skipped down the stairs.

I continued to get dressed, pulling my conditioned hair back in a tucked-under ponytail. A spurt of steam grew inside. She could have told me not to rush. I should have stayed in there until I rinsed out the conditioner. With a quick glance at the timetable, I discovered I could make a two-minute dash to catch the next bus.

'You don't look your usual bubbly self today.' Shelly greeted me when I arrived.

'Yeah?' I still had half-washed hair and Steph on my mind.

'Come on in. I'm sure you'll feel better after the service.'

The music began and the lighting dulled. Peace rested on my shoulders and the tension fell away. I sat with Shelly, Priscilla and a few other girls who were including me in their lives. They were always inviting me to join them when they met up through the week. Until now, hanging out with them twice a week had been enough to boost me through everything else going on.

'Would you like to join us for lunch?' Shelly asked after church.

It would mean I didn't have to face Stephanie for a bit longer. I could always get my assignments done later. 'Sure.'

They took me to their favourite coffee shop, which was within walking distance of the church. Conversations flowed from living a fulfilling life to the freedom they had with Jesus. There weren't any discussions about parties or boyfriends or school. My whole perspective began to change. I started to see the lack of control I'd had over the little green-eyed monster that dwelled within me. How had I become so self-centred? When did that happen?

Shelly dropped me home a few hours later. I settled onto the couch for an afternoon chat with Mum, but was interrupted when the landline rang.

'Stephanie, it's for you,' Mum called.

Stephanie raced down the stairs like she'd been anticipating the call. Mum handed the phone to Stephanie and left the room. Stephanie's face bloomed. This time I made a conscious effort to keep my green-eyed monster in check.

'Yeah, I've missed you too.' With a wide smile, her voice took on a fresh tone.

I waved, trying to get her attention. I don't know why, but I wanted confirmation that it was Jason. She answered my question by turning away from me.

'I don't know when I'll get back to Toowoomba. I'm really busy. I've got a job.'

I knew I should stop listening. But I lingered, urging myself to leave the room.

'Yeah, I'm back at my old school. It is good being around my friends again.' She turned around and smiled at me.

At that point I knew I needed to give her some privacy. I found Mum in the kitchen washing the dishes, so I grabbed a tea towel and dried.

Chapter Seventeen

'Stephanie seems pretty keen on Jason.' Mum sloshed water over a pan.

'Yeah, she really likes him.'

'Are they serious?'

'They were pretty serious before he went overseas. And it seems he's back again.' I wanted to change the subject. Steph was in the next room and could walk in any minute. 'Does—'

'I hope he doesn't distract her too much from her school work.'

'Yeah, me too.' I dried the last pan as I heard Stephanie say goodbye.

I darted towards her. 'Well? Spill.'

Her smile told me before she spoke. 'He's coming to Sydney.'

'When?'

'Next week. He chose Sydney. He had other uni offers, but he chose Sydney to be near me. Did you hear that, Tabbie? He's coming to be near me.'

'I was wrong?'

'I think you were.'

'I'm sorry.' Maybe now was a good time to stop hoping they'd never see each other again and just accept that my best friend had a boyfriend. 'Wow, that's exciting.'

Stephanie beamed a wide smile, nodding.

I tried to stay in the moment as long as I could but reality hit. We had work to do. 'How are you going with that ancient history essay?'

'No go. Can't get focused. How about you?'

'I can't find enough information. Maybe we should work on it together?'

'Great idea. Let's get to it.' Stephanie pulled her ponytail tighter.

We laughed like we did before she'd met Jason, the way we had before she'd moved away. Could we finally be rebuilding our friendship?

I set my alarm to go off twenty minutes earlier than usual so I could shower without rushing. I wanted to keep things sweet between Steph and me. But when the alarm clock sounded, my eyes stung and I felt far from sweet. I squinted as I shuffled to the bathroom and let the hot water steam my eyes open.

'Happy Monday,' I said after my shower as I passed Stephanie in the hallway. 'Shower is all yours. Thought I'd get up a little earlier so we weren't fighting over it.'

'Thanks, Tabbie. You're one in a million.'

Yeah, sometimes. 'This year is going to be great.'

'I think so too.' Stephanie leant against the wall.

'I've decided not to get back into dance. Do you think you will?'

'No. But you were going really well. Why would you stop?' Stephanie pulled her lip between her teeth.

'Because I stuffed my ankle.'

'It's healed now, isn't it?'

'Yeah, but it's weakened.'

'So what's stopping you from strengthening it again?'

'Dancing was always your dream, not mine.'

Stephanie didn't reply. I didn't understand why she would completely drop her dream to become a professional dancer, but that's exactly what had happened.

On Friday night, Steph and I went our separate ways. She headed to work and I went to youth group. I arrived home with blood rushing through my body and cleaned my room, then Steph's.

As I was almost asleep, Stephanie trudged home and fell into bed. Unlikely even noticing the effort I went to. The following morning Shelly arrived at nine to take me to the beach. 'Who else is coming?' I asked.

'Mostly the music team. I'm just tagging along on Priscilla's invitation.'

'You mean the music team from church? The whole team?'

'I don't know who'll actually turn up.'

The hairs on my neck prickled. I'd become used to seeing Danny on stage, playing his bass while I admired his biceps and good looks from a distance. Other than that crazy incident at the pool, which I'd squished into a dark hole in my mind, I hadn't come face to face with him again.

I reminded myself he was a complete nerd and, in all seriousness, looks were a very small part of a complete attraction.

We arrived to perfect weather and crystal-clear waves crashing on the sand. There were a bunch of familiar faces, some playing beach volleyball and others lying on their towels. After a quick scan, I couldn't see Danny anywhere. That was probably a good thing.

'Come on, let's play some volleyball.' Shelly dumped her towel and headed towards the others.

'Thanks, but I don't want to risk stuffing up my ankle again.'

'Why don't you strap it?' Priscilla jogged over to her bag.

'Do you have some tape?' I raised my eyebrows.

'Yes. I have a weak ankle too.' She pointed to her strapped ankle and pulled out a roll of tape.

'Thanks.' Her kindness flooded my heart with warmth.

I'd only ever played beach volleyball a handful of times. It was a thrill, with sand flying everywhere and high fives all round. What made it even more fun was being on the winning team. After the game, most of us hit the surf. I did my usual walk-jump-paddle-paddle until I reached the calmer water just past the wave break. I bobbed up and down while Shelly rode along the crest of a wave on her bodyboard.

Before Shelly had paddled out again, my eyes were drawn to some very attractive boys on surfboards down the beach a little. The surf was pumping and there were dozens of surfers floating on their boards, waiting their turn to catch a wave. Many of them surfed right into the shoreline. I was in awe. I couldn't even bodysurf. While I was focused on them, a tidal wave crashed over my head, tumbling me over and over until my head hit something hard. Paddling and kicking hard, I found daylight again. The world spun and I spat out a mouthful of sand.

I rinsed my mouth with salty water and tousled my hair out of my eyes before paddling back into deeper water. When I returned to my spot on the calm side of the waves, my gaze fixed on what looked like a dream ride for a surfer. The guy flicked his messy sun-bleached hair as his ride cruised from way out in the ocean, right in to the sand.

My heart raced as he picked up his board and walked towards our towels. He was with our group. He speared his board into the sand and jogged towards me in the flagged swimming area. I recognised him before his feet hit the water. *Danny.* A quiet gasp escaped my lips. He was looking in the other direction and didn't see me. *Phew.* I searched for Shelly or Priscilla. Another large wave splashed my face. I hoped it would cool my overheating cheeks before anyone noticed. I couldn't believe I'd been checking Danny out. When the heat receded from my face, I returned to my towel.

'We'll get going in around ten minutes.' Shelly smiled as she dried off.

I nodded.

'You must be Tabbie.'

I turned, startled at a male voice I'd never heard before. The guy plonked himself right down beside me. So close, he may as well have shared my towel.

'Yeah. Are you part of the music team?'

'Oh no, not me. I'm Rhett. I go to school with Danny. He told me about you.'

'Really?' *What did Danny know about me?* I hoped the breeze would stop my face turning completely red, but a tingle of warmth rose up my neck. 'What did he say?'

'That you were a great chick, so I thought I should get to know you.' He brushed sand off my towel, making slight contact with my thigh. I crossed my legs, trying not to be obvious. But he was way too close.

'I barely even know D—'

'He tells me you're a great swimmer. Do you do all the strokes?' Rhett raised his eyebrows then winked.

I looked away. He was seriously flirting with me!

'Well, I don't do much dog-paddling.' I stood and shook my sandy towel out, allowing the wind to blow the sand in the air.

'Hey, you're covering me in sand!' He jumped up, dusting himself off.

'Oops, sorry.' *But not really.*

'I was thinking, maybe you and I could see a movie sometime.'

Wow, he was quick. I smiled and shook my head. As I walked away, a slight nervous giggle escaped my lips. He was average. Nothing stood out about his looks. Sure, he had muscles, but so did every other guy on the beach. I didn't expect a friend of Danny's to be such a painful flirt. I slid into the front seat of Shelly's car.

'Do you want to come in and have lunch?' I asked when she pulled up outside my home.

'Thanks,' she said, 'but I promised Mum I'd have the car back. See you in the morning.'

     Spiralling Out of the Shadow

I waved as she drove away. No one had said anything about my gawking at Danny. As long as no one noticed, I could be free to get my fill of eye candy and no strings would be tangled.

A knot pulled my stomach as I plonked myself on the couch with Mum and Dad to watch cars driving around a track. Something about Danny's friend unnerved me. I was thankful Shelly had to leave so I didn't have to continue the conversation with him.

Stephanie arrived home only a few minutes after me. A very good-looking guy followed closely behind her. So here he was. He did have amazing dreamy-brown eyes, and they followed Stephanie's every move. His T-shirt clung to his broad shoulders. *Wow, he'd stand out in any crowd.*

'Jason, this is Tom and Francine. And this is my best friend, Tabbie.'

Dad flicked the TV off and stood. Mum joined him.

'Pleased to meet you.' Dad offered his hand to shake.

'Hello.' Jason's smile was slightly crooked.

I went to invite them to sit down and chat, but Stephanie whisked Jason up to her bedroom before I took a breath.

'Mum, are you okay with that?'

'No, love, but I won't embarrass her right now.'

Jason left before dinner. I waited to see how long Mum and Dad would wait until they addressed the bedroom situation. Dad broke the silence. 'I think we need to make some rules if Jason is going to be visiting regularly.'

Mum nodded.

Stephanie opened her mouth but closed it again without speaking.

'Now …' Dad cleared his throat after everyone sat around the table. 'The rule in our house is that we've never allowed boyfriends or girlfriends in the bedrooms.' He picked up his knife and fork, looking at his plate then back at Stephanie. 'What's been the rule at your home?'

'We never had one.' Stephanie pushed the food around on her plate.

I sat at the table playing eye ping-pong, not game to speak in case I put my foot in it. Mum and Dad were pretty fair on her. They said Jason was allowed in her room during the day as long as the door was open. There's no way they'd ever be that relaxed with Peter or me.

Stephanie agreed to Mum and Dad's rules. I checked her body language and hoped they could trust her—I had my doubts. I wanted to suggest she keep her relationship a little less intense. But I knew I couldn't control her. She was a free spirit, focused on her boyfriend.

I recalled a conversation I'd overheard between Mum and Dad after Dad had spoken to Stephanie's father on the phone before Stephanie had arrived. Mr Stronge wouldn't allow them to take on Stephanie's guardianship. He said it wouldn't be necessary as they didn't want to hand over the responsibility. The arrangement was for boarding only. The Stronges planned to keep in touch and follow up with the school and Stephanie on a regular basis.

I didn't understand where they were coming from. And from Mum's reaction, she didn't either.

Chapter Eighteen

'Hey, Tabbie, are you coming back to dance?' Joey rang out of the blue.

'No, I'd rather do something else this year.'

'What? Like hang out down at the beach?'

'Y-e-s.' I drew the word out. 'That and other things.'

'What about your friends?'

'Do you mean Suzie? She'll be back if her parents let her.' I smiled and let the silence linger. I wished one of them would make a move.

'Oh, ah ... that's good. Anyway, do you remember my mate, Danny?'

'Yeah.' I tried to sound aloof in my response, but just the mention of his name sent visuals of him walking along the beach. His biceps. His sun-bleached hair. His wide smile.

'Apparently you really wowed a friend of his today and he's asking for your number. I didn't want to hand it over before checking with you first.'

'Thanks, Joey. Some guy did come up and talk to me, but I don't remember his name.'

'Rhett. Does that sound familiar?'

'Mmm.' I repeated his name in my mind and cringed. 'Yes.'

'Well, he's been nagging me all afternoon. Is it okay if I give him your number?'

I could say no and wonder if I had the wrong first impression. Or I could say yes and actually get to know a guy who might be interested in me. 'Sure. That should be okay.' I hung up but didn't dare move away from the phone. I half expected Rhett to ring back immediately. Hopefully I'd made the right decision. My stomach knotted up. Maybe I should have said no.

Leaning against the wall, I looked out the front windows at the night lights and tried to remember exactly what he looked like. But all I could see was Danny. I blinked a couple of times to remove his surfing image from my mind. I should have got straight back into study. The phone was silent for the rest of the night.

'Hey, Tabbie.' Mum stopped me as I went to climb the stairs. 'I know Stephanie's your best friend, and her parents seem to be okay with her having a boyfriend, but it's still the same deal for you. Your father and I still want you to wait until you are at least sixteen before you start dating.'

Groan. I couldn't believe the timing of the conversation. 'But Mum, my birthday is like, a couple of weeks away.'

'More like a few months. A rule is a rule. And that's what we've decided is right for our family. And if you do start dating after you turn sixteen, zero bedroom entertainment.' She gave me a hug and that warm caring smile that made me wish I could just be happy with how things were.

The next morning, Steph flew past me on the staircase. 'See ya later. I'm running late for work again.'

'Steph,' Mum called from the kitchen. 'Let me wash my hands and I'll drive you.'

I watched the door close behind them and was happy to be home alone for a while. Dad had gone for a walk to buy the Sunday paper, and Mum wouldn't be back for at least twenty minutes.

I sat on the couch and flicked through the channels, unable to focus on anything, wondering if Danny's friend would call. Or maybe even Danny. After five minutes had passed, my stomach twisted in knots until I hoped no one would ring. Everything would stay simple if no one rang. I turned the TV off. Church would be starting soon. Just as I turned the door knob to leave, the silence broke. Ring, ring. Ring, ring. The landline.

'Hey, hello,' I answered out of breath. Not that I'd been running or anything—my breath just seemed to disappear.

'Is that Tabbie?' A slightly familiar, yet over-the-top-confident voice asked.

'Yeah.'

'Rhett here, we met on the beach yesterday. I'm sure you've been dreaming about me since then.' I couldn't help but laugh. I didn't know if he was joking or if my nerves had taken over. 'Well, you have to admit, you couldn't keep your eyes off me. I saw you watching me walk out of the surf and along the beach.'

'No, I don't remember that.' I was watching Danny. But Danny wasn't the one on the other end of the line.

'Oh.' He was silent for a moment. 'Well, it must have been me who couldn't keep my eyes off you.'

Whoa. His straightforward flirtatious way was something that only an ant might enjoy.

'So, what do you say to a movie this Friday night?'

'I go to youth group on Friday night. Maybe another time.'

'I've heard about your youth group. How about if you come to the movies this Friday, I'll go to your youth group the next week.'

That sounded okay. *Oh, where was Steph?* I wished she was beside me to help with my decision.

'Okay,' I said, because I just didn't know what else to say.

Maybe I should have said no, but he was already making arrangements to meet at the cinema. I rubbed my stomach as it pulled into a cramp.

He wanted to meet at seven just in time for the movie.

I hung up as the sound of car wheels hit our driveway. *Mum.* With my bag over my shoulder, I ran out the door as she came in. 'See ya. I'm off to church.' I didn't dare look back.

'Oh, you should have said, love. I could've dropped you while I was out.'

'Never mind.' The walk to the bus would hopefully help clear my mind and relax my stomach.

During church, Danny's muscles flexed as he played music with the band. I looked away. He was a nerd. Plus, his friend Rhett had just asked me out. I was still trying to get my head around the possibility of my first date, so I didn't mention it to Priscilla or Shelly. They went out to lunch with a bunch of girls, but I decided to enjoy the long walk home. I surrendered myself to the delicious warm day as the slightest breeze lifted the leaves on the path. The gust carried my steps and my thoughts. Maybe it was time to challenge the dating waters. *What do I have to lose?* I'd already said yes. *No turning back now.*

When I arrived home the house seemed empty, until the echo of voices rolled down the stairway.

'Stop it,' Steph said in a raspy voice.

A deep male voice rumbled with laughter. *Jason?*

'Hi, Stephanie,' I poked my head through her open doorway trying to put on a spontaneous didn't-know-you-had-company face. 'Oh. Hi, Jason. Sorry. Didn't realise you were here.'

Stephanie raised her eyebrows and eyed my doorway across the hall. My arrival was obviously bad timing in her eyes.

'Okay, we can chat later then.' I clenched my jaw and turned to leave.

'Is there something you wanted to talk about?' She followed me into the hallway.

     Spiralling Out of the Shadow

'No, no. It's nothing important. Just come and chat when Jason goes.' I only had boy problems, but she had a real, tangible boyfriend.

'Won't be long. He's about to leave.' Stephanie smiled and returned to Jason.

I pulled out my folder and tried to work on the most pressing assignment. But my gaze kept heading out the window.

Stephanie took her time seeing Jason off before she came to my door. 'What's up?'

'You didn't have to kick him out because of me.'

'It's okay. He was about to leave.' Stephanie sat on my bed and inspected her fingernails. 'So what do you want to talk about?'

'Rhett asked me out on a date.'

'Wow, that's exciting.'

'If Mum and Dad would let me go out on a date, it would be exciting.'

'And … who is Rhett? Where did you meet him?'

'At the beach yesterday.'

'And why won't your parents let you go?' asked Stephanie. 'I knew they were strict, but you'll be sixteen soon.'

'Not for another two months. They said I have to wait.'

'What if you just go on a date without them knowing?'

'I can't lie to them.' I'd never lied to my parents.

'Or …' Steph paused for a moment. 'Just tell them something like … you're staying at a friend's house, but then go on the date from there. You just have to ask a friend.'

'How is that not lying?' I bit my lip, squinting.

'Do you want to go or not?'

'I do.' My shoulders tensed. 'But I'm not a liar. I don't want to lie to Mum and Dad.'

'Well?' Stephanie raised her eyebrows.

I lifted my head as we communicated a silent conversation that would have sounded like. Me: *Maybe I could.* Steph: *Yes, why not. Go for it.* Me: *But I don't really want to lie.* Steph: *Just this time.*

When I couldn't stand the silent chatter between our eyes a moment longer, I asked, 'Do you think Suzie or Jaya would be okay with me staying at their house for a night?'

'You can only ask.'

'What if you come and stay too?'

'Which night?' Stephanie pulled her hair into a ponytail.

'This Friday.'

'What about youth group—won't you have that Friday night?'

'It's only once, and he said he'd come with me to youth group next week.'

'I'm working Friday night. Plus, Jason has asked me out.' Stephanie looked at me through the corner of her eye. 'But I guess I could go there with you straight after school.'

'How would that work? Would you get Jason to drop you back?'

'Um ... I think ...' Stephanie paused.

She wanted to hide it from me, but I knew. 'Are you sure? I thought you said you didn't want to—'

'Yeah, you're right. I'll get him to drop me off—probably after midnight. We'll just have to get one of the girls to agree to help you out.'

Chapter Nineteen

THE NEXT DAY, STEPH AND I found Jaya and Suzie talking in the school grounds. I was pretty sure Suzie would say no straight away.

'As if …' Suzie shook her head. 'You're still in Mum's bad books.'

'Mum and Dad said you guys are welcome any time.' Jaya eyeballed both Suzie and me. 'They think your parents are way-over-the-top-too-strict.'

'Too easy.' Stephanie beamed a wide grin. 'Now all Tabbie has to do is ask her parents and it's all sorted.'

'You mean you haven't asked them yet?' Jaya screwed her nose up and looked at me.

'That's not like you,' Suzie said, with a soft tone.

Talk about stating the obvious. I was still coming to terms with the fact I was about to lie to my parents. I put it off as long as I could.

A shudder ran down my spine that night as I asked Mum and Dad about staying at Jaya's house. They thought it was a great idea because they were going out to a fiftieth birthday party and were happy they weren't leaving me home alone.

My stomach churned. I'd lied.

'Now, you'll call me anytime if you want to come home, won't you?' Mum insisted when we left for school on Friday morning.

'Mum.' I rolled my eyes.

'Sure, Francine, we will.' Stephanie lifted her overflowing school bag onto her shoulder. 'Won't we, Tabbie?'

'Have a great time, and be careful.' Mum smiled in her protective way.

The final bell rang Friday afternoon and I trembled. I took a long deep breath to calm myself. The three of us caught the bus back to Jaya's. Soon after we got there, Steph wished me well and left to go to work.

'She didn't hang around for long.' Jaya pointed to the door after Stephanie left.

'She had to get to work. You know that.'

'Why did she even come here in the first place? Wouldn't it have been easier for her just to go to work from your house?'

'Yes, it would. But she came to support me.'

'To support Miss Goody Two Shoes?' Jaya raised her eyebrows.

I frowned at her, and a shudder ran down my spine. *How am I going to make it through? That's it. No more lies. Ever.*

'Do you think she'll come back here or go to your place after work?'

'I don't know. We'll just have to listen for her.'

'Okay, let's get started.' Jaya pulled out a make-up case and hair straightener. 'Hair and make-up for your big date.'

I swallowed. I swallowed again. I tried to downplay the date and not make it a big deal. The last thing I wanted was Jaya swinging from the highest tree shouting about Tabbie going on her first big real date. I sat on the bed watching her with the straightener in the mirror. My face looked long with straight hair.

'You have that concerned look in your eyes. What's up?' Jaya put the straightener down and sat beside me.

'It's just ... I look so different. What if he doesn't recognise me? What if he thinks I look ugly like this?'

'Tabbie, you're so pretty, it wouldn't matter what you did with your hair. You could shave your head and still look amazing.'

Even though I still wasn't sure about the straight hair, one thing I was pretty sure of—I wasn't about to try the bald look. She finished with my hair and went to apply make-up.

'Jaya, thanks, but I can do that myself.'

I brushed a little mascara across my lashes and smudged on some brown eyeliner. I wiped watermelon lip gloss across my lips and put it in my pocket for another application later.

Mum would be beside herself if she knew I planned to walk the couple of blocks from Jaya's by myself. But this time, just for once, I wanted to be the girl who could go out on a date and not have Mum and Dad clucking over me. A shivery tingle went up my spine at the thought, so I left while it was still light and hung around the front of the cinema, people-watching.

I checked the times and hoped Rhett would arrive early. The next movie started at six-thirty and the next sessions didn't start 'til late.

Leaning against a pole I checked the time for the fiftieth time. Just after seven, a plain-looking lanky boy walked around the corner and straight up to me. When he kissed me on the cheek and handed me a bunch of red carnations, I recognised him. *Rhett.* My cheeks burnt hot. I was sure they'd flushed to the same colour as the carnations. I wouldn't have recognised him if he didn't find me first. He looked different in a shirt.

Awkward. I didn't know where to look, so I stuck my nose into the flowers and smelled them. They had no scent. 'Thanks,' I said.

'What movie are we seeing?' He started walking towards the counter.

'A good one just started.'

'Oh, damn.' Rhett cursed a string of unsavoury words under his breath. 'We could still go in.'

'No, it's too late now. I hate missing the beginning.'

He cursed again, kicking his toe into the tiles.

'Did you want to just get a milkshake?' My mouth was dry and I felt awkward, just standing there.

'Good idea. Then we could catch one of the late movies. What flavour would you like?'

'Caramel, please. But I'd rather not stay out that late, so how about just a milkshake.'

He winked and ordered at the counter. I slipped into a booth and found myself staring out the window. How could he be so inconsiderate to be late? And how could I be so dumb to agree to a date with a guy I wasn't the least bit attracted to? And even dumber, I'd suggested a milkshake. More time with him when I could have gone straight back to Jaya's house.

I expected Rhett to sit opposite me, and almost jumped out of my skin when he slid in so close he nudged my arm. I couldn't work out if he was just overconfident, with a straightforward manner, or a painful flirt. He draped his arm around my shoulders. I wanted to remove it without coming across completely rude. Sitting up a little straighter I cleared my throat.

'Not comfortable?'

'Ah, not really.' I lifted one shoulder then the other, trying to shake free.

'Do you want me to move my arm?'

'That would be great.'

Before I'd taken a sip of my milkshake, Rhett put his straw in. 'Let's drink it together.'

'Gross.' I did not want to share anything with him. I wanted to get away but I was sandwiched between Rhett and the wall. He pulled his straw out, dropped it into his milkshake and grabbed my thigh. I pushed his hand away as his other hand grabbed my chest.

'Rhett!' I shoved him away again and slid under the table, crawling out into public view.

'Hey, what's up?' he asked with questioning hands.

'I'm going.'

'You can't walk home alone.' He slid off the seat and followed me.

Walking alone seemed a whole lot safer than walking with Rhett. I hurried. But he was close behind me. I quickened my pace. The thud of his footsteps followed me. I turned. 'Stop following me.'

'Hey, babe, don't be like that.' He groped at my waist.

'Urgh.' I swiped his arm away and ran.

The scuff of running feet followed me. I shuddered when I saw the street was deserted. *Just me and him.* I raced towards Jaya's. Until ... I tripped.

My weak ankle buckled, and I crashed onto the concrete path. I was too freaked out by the way he kept following me to stop and check the damage. I scrambled up, hoping my ankle would work again. It hurt. But I ran on it anyway.

Rhett's laughter rumbled behind me.

'Shut up!' I yelled but didn't turn back.

Thankfully Jaya's doorknob turned. I flung it wide and locked it behind me.

'Jaya, he's gross! Check through the window. Please tell me he's gone.'

'There's someone walking the other way. Is that him?'

'Yes.' I glanced through the window as he crossed the road and kept walking without turning around.

'Didn't go too well I take it?'

'It was a nightmare, Jaya. He's a complete creep!' As I spoke, tears swelled in Jaya's eyes. 'Hey, what's up?'

'Mum and Dad had another huge fight. They both took off. Mum thinks Dad's been having an affair.'

'Oh.' Was this when I was supposed to say something about the noises I heard the night Jaya was paralytic? *Probably not.* I didn't actually see anything. It would be devastating if I was wrong. I leaned over and hugged her. About now would have been a nice moment to pass her my bouquet of carnations, but I'd left them at the café. Hopefully they were brightening someone's night.

We drank hot chocolate with marshmallows and camped out in the lounge room in case Stephanie arrived home.

When I woke up, it was just the two of us and Jaya's mum. She looked miserable. I needed to get out of their house so they could deal with their family crisis.

Chapter Twenty

'How did it go?' Stephanie whispered when everyone was silent at the dinner table.

Mum and Dad looked at me.

'What was that? Is there someone at the front door?' I scraped my feet across the floor and looked towards the front of the house.

'Not sure.' Dad pushed his chair out. 'I'll check.'

'Everything okay, love?' Mum called out to Dad.

'Later,' I whispered, glaring at Stephanie with wide eyes.

Sorry, Stephanie mouthed when Mum wasn't watching.

'No one there.' Dad returned to the table. 'Must have been a cat or something.'

Once we'd cleaned up after dinner, Stephanie followed me to my bedroom. 'Tell me. I want all the details.'

'Yuck!' I fell onto my bed with my hands over my eyes, not wanting to replay the sordid event.

'Bad, huh?'

'Yes. Urgh. It was horrible.' My stomach churned. 'Like spew horrible.'

'Why? What went wrong?'

'We were going to go to the movies but Rhett got there late. The movie had already started-and-it-would-have-been-too-late-to-go-to-the-next-one-so-we-sat-in-the-coffee-shop-and-had-a-milkshake.' I knew my words had run together, but I just couldn't get the story out quick enough.

'That doesn't sound too bad.'

'The whole time I struggled to keep his hands off me. Eww. It's gross just thinking about it.'

'Oh, no.'

'He turned into Mr Octopus Arms so I took off. Look what I did on the way back to Jaya's.' I pulled up my jeans to show the grazed and bruised knee.

'Ouch! Did you get inside okay?'

I nodded.

She said she was sorry I had to go through the ordeal. It seemed like she meant it because she didn't push for any more details. I was so caught up in my own grief I almost didn't ask how her night went. I was sure she'd had a blissful time. It was hard keeping that green-eyed monster at bay. But in a moment of silence, I asked, 'Anyway, how was your night—amazing, I'm sure?'

'Ah, pretty average.' She turned to the window with slumped shoulders.

'But you stayed, with Jason for the night ... somewhere?' I asked, knowing the answer.

'Yeah, slept in and got in trouble at work. I have to find another job. George and Bridget are horrible.'

'Steph, did you ...'

'Yeah. We did. I'm off to get some more sleep.' Steph stood up and trudged to the door. 'Have you got church in the morning?'

'Yes. I wish you could come sometime. You'd love it.' But I knew she didn't want to come. I was sure she saw God as an angry father, wanting to tear shreds off her. But he wasn't. Steph turned and blew me a kiss before shutting the door. She looked like someone else.

Her body language had changed. She would never have blown me a kiss like that before. I prayed silently for her safety.

Priscilla stopped me after church. 'Weather is so good. We're heading to the beach for lunch. Want to join us?'

Cringe. I shuddered at the thought of Rhett being there with Danny. 'No, thanks. I've got to get some homework done.'

It was the truth. I was already sinking under the avalanche of assignments. After last year's results, I wanted to blitz the year as an A-plus student. As long as life didn't get in the way.

'Hey, Steph.' I stopped her as she arrived home. 'Can I bounce some ideas off you for this assignment?'

'Sorry, Tabbie, I'm not in the right frame of mind.'

Stephanie left the house for the afternoon, and Mum and Dad were catching up with friends. I was home alone, listening to my own thoughts, which weren't pleasant after Friday night. How was it that I got a dud first up? I couldn't even go on a regular date with a guy and get all gooey-eyed after the fact. Stephanie's life just cruised along even when she lied. I told one lie to go on a date and thwack—I ended up on the horror date of the century. Maybe I'm the girl who just shouldn't lie. Maybe I'm just meant to be the nice person and never have any fun.

The landline interrupted my mind battle.

'Tabbie?'

'Yes?' I didn't recognise the voice.

'Rhett here. Maybe we could try the movies again this week.'

'No. Not in this lifetime. Don't call me again.' I couldn't get the phone out of my hands quick enough. I stepped back, staring at the handset sitting on top of our old-fashioned phone and shook my shoulders and hands to rid myself of him. Before I could return to the couch, the phone rang again. My heart thrashed. My skin shivered. Surely he wouldn't ring back. 'Hello?'

'Look, Tabbie, I think we got off on the wrong foot.'

'No.' I flexed my strained ankle.

'I'm not that bad.'

'I said no! And don't ring again. Just go away.' I slammed the phone down and pulled the cord out of the wall. *Creep.*

How was I going to get through the next week after such humiliation? I was sure everyone would be laughing at my attempt at dating. Perhaps I could shake it off by making a joke out of it by saying, *Ha, can you believe I even went out with him?* I could hear everyone's laughter already. But the truth was, I went out on a date with a complete dweeb. I made the choice to go. My error.

As I meandered into the school grounds on Monday with Steph, I saw Jaya, and my perspective changed. What she was going through was a whole lot more intense than my dumb-arrogant-boy date. My issue would blow over and be forgotten in a couple of days. Jaya had to deal with the possibility of major changes in her family. 'How are you?' I asked. 'Did you talk to your parents about what's going on?'

'It sucks.' She spat the words like she had a bad taste in her mouth. 'They both need help.'

I was lost for words. I wanted to console her but what could I say?

'So, Steph,' Jaya said. 'Are you sleeping with him?'

'What?' Steph asked.

'You asked if you could sleep over but you didn't return. Great friend you are.'

'You're pretty torn up about your parents, aren't you?' I interjected a moment too late.

Stephanie tried to apologise as Jaya stomped off in a huff.

It seemed my horrendous date didn't make it to the school gossip chain. *Phew*—saved from that humiliation. Jaya, on the other hand, was lashing out and putting everyone offside.

 Spiralling Out of the Shadow

'You have to dance with me again this year.' Suzie rushed towards me during lunch with the sign-up form in her hand.

'No, Suzie, it's your chance to shine. My ankle is still weak. And to tell the truth, it's not my thing. I'd rather go for a run or a swim. I only started dancing because everyone else was doing it.'

'Please, Tabbie?' Suzie begged with puppy-dog eyes. 'It won't be the same without you. I'll go insane.'

'You'll be fine.' I promised her I'd drop in from time to time and was about to mention Joey but stopped myself. Her parents were way-over-the-top stricter than mine. It was pointless even suggesting Joey might have a thing for her.

'You and I have hardly done anything since Stephanie returned. I hoped you'd do dance so we could hang out again.'

'What do you mean? We have classes together.'

'I mean, like, out of school.'

She had a point. I hadn't been to her house since before Christmas. Not that I was welcome there.

'And you know Mum and Dad never let me do anything outside of routine. I'm lucky they actually let me take dance classes.'

'I'm sorry, Suzie. I'll check what I've got on. Why don't you come to the beach with us on Saturday?'

'No way the parentals would let me.'

'Leave it with me. I'll find time to come and hang out or something.' I parked a mental note, to make an effort to see Suzie outside of school. I could only imagine how isolated she felt.

Chapter Twenty-One

ON SATURDAY MORNING, I WOKE well after dawn, strapped my ankle and headed out for a run. Stephanie's door hung ajar and her bed hadn't been slept in. My heart nearly stopped. The best friend I was hoping to reclaim seemed to be slipping further away. I had to deal with my frustration. I ran for half an hour before returning home to shower and head into the mall for a little retail therapy.

Entering my favourite jeans shop, I tried on a couple of pairs. They accentuated my pear shape which seemed to become more obvious every day, so I hung them back on the rack. All I came home with was a new top.

My best friend, the beautiful, sophisticated and elegant one, still wasn't home when I walked in.

'Have you spoken to Stephanie, love?' Mum asked.

'No, I thought she'd be home by now.'

'So did I. Maybe we should give the *Tiger's Eye* a call and see if she's there.'

'Yeah, maybe.'

Mum's phone call uncovered the fact Stephanie hadn't made it into work that day. I waited in the room while Mum rang Stephanie's mum.

'That was quick,' I said.

'She said she was busy, and she'd ring Steph later.'

'Is there anything else? Study is calling me.'

'No, love, you go. Maybe we should get Steph a mobile phone. I'll talk to her about it when I see her.'

Hmm, that sounded ominous. I trudged upstairs and opened my books.

When Stephanie arrived home, I pulled my door open a little, waiting for Mum to question her. I hoped Mum wasn't about to send her back to Toowoomba. When they spoke, I heard bits and pieces of Mum voicing her concerns about Stephanie staying at Jason's. Within minutes, Stephanie stomped into her room and closed the door. After half an hour, I couldn't resist any longer. I knocked on her door and opened it wide enough to see her.

'Hi, how's it going?'

'Not learning much.' Stephanie's books were open on her desk, but she was lying on her bed.

'How was last night? You stayed at Jason's again, didn't you?'

She raised an eyebrow.

'I overheard Mum before. Steph, what will you do if she talks to your mum and dad, and they want you to go home or something?'

'I don't know. I don't think Mum and Dad actually want me to come back anyway.' She sat up. 'What if … the next time they ring, I stay in the room so your mum hears and continue the conversation when they hang up to make it sound like they're fine with me staying at Jason's. That'll work.' She nodded.

'Or you could just come home instead of staying with Jason.'

'But that would be boring.' Stephanie swung her legs off the bed. 'I'm living on the wild side.'

I looked down at my new shirt, a conservative T. Maybe I was boring in her eyes. 'Just tell me you'll be safe. You know Mum is okay with you ringing at any time of night.'

'Maybe they'd be okay with you ringing, but I think I'd be stretching the friendship if I rang at four in the morning. Anyway, Jason loves me. He won't let anything bad happen.'

I wanted to say to her that he may say he loves you, but he's only seventeen and has all the hormones of an average teenager. But I ran my fingers through my hair and said nothing. Would it make me an accomplice now I knew her plan? Sometimes best friend codes were hard to work with.

Steph and I were watching reruns of an old TV series when her mum rang. She jumped from the couch, ready to follow through with her premeditated lie. She was ridiculously convincing, and I would have believed the fib if I didn't know what she was doing. I wanted to run into the kitchen and tell Mum the truth. My stomach churned. Yep, I was guilty of enabling her. I was an accomplice. But, it was her life. Everything felt messy.

'I couldn't help overhear,' Mum said, standing beside the TV after Stephanie hung up. 'Just be careful, okay?'

Steph nodded.

'I need to head out for a couple of hours. Call if you need me.' Mum grabbed her keys and left the house.

My blood started to boil. 'You're getting a bit too good at lying, don't you think?'

'Don't go getting all judgmental on me now.'

'I'm not judging you, just stating a fact. It just isn't the right thing to do. Wouldn't it be better to 'fess up and tell the truth?'

We both stared at the TV. I was still steaming, and aware of Steph's stony face in my peripheral vision. When the show finished, she left the room and I went for a walk.

She was the one lying. It was her decision to lie. Her life—not mine. I wanted to talk to Mum about the whole situation, but the loyal-best-friend in me urged me to keep quiet. After walking a

          Spiralling Out of the Shadow

block, I began to run, pounding my feet into the path. My ankle held my weight without wobbling. I wanted to punch the air and scream: *about time!*

When I returned, I stopped at Steph's room before showering. 'Hey, sorry if I upset you before.'

'You were just being honest. Apparently, that's something I could get better at.'

I smiled. *Yep, something she could get much better at.*

'I know you're right. I'm stuffing up, aren't I?' Stephanie pulled her bottom lip between her teeth.

'You need to spend more time on your schoolwork if you want to pass.'

'I'm too tired most of the time.' Stephanie covered an escaping yawn with her hand.

'Have you looked for another job?'

'Haven't really had time.'

'Maybe I could help you find one?' I went to grab the newspaper from downstairs.

'No, it's okay. I'll get to it, eventually.'

She didn't want my help. 'What are you doing with all that money you've earned?'

'Yeah, I do have a bit in the bank.' She smiled. 'Let's go shopping tomorrow. I'll buy you some new clothes—a peace offering.'

'What about school?'

'Stuff school.'

'I can't, Steph, and you shouldn't either. We've got millions of assignments to do.'

'I guess. It was just a thought. You're just too good. You do all the right things.'

I shook my head. 'Right now, I stink. I need a shower.'

I had to get out of her room. I didn't do all the right things. If I did, I would have called her parents and dobbed her in. I would have told Mum and Dad the truth. I would never have gone out with Rhett. But no. I kept Stephanie's secrets to keep in line with the best friend code. And I had a scar on my knee reminding me to be honest.

On Tuesday, when Shelly rang to invite me out to the movies, I jumped at the chance. A night with a bunch of fun people who didn't seem to hide secrets and tell lies was what I needed. When they invited me to the beach the next Saturday, I shook my head. Then I cringed, knowing my face hid nothing.

'What's up?' Priscilla asked

'I've got some homework to catch up on.'

'Spill.' Shelly leaned in. 'Tell us. You enjoyed coming last time. What's going on now?'

'It's about one of your friends but I really don't want to bad-mouth him.'

'Him?' Shelly asked.

'Who?' Priscilla's eyes opened wide.

I told them the whole sordid story.

'That was the first time Rhett joined us at the beach,' Priscilla said. 'He was there again last week.'

'And that's why I don't want to go.'

'But that's crazy.' Shelly shook her head. 'You'll be with us.'

'That's right. We'll protect you.' Priscilla flexed her tiny arms.

'I don't think I could face him. I don't ever want to see him again.' Thought of Rhett gave me chills.

'I think he came with Danny, so I'll have a chat with Danny this Thursday night at music practice and ask if he's coming again.'

'Are you sure?' Heat prickled in my cheeks.

'Yep.'

Shelly drove me home and before I climbed out of the car she said, 'We'll talk again Friday night, okay?'

'Sounds good.' *Could they really protect me?*

     Spiralling Out of the Shadow

Chapter Twenty-Two

'HE'S HERE,' I GASPED when I saw Rhett as we walked onto the sand. He was sauntering towards the surf with Danny, both with boards under their arms.

'Danny rang Rhett in front of me.' Priscilla linked her arm through mine and kept me moving forward. 'I listened to the whole conversation on speakerphone. Rhett told Danny he had other plans and wouldn't be coming.'

'It'll be fine.' Shelly spread out her towel on the sand a good distance away from the crew. 'We're here to protect you.'

'Yes, we are. It's warm—let's swim,' Priscilla said.

With a wave of hesitation, I lifted my gaze to the surfers paddling out to catch a wave. Priscilla stood on one side of me and Shelly on the other as we entered the water. They left their boogie boards behind and swam with me. Once we were past the wave break, I searched the deeper water to see if the boys were still there.

Shelly held imaginary binoculars to her eyes and two-way radio in the other hand. 'Ksh. Yes, err, I have visual. Tabbie need not look. Relax and enjoy the water. I'm on to it. Over. Ksh.'

I giggled and splashed her.

After a swim, we returned to our towels. When I looked up, Rhett was leaving the surf with his board under his arm. Shelly and Priscilla ushered me back into the waves. He joined the others playing beach volleyball. Shelly and Priscilla were quick to march me in a wide arc back towards our towels as Rhett and a few others raced towards the water for a swim. Before we had a chance to relax on our towels, Rhett came out of the water and made a beeline for me. Shelly and Priscilla packed up and rushed me off the beach before he could reach us. We piled into the car and burst into laughter. The knots that had grown in my stomach during the morning unravelled.

After a week of focusing on good results and sticking to my planned study schedule, I needed a break. I took Shelly and Priscilla up on their offer to head to the beach again the following Saturday.

I released a breath of relief when I saw Danny surfing with some other guys. Not Rhett.

'Next time you think about dating someone, take some of us as chaperones,' Shelly said as we left the water for a game of volleyball.

I'd never heard anyone in the group talk about dating. I wondered what that might actually look like—to have them come along. I hoped to find out one day.

Danny was on the other team. I fumbled the ball every time it came to me. Such a klutz. It wasn't like I was trying to impress him or anything. But it would be good to hold my head up and actually play the game with some skill. Perhaps another day. I gave up and left the court to lie on my towel.

I sat on the couch with books open around me and the TV on for some background noise. My mind wandered, wondering whether my best friend—the beautiful, sophisticated, and usually intelligent one—had actually spent all of her savings on a car for her perfect boyfriend. She'd told me last night she wanted to blow his mind with an amazing present.

Just after I refocused on my schoolbooks, sniffling and breath-gasping hiccups interrupted me. I jumped up and moved to the front door. 'Steph! Oh my goodness, you look like a train wreck! What's happened? What's he done to you?'

'Nothing. Well, not nothing. He hasn't done anything to me. He just ... doesn't want to be with me. And it's his birthday!'

'Slow down. Weren't you going to look at cars with him?' I pushed a tissue into her hand.

'We did.' She blew her nose. 'And I bought him one.'

'And he made you walk home? What a creep!'

'No, I got so angry ...' She grabbed another tissue and blew her nose again. 'I yelled at him and left.'

'Why? What were you so angry about?'

'He's going clubbing.'

'And you can't go.'

'But I want to.'

'You're too young.' Was she really hoping he'd take her clubbing?

'I know. I just wanted to celebrate with him. But he chose his friends over me.'

'Oh, Steph.' I wrapped my arms around her. She wanted to be with her boyfriend on his birthday. I couldn't blame her for falling apart.

My best friend soon became an ugly person to live with. Miserable, bitter, and angry. I did my best to hide it from everyone. Afternoon visits to the library to avoid her helped me cope with the changes.

By Easter, we needed a break from each other. Stephanie's visit to see her family came at the right time.

It would have been great to catch up with Peter when he returned home for a couple of days, but he spent most of his time with his ex-girlfriend, Phoebe, and the rest of the time with his head in textbooks. I finally found a moment to chat to him as he made a sandwich before he left to see Phoebe again. 'I thought you said at Christmas that it was over.'

'Tabbie, it's hard to explain.' He picked up the sandwich and grabbed his keys.

'You could try.'

'She started ringing me. And well ... we've talked a lot over the past few weeks.'

'Didn't you say, long distance relationships don't work?'

'Or maybe it's just that ... absence makes the heart grow fonder,' he said over his shoulder and jogged to his car.

Maybe the whole situation would make more sense if Phoebe came around sometimes and I actually got to see them together.

'It's your birthday next week, isn't it?' Shelly asked as the regular Friday night crowd began to dissipate.

'Yeah, how did you know that?'

'You mentioned it when we were at the beach.' She laughed, pointing to her forehead. 'I parked it in my very trusty memory bank.'

'Let's do something fun,' Priscilla said. 'How about bowling?'

'Do you like tenpin bowling?' Shelly asked.

'Sure. Sounds good.' I was relieved. With my best friend out of town for a couple of weeks, Suzie's parental restrictions and Jaya's idea of a party involving vomit, I welcomed Shelly and Priscilla's plans. Maybe Jaya and Suzie would join us.

'Sorry,' Jaya said. 'Mum and Dad have split up again, and I'm being shipped off to Grandma's at Penrith for the rest of the holidays.'

I found it hard to keep up. Jaya's parents' marriage had become a yoyo—on, off, apart, together, fighting, happy—*gah!*

'I'm sorry,' Suzie said when I rang her. 'You know I'd love to come. But Mum said I had to get these assignments done, clean out the garage, and wash all the windows and curtains before I can go anywhere. But I'm sure even when I've done all of that, she'll find more for me to do. I miss you.'

I recalled the mental note I'd made to make time to visit Suzie. She was even more isolated during holidays. 'I'll come over tomorrow and help you.'

The next day I swung by Suzie's home and knocked on the front door.

'Suzie said you might come by.' Mrs Peters pursed her lips.

'I thought I might be able to help her do some chores.'

'She won't be needing any help. I think it's best you leave.' She closed the door in my face. I couldn't understand why they were so intent on isolating their daughter. When Suzie didn't return my calls, I made another mental note to keep trying, praying she'd answer the phone and not her mother.

Shelly parked out the front and came to my door. 'I hope you don't mind, but I invited a couple of other friends.'

'Like who?' My shoulders arced a little.

Please don't say Danny. It would ruin my birthday if I had to hang out with him or any of his lame friends. *Really.*

'Jacinta and Lucy. I hope it's okay. I guess I should have checked with you first.'

'Oh, no, no. That's fine. The more the merrier.' I smiled in relief.

A girly day with bowling and drinking way too many bubbly sugar-filled drinks was just what I needed.

Jaya sent me a text message, 'You know I wish I was there. BTW Happy Birthday.'

When I arrived home Mum replayed a birthday message on the answering machine from Suzie for me.

That night Peter actually pulled himself away from Phoebe to eat with us.

'Where's Phoebe?' I raised my eyebrows.

'She's catching up with friends.'

'She could have come too.' I was wondering if she would ever join us for a meal.

'But—'

'Is she still scared of Mum and Dad?' I laughed.

'You're joking, aren't you?' Dad raised his eyebrows.

'Who'd be scared of us?' Mum laughed.

'My girlfriend.' Peter smiled. 'Don't worry, I haven't told her any nasty stories. She's just quiet.'

We continued to laugh while Peter's cheeks flushed.

'Perhaps I should invite her shopping sometime and get to know her a little.' Mum poured a glass of water.

Peter shrugged.

If anything, my parents were too kind, not scary.

After dinner, they presented me with a new mobile phone and a bling accessories pack. I lay in bed that night, setting up my new phone and it hit me—my best friend, the beautiful, sophisticated, and mostly considerate one—didn't call me. She'd never forgotten my birthday before. It wasn't the first time we'd been separated on my birthday, but it was the first time she'd forgotten to call me. Guess her life really was self-centred at the moment.

The next day I went for a run and pulled out my phone to call Suzie. Thankfully she answered. 'Guess where I am.'

'Ah, it's noisy … and you sound a little out of breath …'

'Yes! I'm outside on my brand-new mobile phone! Way better than Mum's old one.'

'Did you have a good birthday?'

'It was great. Wish you could have joined ...' I could hear Suzie's mother yelling in the background. 'What's she yelling at you for this time?'

'I've got a stack of jobs to do around here.'

'Still? Did your mum tell you I came to visit?'

'No. When was that?'

'When you were busy doing chores.'

'That's life.' Suzie's voice was low and miserable. 'See you next week at school.'

Was there anything I could do? She was so isolated, almost imprisoned, yet I was so free. It didn't seem fair.

People rushed around us while we waited for Steph's plane to arrive. I was still irritated that my best friend had forgotten my birthday. I couldn't let it go. I had to ask why she hadn't made time to wish me a happy birthday. Was I self-centred because it bothered me that she hadn't remembered?

She emerged from the pool of people, looking as glamorous as ever.

'Have you forgotten something?' I asked as we pushed our way through the swarming airport.

'No, I think I packed everything.'

'I mean—'

'You had your hair done or something?'

'No, it's just—'

'What? Just tell me, Tabbie.'

'Did you forget my birthday?'

'No! No way.' She stopped walking and the person behind her bumped into her back. 'I've never forgotten your birthday. How could I have?'

'You really did forget it?' I felt like the wind had been knocked out of me.

She shook her head and strolled forward. 'Yeah, sorry.'

'I thought you might have been planning to surprise me or something,' I blurted.

'Sorry.'

I averted my eyes as tears swelled. When she was silent for a moment too long, I glanced back at her. A dazzling shimmer at the side of her face caught my attention.

'Are those earrings new?' I asked.

'Yeah.' Stephanie paused. 'My family gave them to me as an early birthday present.'

'Oh.' *How lovely.* She celebrated her birthday without even thinking of me.

'I'll make it up to you. Let's catch a movie tonight.'

'We've got school tomorrow.' The automatic doors opened, and I stormed off to find the car.

'It doesn't have to be a late one.'

'No. Don't worry about it.'

I turned away from her after we climbed into the car and watched the traffic flash past the window for the entire drive home. She didn't seem sorry. Just guilty.

Chapter Twenty-Three

In second term our schoolwork increased and Jaya's parents were on and off like a jumper in autumn. Suzie was only allowed out for school and dance classes and Stephanie spent hours crying in her room. Even though Jaya and Suzie had major problems going on, Stephanie was the one I had to live with. I couldn't control Jason's moves and tell him to fix the problem any more than I could control Stephanie. I hoped after her break in Toowoomba she'd be ready to move on and stop moping. But pillow-muffled sniffle sounds slipped under her door every night.

After all she'd been through, I wanted to do something for her birthday. Just to make her feel special and take her mind off Jason. I bought some helium-filled balloons and hid them in my wardrobe overnight.

'Happy Birthday!' I woke up and bumped the balloons through the doorway.

'Thank you.' Tears sprung from her eyes as I handed her a small gold-foil box.

'Here.' I passed her a wad of tissues. 'Enough crying. Let's have a great day.'

'I can't believe you've done all this when I totally forgot your birthday.'

'Don't worry about it. It's in the past.' I'd let go of the fact she'd forgotten my birthday, so she may as well let it go too.

'Do you want to ditch school for the day and hang out?'

'I can't. You'll have fun at school. Wait and see.' It would have been nice to take a day off, but I had a maths quiz and I knew Steph was already in the bad books with most of her teachers.

She opened the present I'd given her—a silver bracelet with a small charm in the shape of a cross. Since going to youth group, I'd found so much peace in the symbol I wanted to give Stephanie a little peace as well.

'It's really pretty. Thank you!'

Stephanie's eyes lit up at the school gate when she was greeted by girls with dozens of balloons. Everyone fussed over her all day. I hoped her day was fun and a timely distraction from her neglectful ex-boyfriend.

Mum and Dad had planned to give Stephanie a family dinner party for her birthday. But then Jason turned up at the school gate and whisked her away. They'd obviously made up because from fifty metres away, I watched her happily jump into his car. The car she'd paid for.

That night, I lay in bed wondering if she'd come home. I released myself to sleep when the front door clicked just before midnight.

Stephanie wasn't in her bed when I woke up. She hadn't come home. The click that had let me sleep was only Dad locking up.

'I quit the job,' Steph told me the next afternoon. 'Jason took me out to a fancy restaurant for my birthday. It was amazing.'

'That's great, Steph. I'm ecstatic for you,' I said, knowing my voice sounded anything but.

'I'm happy I won't be going back there, but I don't think I'd go as far as ecstatic. I'll have to find another job.'

'Surely you can wait a bit?'

'Perhaps a week or two ...'

I waited for her to go on. She opened her mouth but nothing came out. I wanted to talk to her about dating. Now I was sixteen, Mum and Dad were okay with me going on a date. But I didn't have anyone to go out with and, well, I wanted to talk to someone about it.

Thursday afternoon was my next opening to chat with Stephanie. But she didn't have listening ears, only talking lips. Whenever I spoke, she responded with vague comments like, 'I thought we were over, but I was wrong.' And, 'He's everything I hoped for.' Then, 'It's not always great, but what relationship is?'

I listened to learn from her, as she paved the way before me.

On Friday afternoon, I again hoped to have a best-friend-deep-and-meaningful about what was happening in my life. I walked out of the school grounds to see Steph lingering at the gate. 'Hey, Tabbie,' she called. 'Come shopping with me.'

'Are you asking or telling?'

'Can you?'

'I guess.' I checked the time on my watch. We'd be back in time for youth group.

'Jason's parked over there.'

Oh, great. I was thinking she wanted to spend some time with me, but he was there. I didn't want to go shopping with Jason in tow. 'Is he coming shopping as well?'

'He'll just drop us off. He's not into shopping.'

I grinned, hoping she was right, and climbed into the backseat. Maybe a shopping afternoon with Steph would be just the way to sort out my life.

'Right, first stop, milkshakes,' I said, as we watched Jason drive off.

'Okay, let me guess. Caramel for you?'

'You've got it.'

'Maybe I should get a skinny shake.'

'Why?' I looked up and down her perfect figure.

'April noticed I'd gained a little weight.'

'No way. Why would she have said that?'

'You're right. Stuff it. Make mine extra thick.' Steph laughed and for the first time in a long time, she looked like my old light-hearted friend.

'It sure is good to see you smiling, Steph.'

She winked at me and grabbed two straws.

'So you've forgiven him?'

'He said he was sorry.'

'How do you trust he won't do it again?'

'I don't know. But he does really care about me.'

I hoped she was right. I wished I had more experience. But my gut told me she shouldn't trust him, and wisdom told me she wouldn't listen to my gut feeling on the matter.

'Right.' Stephanie slurped the last drop of thick shake. 'Let's check out some clothes.'

She was drawn to the shops with clothes fit for nightclubbing. I wondered if the whole 'making up' business meant that Jason was going to drag Steph out with his friends. It seemed like she was after the shock factor with the clothes she tried on.

'That's trashy, Steph. Where would you wear it anyway?'

'It's how they all dress.' She turned to look at herself in the mirror from every angle.

'Who? The girls at those parties you've been going to?' *Who's she hanging out with?*

'Yeah, I feel so out of place and young.'

'You're sixteen.' I couldn't control what she wore, but ... 'Here, what about this, and this top ... and here, try these.' I passed her a few pieces that would leave a little to the imagination.

'Okay, I'll try them on.' A few minutes later she walked out of the changeroom with wide eyes.

'I love that.'

'Me too.' Steph smiled. 'I knew there was a reason I brought you. Why don't you find something new too?'

'Ah ... not from this shop.' I looked around. I couldn't see anything that I would wear. 'Where would I wear clothes like these?'

'Maybe you could come to a party with us sometime.'

'Oh, you're funny.' *That'd be really crazy.* I couldn't believe she even said it. 'Three's a crowd.'

'Let's find you something.' Steph paid for her clothes at the counter. 'Next shop is your choice.'

I chose to hit a shop where I always found something I loved. Steph bought me a top, two pairs of jeans that didn't make me look like a pear, and a cropped cardigan.

'Thank you.' I hugged her. 'I can't believe how generous you've been.'

'That's okay.'

'But are you sure? I could pay you back for them.'

'No way. I wanted to buy them for you.' Steph had a yearning in her eyes I'd never seen before. 'Do you want to come back to Jason's and he can drive you home?'

'Are you going back there now?' I was hoping we'd head straight home.

'He's expecting me. We're going out tonight.'

'I'll be fine getting the train home by myself.' I sighed, hoping she didn't hear my disappointment.

'Come back and have some dinner with us,' Steph said. 'I've had so much fun this afternoon. I think we're getting pizza. Please say you'll come.'

It didn't sound like the most fabulous invitation, but we'd had such a lovely afternoon I didn't want this time with Steph to end. 'Okay. But I want to get home for youth. Can we eat soon after we get there?'

'Sure.'

As we walked up the stairs towards Jason's apartment, laughter and music rumbled down to meet us. 'He must have invited some friends,' Steph said over her shoulder.

'Should I just go home now?' I wanted out of there. Hanging out with a bunch of uni students in party mode was not my idea of fun. 'If I get the next bus, it'll still be light when I get home.'

'It'll be fine. Just come in for a minute.'

Bad idea echoed in my head but I ignored it. 'Alright, but if I feel uncomfortable, I'm ringing Mum.'

'Okay.'

We had to push our way through people dressed in trashy clothes, drinking beer, and smoking. 'Babe, how did you go?' Jason spoke to Steph.

How can I get out of here? Where's the quickest and easiest way? 'Is it okay if I use your bathroom?'

'Sure, down there, to the left.' He pointed.

High school kids drinking at a party was one thing. This was a whole new level. I could only pretend to pee for so long before someone came knocking, needing to use the toilet.

'Are we still getting pizza?' Steph was asking Jason when I returned.

'Yeah, sure, we'll order them later,' he said.

'Can we get some now?' she asked. 'I invited Tabbie to hang around for dinner.'

'Great. Tabbie, grab a beer from the fridge.' He walked away.

'Steph, are you drinking?' Because it pretty much looked like she was, as she clung to a beer bottle with her left hand. Visions of Jaya throwing up flashed in my eyes. Could Stephanie now be acting the same way?

'It's only beer,' she said. 'And Jason's already had half of it.'

'But you're only sixteen.'

'Don't get so stressed. I'm careful. Like ... it's just one.'

'Hi, I'm Jules.' A tall girl introduced herself, pushing past us in the hallway, with all the glamour of a supermodel. I hung my head, in awe of her beauty.

'I'm Steph, and this is Tabbie.'

Jules smiled and continued down the hallway.

'I think it's time I rang Mum.' I wished I'd remembered my mobile.

'You won't tell her about the drinks, will you?'

'Are you trying to hide it?'

'No.' Steph shook her head as she put the bottle down. 'Just rather they didn't know.'

'Okay. I won't tell them, but it might be a good idea to leave the beer up here if you come downstairs with me.'

'Sure.'

I watched Steph take another swig as I called Mum. I needed to get away from the place. Something gave me the creeps. 'I'm going to wait downstairs.' I said when I hung up. 'Mum's only ten minutes away.'

'Sure you don't want a cuppa or a soft drink?'

I wanted to say, I'm going downstairs with or without you, but instead I managed to force the words, 'Stephanie, I want out of here.'

'Okay, okay I'm coming.' Stephanie sculled the rest of her beer, grabbed one of my shopping bags, and followed me.

'Promise me Jason doesn't drink and drive.'

'He gets a taxi if he goes anywhere.'

'Promise me, no matter what time of day it is, if you're ever in trouble, you'll ring us.'

'I'll be fine,' Steph said.

I held her hand, pulling her close until her nose nearly hit mine.

'Promise me.'

'Okay.'

'Mum and Dad would rather you were safe than have anything happen to you. You are family to us.'

'Alright, I'll call if I need them. But everything will be fine.' Steph swayed a little, then vagued out on me.

'Are you okay?' I reached out to steady her.

'Yeah, just thinking about what you said before. Oh good, here's your mum.'

'Be careful!'

'Bye.' Steph hugged me, waved and ran back upstairs before Mum stopped.

I prayed for her safety as we drove away.

Chapter Twenty-Four

I WAS RUNNING SO LATE, it would have been easy to just stay home. But I'd told Shelly I'd meet her there.

'Love, take a night off,' Mum said when she saw me panic about the time.

'I'd really like to go. Can you take me ... please? It's too late to get a lift with anyone. They'll be there already.'

Thankfully Mum said it was no problem. When I walked into youth group, music was already playing in the auditorium. I found a seat, aware of how tense my shoulders were. Still, I allowed my mind, body, and spirit to be refreshed. Danny was on stage, but I didn't stare at him. Instead, I kept my eyes closed. Tears rolled down my cheeks as I prayed for my three school friends. Soon, the burden of their worries was lifted and I relaxed.

It was exactly what I needed. The music and the lyrics of the songs washed over me, cleansing me. I sat through the rest of the service with a strange kind of peace—like everything might not turn out great—but it would still be okay.

'We're all off for a walk early tomorrow morning. Want to join us?' Priscilla asked.

'Sounds great.' I could do with some time away from my books.

'I'll pick you up at seven.'

We drove to a lake far from anywhere. The usuals were there, Danny included, but thankfully there was no sign of Rhett. The beautiful, serene, and seemingly untouched nature surrounding the area relaxed me. We sat around wooden picnic tables to eat morning tea before we set off on a man-made boardwalk around the lake. When we got back, we jumped into the freezing water for a swim. Well, most people jumped in. I waded up to my knees.

'Is this where you come when you're not at the beach?' I hoped the sun would dry my legs, and quickly. I was sure my lips were turning blue.

'We come here sometimes for water baptisms.' Shelly picked up a stone and skimmed it across the lake.

'Oh?' I was intrigued. Weren't most people baptised as babies?

'It's nothing weird or anything.'

I glanced back at her, nodding. I believed her. I was sure it wasn't anything weird. I'd just never seen anyone other than a baby being baptised.

'I'll invite you out here next time. You'll see ... it's beautiful, not weird.'

I smiled. She was pushing the not-so-weird factor. I wasn't about to be water-baptised myself but coming to watch might be good. Anyway, I'd already been baptised as a baby.

I did my best to keep my eyes averted from Danny all day. Seriously, my only attraction to him was nothing more than a passing lustful thought because of the similarities between him and that guy with amazing biceps I saw on the plane. A fantasy.

A group who'd jumped straight into the water obviously thought we all should be wet and splashed us, laughing. This group had my kind of fun. Active, with lots of jokes, mixed with food. Good times.

I didn't arrive home until it was getting dark. Mum pulled a homemade pizza out of the oven, and we ate in front of the TV. Just Mum, Dad, and me. My best friend didn't come home last night and hadn't been home all day. She'd left a message to say she was busy. With what, I didn't know. Busy with Jason? Busy with parties? She didn't have a job. I didn't know what she was up to. But there was no answer at Jason's and his mobile was turned off.

The next day, I woke up before the sun lit up my room. I used the extra time to walk to church. It took a while, like a whole hour, but after the fresh air yesterday, my body moved with ease and energy. During the service, I kept having visions of Stephanie crying. I opened my eyes to force the pictures away, but each time I closed them she was crying again. By the end of church, I was pretty shaken by the visions, so I hung around to ask Shelly and Priscilla to pray for Stephanie.

Mum looked concerned when I stepped through the door. 'Tabbie, Steph dropped in. She said she'd call later.'

'Is something wrong? Is she coming back again today?'

'I wondered that myself. But she didn't say. She left in quite a rush,' Dad answered, also with concern in his voice.

The visions of Stephanie crying crossed my mind again. 'I hope everything is alright.'

'So do we.'

'I have ridiculous amounts of school work to get through. I'll be upstairs.'

I had to push myself to write an essay, do maths homework and get a geography assignment drafted. It was a struggle to keep my mind on study and off Stephanie's business.

   Spiralling Out of the Shadow

By Tuesday, Stephanie hadn't returned my calls or been at school for two days. I checked with Mum to see if she knew anything.

'She was only here for a moment on Sunday ... sat down to watch the TV with Dad while I was in the kitchen. Dad said she seemed to jump out of her skin when they reported on the death of a young girl.'

'Huh?'

'Didn't make sense to Dad either.' Mum shrugged.

I sat down at the computer and searched *weekend news, Sydney*.

'Diane hasn't been able to contact her,' Mum continued. 'The school rang them wondering why she hadn't turned up for the last few days.'

I scrolled through a couple of pages, but nothing stood out at me. 'Morning Show?'

'Yes, your father was watching his usual shows.'

I read headline after headline. Some idiots were caught drag racing on the freeway. A drunken buck's night got out of hand when they left the groom strapped to a light pole. I scrolled down a little further, and there, staring back at me through the computer screen, was Jason's friend, Jules. Dead from taking ecstasy. My heart raced. A lump caught the saliva in my throat as I tried to swallow. I waited a moment until I could speak with a steady voice.

'Could you drop me over to see Steph?'

Mum agreed.

I didn't want to alarm her. I didn't know the whole story. I'd hate to highlight something then have it all blow over. I wanted to get the facts before I set off the alarm bells for my parents.

Mum parked the car along the kerb. 'Do you want me to come up with you to see if they're in?'

'You can wait a minute or two, but I've got my mobile. I'll call you later to come and pick me up, if that's okay?'

Mum regarded me for a moment then said, 'Sure. Just take care, okay?'

Even though they weren't home, I decided to wait. I sat on the top step, checking my watch every five minutes, hoping someone would eventually turn up. Finally, thirty minutes later, Stephanie edged her way up the stairs.

'Where've you been?' I asked.

'Hey, what are you doing here?' She gazed at me through red eyes in a vague trance, like she was on another planet. But not in a drugged kind of way. She'd been crying.

'Mum said you came by on Sunday, but you haven't returned my calls and you haven't been at school. Your mum's been ringing. She wants you to ring her back ASAP.' I knew I'd raced my words. My breath came in short bursts.

'Whoa, hold on. Sunday?' Steph unlocked the door with a key from her handbag. 'Yeah, felt like hanging out.'

'You have your own key to Jason's now?' Had she forgotten to tell us? 'Have you moved in?'

'No, no—'

'Well, you haven't been home much.'

I grabbed my nose. Stale cigarette smoke. *Gross.* Obviously Steph noticed the stench as well. She rushed to open up the windows. 'Don't get all weird on me. There's just been stuff going on because of my birthday—you know?'

'No, not really. Mum said you ran out in a rush on Sunday. It was Jules ... who I met the other night, wasn't it?'

Steph glanced at me, startled.

'And she's dead?' I looked her in the eye. 'Who are these people you're hanging out with? What are you doing with them? Are you really going out with that kind of guy?'

She said nothing.

Oh, no! 'Did you take that drug too?'

The guilty glint in her eyes answered my question.

'Are you going out to nightclubs as well?'

Steph's gaze darted from side to side.

'Oh, Steph.' I had to stop judging her. She looked fragile. She needed someone to help her pick up the pieces. 'There's so much more for you.'

'What do you mean?

'I know God loves you.'

'Don't go getting all religious on me now.'

'Come back home with me now, Steph. Please.'

'Jason's expecting me to be here.'

'Leave him a note. He can always come over to our house.'

Thankfully Steph gave in to my begging. I read over her shoulder as she wrote a note—something about Jason finding her a new job. 'You looking for work again?'

'Yeah.'

'Have you tried Maccas or Woollies?'

'No, I'm hoping for something with better pay.'

I wondered what kind of job Jason was sussing out for her.

'Are you going to tell your mum anything?' Stephanie asked on the way home.

'She probably should know, but I won't say anything. That's up to you. What about your mum and dad? They're the ones you really need to talk to.'

'No way!' Stephanie clenched a fist. 'They'd make me go back to Toowoomba. I'd rather die.'

She looked at me for a moment then looked away. *Does she really mean what she just said?* 'I may not agree with the way you are living right now, but I am here for you.' It was up to her, but she needed to be honest about her life.

The urge to tell Mum and Dad everything raced around my mind. But I had a feeling Steph would run away, vanish, or do something even more stupid if I opened my mouth. Somehow, I justified my silence. I was glad to see my best friend at home for a couple of nights, away from her boyfriend. But she was a mess. I had a feeling it had something to do with that girl's death.

Chapter Twenty-Five

On Friday, Suzie and Jaya edged in on me.

'What's going on with Stephanie?' Suzie flicked her hair. Her sweet disposition seemed to be crushed by an invisible mask.

The bell had rung, but Suzie and Jaya had me cornered.

'She's got some stuff going on.' I tried to brush them off and move towards class. If they really wanted to know, they could ask Stephanie themselves.

'Don't we all?' Jaya screwed up her nose.

'Guess so.' *Am I the only one without major issues?* One dodgy date was the single biggest drama I'd experienced.

'Steph's changed.' Suzie turned to walk away.

'I agree. She's a completely different person this year.' Jaya turned to follow Suzie.

'Jaya, Suzie!' I followed them. 'Just go easy on her, hey?' I wasn't sure if any of them wanted to fix the deep rift that had grown between Stephanie and all of us.

'Are you able to come to youth group with me tonight?' I asked Stephanie during our lunch break.

She glared at me like I had two heads. I knew she didn't want to come but this time I wanted more than a lame excuse. I wanted a reason. 'What do you have against it?'

'Everyone seems so nice. It's like they have it all together—my life just isn't that easy.'

'Yes, they are nice. But once you come a few times you'll realise they struggle with stuff, just like you.'

'Guess I don't have anything else on. Okay, just this time. Then will you stop asking me to come?'

'Agreed.' I was so excited she said yes that I had to refrain from jumping up and down.

As the day went on, the fear of Stephanie running off straight after school gripped me, so I waited outside her classroom. 'Tonight will be fun,' I said as we walked away from the school building.

She pulled the corner of her mouth back in an attempt to smile.

'I've got some great friends there. Perhaps I can find someone who you can talk to, you know, about Jules.'

'I told you, I don't want to talk about it,' she snapped, then looked towards the gate. 'Jason!'

He was leaning against the school fence. I didn't hide my disappointment. 'Oh, hi, Jason.'

'Hello, Tabbie,' he said with forced politeness. 'Steph, I got you a job.'

'Really?' She skipped towards him. 'Where? When do I start?'

'At *The Groove.* You start tonight.'

'Isn't that a hotel or something in the city?' I stepped towards Steph.

'Yeah, that's the one,' Jason said.

'Don't you have to be eighteen to work somewhere like that?' I asked.

Stephanie shook her head, fobbing me off. 'Guess I won't be able to come with you, after all. Can you let your mum know I'm starting a new job in the city?'

I hugged her before she could run away again. 'Be careful, Steph.'

'I will.' Steph beamed a wide smile as she left with Jason.

I kicked a rock off the path to avoid watching them drive off. I'd been dumped for the boyfriend.

'I'm concerned about my best friend,' I said to Shelly soon after I walked into youth group.

'Why? What's up?'

I told Shelly bits and pieces, trying to honour my friend and not paint her out to be some kind of crazy teen. 'I'm not sure what I can do.'

'You can pray for her. Have you invited her here?'

'Yeah, it's the friend I asked you to pray for last week. I'm always inviting her here. She came to that big concert night last year and doesn't want to come back.'

'I can understand that. Coming to a night like that can be pretty overwhelming.'

'I thought it was great.' I smiled as I remembered the night.

'I know you enjoyed it, but you'd been to youth group and already loved it here. I'll keep your friend in my prayers this week.'

'Thanks, Shelly.'

At nineteen, Shelly didn't treat me like a young school girl. She was becoming a really good friend. Because my actual best friend was so self-absorbed, and Jaya and Suzie had issues of their own, I found myself relying on Shelly more and more.

We started to play poison ball outside the building. One of the leaders did a crazy leap and came down on top of the ball, twisting his ankle. It looked hilarious. Everyone was in hysterical laughter. He laughed at first but we soon discovered he was in quite a bit of pain by the end of the night. I guess it wasn't that funny. I knew all about twisting an ankle and prayed his would heal quickly.

The following day, when Steph arrived home, I ran downstairs to greet her. 'How did the new job go?'

'It was great. The money is good.' Steph didn't look at me. 'I'll be working less hours.'

Mum wanted to know all the details of Steph's new job, but Steph was careful not to mention it was in a hotel.

'Do you want a study partner?' I asked when I could see their conversation was going nowhere.

'Yeah,' Steph said. 'I might have to use some of your notes.'

'Why?'

'I forgot to bring my school bag back from Jason's.'

Was she completely losing it?

'So, did I miss much last night?' Stephanie looked at her reflection in my mirror and scrunched her hair into a messy knob.

'It was fun.' My face grew warm as I tried not to laugh. 'We played poison ball and one of the leaders twisted his ankle. It was really funny—not that he got hurt, but it was a fun night.'

Steph looked at me like I'd grown an extra limb. I smothered the laugh behind a hand. 'Guess you had to be there.'

'So you just played games?' She stopped fussing with her hair and sat beside me. 'What about all the religious stuff?'

'We don't do religious stuff,' I said. 'But we do spend some time singing, then one of the leaders speaks—'

'Like a homily?' Steph rolled her eyes, shaking her head.

'Not really. It's a lot different to the churches you've been to.'

'Churches are all the same. Full of rules and people breaking them.'

There was something else bubbling under Steph's skin. She wasn't herself.

'Go,' she said with a click of her fingers. 'Teach me all you know.'

'I can't do all the work for both of us.'

'I'm so sick of school.' Stephanie closed her eyes and lay on my bed. 'I wish you could finish for me.'

'You know you'll kick yourself if you don't finish year twelve.' I didn't want to cheat her out of an education. 'We've got a maths quiz tomorrow. Do you know the formulas?'

'Bed plus Steph equals sleepy.' She laughed.

'What did you do last night?' My shoulders tensed.

'Why?'

'You are in one fine mood.'

'I'll leave you to it then.' Stephanie flung herself off the bed.

'Wait.' I grabbed her arm to stop her from leaving my room. 'How's Jason?'

'Why do you ask?'

I raised my eyebrows in a tell-me-because-I'm-your-best-friend kind of look.

'We kind of had an argument. We'll get over it—we always do.'

'You argue a lot then?'

'A fair bit. I'm sure it's like any other couple.'

'As long as he doesn't hit or hurt you.'

'Yeah.' She looked at the floor.

'Having a boyfriend sounds like too much work.'

'Probably looks that way.'

I'd changed my mind about asking her to help me find a boyfriend. I no longer wanted one. Steph's life seemed to revolve around Jason. My life was fun and exciting and I was in control, making all the decisions. I didn't want to give that up. Did that make me self-centred?

Chapter Twenty-Six

THE WEEKEND SEEMED TOO RUSHED, like I'd blinked and it was Monday morning already.

'Tabbie.' Steph poked her head into my room. 'Can I wear one of your uniforms? I've left mine at Jason's.'

'Steph! You mean to tell me you have no uniforms here?'

'I know, I know. I'll be more careful next time.'

'Where are you living?'

'Here.'

'But you've been at Jason's—'

'I know, don't lecture me about it. Can I please borrow a uniform?'

I shoved a uniform at her, pushing her backwards, out of my room. 'It's not going to fit you properly.'

I had to get my uniforms adjusted, sewn right in at the top seams and let out as far as possible on the skirt. Thankfully they made them with extra wide seams for my pear-shape.

Stephanie looked as uncomfortable as a cat in a doghouse. I couldn't work out why she didn't call Jason and ask him to drop her things home. Perhaps their argument was heavier than she wanted me to know.

I saw her around school a couple of times, and she seemed vague and totally off with the fairies.

We both had to sit a maths quiz. I blitzed it, remembering every formula I needed. Just as I finished the last question, Stephanie stood to leave.

She threw her test paper on the teacher's desk. It was blank. Part of me wanted to call her back, hand her mine, show her the answers, and help her out. But she was gone before I had a chance. It wouldn't have been the right thing to do anyway. Stephanie's chances of passing were about the same as getting frostbite in summer.

On the way out of school, I found my almost-neglected friend, Suzie, sitting under a small tree with her hands over her face. Shoulders shuddering.

'What's up?'

'It's that guy from dance—Joey. You remember.'

'Sure.' Yeah, of course I remembered him—and how he introduced me to Danny, who reminded me of Mr Biceps but was a complete nerd, who in a roundabout way introduced me to Mr Creepy Rhett.

'Yeah, well he asked me out on a date, but Mum and Dad said no way.'

'I get that, Mum and Dad were crazy strict until I turned sixteen.'

'But my mum and dad want me to wait until I'm eighteen.'

A noise escaped from the back of my throat.

'I know! Can you believe it?'

'I know you want to start dating, and Joey is a pretty cool guy, but do you remember what happened on my first date?'

'As if Joey would be like that.'

'I'm sure he wouldn't either. But I lied to Mum and Dad, and felt guilty about it, and then I had a bad night anyway. You don't want to lie to your parents just so you can go on a date, do you?'

'I don't know.'

'Why don't you just ask him to meet you out with a group. Something like ... catching a movie together.'

'You know my parents will want to come too.'

'Hmm.' I stopped to think for a moment. 'Let them.'

'Are you serious?' Suzie leaned away from me.

'Yeah.'

'No way!'

'If we're all out together and they see you acting responsibly and normally around Joey, like you do, then they might come round and let you date him.'

'Urgh! Why do I have the strictest parents in the world?'

'Just lucky, I guess.' I wrapped my arm around her and squeezed her shoulders.

I had nothing else for her. Sure, my parents were pretty strict, but hers were over the top. It would be fun to have a boyfriend. But when it came down to it, I realised I didn't want one, not really. I was happy the way I was. Single and free.

When I reached home, I sent out a text message, inviting a bunch of friends to the movies on the weekend.

'Yes,' Shelly replied straight away.

Priscilla suggested we should mix it up so Joey wasn't the solitary guy there. She had a good point. So far, I'd only invited girls. I thought of Danny. My heart raced, not with excitement, but with the pull of anxiety. I waited until I saw them the next day to discuss it further.

'Remember Rhett, Danny's friend? I'd rather not see him. What if Danny invites him?'

'Leave it with me.' Priscilla winked. 'I'll make sure he comes without that friend.'

'That would be great.' I knew I could trust Priscilla.

I called Jaya, but she was non-committal. I knew she wasn't going to turn up. She probably had another party to go to with her drinking friends. I visited Suzie at home, unsure if I'd be more help or hindrance. Both Suzie and her mother met me at the door.

Thankfully time seemed to have dissolved her mother's hate towards me. I asked if Suzie could come to the movies, her big-cow-pleading eyes looked towards her mother.

'Mum, I'd really like to go.' She paused. I didn't know if she'd continue. I took a breath, and was about to speak when she went on, 'I'd love you to come along, Mum, and Dad is welcome too.'

'Oh, what movie will you see?'

'There's a new one with Tom Cruise.' Suzie raced her words.

I hoped Tom Cruise would grab their interest, being that he was from their era.

'It's not one of his smutty ones, is it?'

Suzie bit into her thumbnail. How long did her parents plan to control everything? My heart broke for her.

Tension clawed the air. I had to break the silence, in language that her mother would understand. 'Mrs Peters, it's an action film. Sure, there'll be the usual romance side—there always is. But I think this one is more about the action.'

Suzie's mum turned so her shoulder cut me off as she spoke to her daughter. 'I'll ask your father. It might be nice to all go to the movies together.'

When I saw Suzie the next day at school, she looked a whole lot brighter.

'See, it wasn't as hard as you thought it would be.'

'Yeah, it looked that way to you. But after you left, Mum wanted to know the name and age of everyone going.'

'Just the name and age? Not the address, parent's names and phone numbers?'

'Well, she did ask where they lived as well.' Suzie slumped over a short post.

I invited Stephanie to join us at the movies when she arrived home after dinner.

'No.' She let her hair down and started climbing the stairs. 'I've got something on.'

Like what? I wanted to ask her, but I was sure if she'd answered, it would have been a lie. So I didn't ask.

'That's a shame. Joey's asked Suzie out, but because her parents won't let her go on a date, a group of us are—'

'Oh.' She looked up, shrugged then closed her door.

She hadn't listened to a word I'd said. Why did I bother explaining?

I wished I was a fly on the wall in Suzie's house Saturday morning. I figured she'd been through the wringer when she rolled her eyes as they arrived at the cinema.

'This is happening. You're here,' I whispered when her parents moved a metre away.

Priscilla, Shelly, Joey, and Danny all arrived at the same time with a couple of other people I hadn't met. Joey walked straight up to Suzie, giving her a small posy of soft pink roses. Her face went so bright the flowers began to reflect off her, almost changing to a hot pink. Mrs Peters raised her eyebrows at Mr Peters.

Suzie had been honest with Joey. She'd told him her parents were over-the-top strict and the only way she would be allowed to go out with him was during the day with a bunch of others, including her parents. He didn't mind. He just wanted to go out with her, even if it meant dating in a group. He was smitten. They looked sweet together, standing side by side, not touching for fear of being reprimanded by the parental chaperones.

I had a huge grin on my face as we walked into the cinema. I wondered where everyone would end up sitting. Mr and Mrs Peters followed their daughter into a row of seats.

'Here will be fine, Suzie,' her father muttered.

'Maybe I should sit over—' Suzie pointed.

'No, sit there, on the end.' It was a command and I could see Suzie wasn't game to sit anywhere else. Mr Peters turned and guided Joey to sit beside him.

I couldn't work out how they got off on crushing her with such control. It was so pathetic it was hilarious. I had to leave the cinema before my bursting-at-the-seams laughter exploded. I was laughing so hard my eyes closed. When I opened them, I stopped, feet planted. Danny had his arms up, as if to catch me. 'What's so funny?' He looked at me with wide eyes and a huge grin.

It was possible that I looked totally ridiculous, laughing by myself, apparently at nothing. When Danny asked me what made me laugh, I laughed even more. I tried a second time to tell him, but the whole scene was too hard to describe as I gasped for air. I shook my head and took a deep breath.

'I wish I was there,' Danny said, looking directly into my eyes.

Suddenly the reality of the fact stunned me. Young Mr Biceps stood in front of me. I was such an idiot.

'We'd better go in. I think the movie is starting.' He gestured for me to go first.

'Yeah.' My eyes lingered a moment too long at his incredible body and his gorgeous face. Heat burnt my cheeks. I broke eye contact and walked back in with Danny following me, thankful for the darkness. Until now, he was the guy who didn't seem to be able to string two words together. Could he actually have a personality?

I didn't dare look in the direction the Peters family were sitting. I glanced around the cinema but couldn't see where Shelly and Priscilla were, so I walked up the aisle and found a seat in the opposite direction to Suzie and her parents.

Sitting by myself didn't bother me. It just meant I was free to cry or laugh without worrying about the person beside me. I slipped into an empty row, only to find Danny still following me. He slid right into the seat beside me. There wasn't anyone else in the row. He could have left a seat between us. There were seats in front and behind. A thud echoed in my chest as he rested that very noticeable

     Spiralling Out of the Shadow

bicep just millimetres away from my arm. So close, his warmth radiated onto me.

'Hmm,' I sighed leaning away a little.

'Oh, sorry. Was I bumping you?' He moved his arm away.

'Thanks.' The claustrophobic moment lessened as Danny increased the air pocket between us.

My eyes had grown accustomed to the darkness and I found where everyone was sitting, though it was hard to see Suzie past her mother. And every time I glanced across, I was sure Danny thought I was looking right at him.

Danny shared his popcorn with me. We reached into the jumbo container at the same time. Our fingers became tangled, and it was so awkward I didn't reach back in for at least another ten minutes. Each time his body connected with mine, my cheeks burnt. *Why am I affected by him?* I wasn't interested in him. He just reminded me of my fantasy guy. Looks, but no personality. That's what I'd told myself until he showed personality potential just before in the walkway. I was happy to stay single. Why was I getting so hot and flustered?

I couldn't even follow the storyline of the movie. My whole body cringed every time there was partial nudity or a love scene. I half expected to see Suzie's parents dragging her out before the end. Eventually the movie credits rolled onto the screen, and I saw Suzie stand up. I went to leave but Danny didn't move. The only way out was past him.

'Excuse me.' I pointed to his legs, completely blocking my way.

'Maybe we can do this again sometime.' He glanced at me then looked away.

'Yeah.' Another fit of laughter began rumbling in my chest. I rushed past him when he moved his legs. This time it was my nerves causing the giggle. I took a breath and managed to smother my laughter behind clenched teeth.

I obviously still looked flustered once we were outside.

'What's up?' Suzie asked.

'Later,' I said with a giggle, raising my eyebrows.

Joey was the complete gentleman and didn't appear too fazed by the whole dating-with-Suzie's-parents process. I wondered where he learnt to be so mature. He never came across that way in dance classes. Hopefully it wasn't just an act.

'Joey,' Mr Peters said when our group had gathered together under the bright lights in the foyer. 'You should come over for dinner one night. How about Friday?'

'Sure, Mr Peters. I'd like that.'

And so began the successful dating life of Suzie Peters within the over-protective parental boundaries. Would my glowing satisfaction over the success be short-lived?

Chapter Twenty-Seven

Mum stopped me as I walked in. 'Jaya rang. She's at a party and wants me to drive you over there.'

'How did she sound?'

'A little nervous.'

'Guess I'll go and change my shirt and get a jacket.'

'You don't have to go.' Mum frowned.

'I reckon she needs me if she's asked you to bring me over. Something over-the-top-strange must be up.'

When Mum parked outside the party house, people were sprawled out everywhere. Most looked half-tanked and it was only just after seven. 'Mum, would you mind staying here for a few minutes? I'm not sure I want to stay. I'll go and see if Jaya will come home with us.'

'Do you want me to come in if you don't return in ten minutes?'

'Umm ...' As if I wanted my mummy following me in. But the crowd did look pretty out there. 'Could you give me at least fifteen?'

Couples lined the walls sucking face, oblivious to the fact that their drunken public display of affection grossed out everyone else.

'Jaya!' I yelled over the music when I couldn't find her anywhere.

'Hi, beautiful. Are you a friend of Jaya's?' A guy stepped in front of me with bloodshot eyes and a crooked nose. 'You'd be a friend of mine too.'

'Have you seen her?'

'Yeah.' He laughed. 'She's down the hallway, first door on the right.'

'Thanks.' I had to step over a passed-out girl, then shuffle around another couple making out.

'But what about me?' the guy called as I walked away.

I shook my head without looking back. The first door on the right was closed. I knocked. No one answered. I knocked again. 'Jaya! Are you in there?'

I opened the door a little. What stood right in front of me was more than my eyes could handle.

'Jaya!' Blinking, I looked away, trying to focus on anything but what was straight ahead. *Eww. Eww. Eww.* She was down on her knees in front of a boy. He stumbled away when he saw me and reached to his ankles to pull up his pants.

Jaya gazed toward me without recognition. She squinted, like she was trying to focus. 'Tabbie?'

'Come with me.'

'We were just—'

'Aah.' I held out my hand. 'Just stand up and come with me now.' Thankfully, she obeyed. I didn't want to have to go in there and drag her out.

'Whad aar you do'n 'ere?'

'What am I doing here? I'm taking you back to sober up at my house.'

'You wanna grink?'

'No, thanks.' I grabbed her around her waist and pulled her arm behind my neck to keep her upright. Her legs buckled under her, and we swayed before I could balance again. For a slight girl, it was an effort to get her outside.

'Sorry, Mum.' I dumped Jaya onto the backseat then climbed into the front.

Mum raised her eyebrows.

'Don't ask.' I closed my eyes and shook my head, trying to shake the scene from my mind.

I was thankful Mum trusted my judgment and stayed silent. But while we drove, I wondered if my judgment was always worthy. Was I kidding myself, thinking I could actually help Jaya, Suzie, and Stephanie through all their issues? Perhaps. But I couldn't bring myself to break their confidences and dob them in.

I ran inside and pulled out our spare mattress and a sheet, then returned to help Mum bring Jaya inside. Once she was snoring under the blanket, I went downstairs to watch TV.

'Are you sure she'll be alright?' Dad asked.

I knew he meant more than just sleeping off the alcohol. 'Yeah. She's just having a hard time with her parents.'

'I slept here?' Jaya blinked, looking around my room.

'Yes.'

'I was at a party.'

'You were drunk.'

'I'd only had a few.' She rubbed her temples.

'You don't remember me bringing you back here? You were drunk.'

'Oh. Was it messy?'

'Yes. Well, no vomit this time. But messy all the same.'

'I don't want to know.' She pulled a pillow over her head.

I pulled it back so I could see her face. 'But I'm going to tell you anyway.'

'Can I get a coffee first?'

'Don't move. I'll bring one up.'

Mum had already brewed a strong pot. I returned within minutes with a steaming hot cup for Jaya. 'So.' I handed her the coffee. 'I walked in to find you in a compromising position.'

'I still had all my clothes on, didn't I?'

'Yes, but he didn't.'

'Who?'

'I don't know. I've never seen him before. It looked like you were about to well, ahem.' My cheeks suddenly warmed up. 'Like ... did you stop to ask if he was clean? He could have just taken a leak and you were about to put your mouth—'

'Stop! I've got it. Just stop. You don't have to explain any more. I get the picture. I don't want to hear another word about it.'

Desired outcome achieved. I hoped she would remember this moment the next time she thought about diving in front of another guy.

'I'm going to church. You can come with me or stay as long as you like. I'll be back at around lunchtime.'

'That was such a great idea.' Priscilla stopped me just before I walked in.

'What was?'

'Setting up a date for your friend like that. It really worked. Maybe you could start a dating service or something.'

'Oh, boy.' My thoughts returned to the party I'd picked Jaya up from. 'I don't think I like all that's involved with matching people up. Anyway, I didn't match those two up. I just helped them get past the strict parent issue.'

'What are you up to today? The music team have planned a barbeque. Want to join us?'

'I'd love to, but I've left a friend at home. I'd better get back to her.'

On the way home, I remembered Danny. Had he actually asked me out, or was he just suggesting we all go to the movies again sometime? Had I misunderstood him? What if I was imagining he had a little bit of personality and he didn't? I could never date someone just for their looks.

Chapter Twenty-Eight

I wanted to rush to my default position and talk to my ridiculously beautiful and increasingly imperfect best friend. But she was missing in action. She hadn't been at school for a couple of days, so I didn't ring her to talk through my crazy weekend. But I did ring to check up on her. Mid-ring, a fuzz of static buzzed through, then the line went blank. *Come on, Steph. Don't hang up on me.* I sent a text message asking her to call back. When she didn't reply, concern clutched at my heart. I rang Jason's home number. No answer. I prayed, asking for her to be protected and tried not to worry.

Just when I felt proud of myself for being able to keep the good friend code, I opened my big mouth without thinking. I mentioned to Suzie that Jaya was drunk on the weekend. That sent Suzie off on a tangent. 'She's just asking for trouble drinking the way she does. Say no more. I don't want to hear about any of the parties she's going to. I'm barely allowed to leave my house, and she abuses her parents' trust.'

It was a good thing Jaya wasn't nearby or it may have turned into a cat fight. I questioned the connection of our circle of four.

Had we been friends by circumstance, friends who never really connected on a deeper level? Perhaps I was also losing touch with Steph. Jaya and Suzie relied on me, but hardly ever spoke to each other. I'd love to pull everyone back together. But perhaps we'd drifted too far apart.

Stephanie turned up at home out of the blue that afternoon.

'I didn't see you at school today or yesterday afternoon.'

'I was so tired, I took an early mark yesterday, and I slept in today.'

'I thought you said this job was much better with fewer hours. If you can't handle school, maybe you should quit this job too.'

'I'll work it out. I'm just getting used to it.' Stephanie chewed a fingernail.

'Are you coming to school camp this year?' We'd just received our consent forms and I hoped she'd come too.

'Isn't that ages away?'

'Only a couple of weeks. Soon after the holidays, but we have to have the forms in by Monday.'

'I think I'll pass,' Steph said. 'It'll be pretty boring anyway.'

'Boring—how? Compared to what you and Jason do?' I cringed at the slip of sarcasm in my voice.

'I'm feeling a lecture coming on.'

'I'm not going to lecture you.' Even though I wanted to. 'I'm just concerned you're making some dumb decisions.'

'Well, don't be concerned.' Steph looked at me square on. 'I'm doing just fine.' She closed her bedroom door on me. I waited in the hallway, listening to her shuffle around on the other side of the wall. I guessed she needed some time to herself, so I retreated to my own room.

I pushed through the next week, heavy with mid-year exams. I looked forward to the reward on the other side. Three weeks off.

By Friday night, I was ready to ditch my high school friends and hang out with my church friends. Everything was pretty normal at youth group until Mr Amazing caught my eye. When I realised I couldn't drag my gaze away from him, I knew this was one guy I'd think about dating just for his looks. His olive skin glowed against the chocolate couch where he sat, and his hair curled over one eye, bouncing against his lashes as he spoke. So blond he could be accused of bleaching it. Every time he blinked, his alluring brown eyes lit up.

'Stop staring, Tabbie.' Shelly bumped me on the shoulder, snapping me out of my dreamy wonderland.

'I wasn't staring.' Straight away, my gaze headed back in his direction.

'He is pretty good-looking, hey?'

'Who?' Okay, so I knew she knew who I was looking at, but Shelly never talked about boys.

'His name is Aiden. Come with me. I'll introduce you.'

Oh boy. My heart was pounding at triple speed.

'Aiden, this is Tabbie. Aiden has just moved here from Melbourne.'

'Oh, like moved here for good?' Like, I wondered if I could have asked a lamer question.

'What are you up to tomorrow?'

Who, me? Was he asking me out right after meeting me?

I shook my head, smiling like a complete ditz.

'I'm playing footy. A bunch of these guys said they'd come along. You're welcome to come too.'

'Aha.' I nodded. I'd fallen under his spell. That night, I left wondering if I'd said yes to going to the moon and back, or just to a local football game.

The next day, Shelly picked me up just after lunch to watch the game. It was AFL. Australian Rules Football League. Aussie Rules. I couldn't work out which to call it. So I tried them all to find which rolled off my tongue the sweetest. I'd never watched a game in my life.

Priscilla seemed to know the rules and gave me a crash course. The ball was mostly kicked. They got six points when they kicked the ball through the two larger posts. They got one point when they missed the main goalposts and the ball went through the side posts.

They didn't throw the ball. They did something called hand-ball, which looked more like punching the football.

'I think I'm understanding the game a little more now. Thanks for the info.'

'No worries. My brothers love the game,' Priscilla said.

Soon after full time, Aiden came over to thank us for being his cheer squad. He walked along the fence and stopped right in front of me.

'Hey, got anything on tonight?' His eyes glistened as he smiled.

'No.' A flash of heat surged through my body.

'Do you want to grab something to eat?'

'Okay.'

'Come over and wait in the clubhouse while I go get changed.' He turned and ran back to his team.

'Hey,' I grabbed Shelly's arm, 'I think Aiden just asked me out. Will you wait over in the clubhouse with me 'til he gets changed?'

'Sure. I think a few of these guys were planning to go over there anyway.'

I grabbed a juice from the counter and sat down at the table Shelly and Priscilla had claimed. Danny joined us. I hadn't even realised he was there, and now he sat right beside me.

'Hey, Tabbie.' He leaned right over to me. 'Would you like to catch a movie later?' His words tickled my ear.

Once again, he had strung more than two words together, and such lovely words ... asking me out words. I was sure no one else had heard. But I had plans. I had to downplay his invitation.

'Oh, is everyone heading out?'

'No, just thought ... umm, never mind.' He mumbled the last words and sat back in his seat.

I grabbed my drink and stared into it, sucking on the straw. I couldn't look at him. This was the guy who couldn't string two words together. He'd probably never speak to me again after my flippant behaviour.

'Oh, great, you're still here.' Aiden walked out in his club shirt, hair still dripping from his shower. He'd exchanged sweat for a fresh soapy scent.

'Yes.' I stood. Now I was the one who couldn't string my words together. I followed Aiden outside, not daring to look at anyone's reaction. Not daring to turn back to see Danny.

Aiden led me to a little Hyundai Excel. When we left the club car park, it rattled around the corner. It sure didn't match his looks one bit. 'Sorry about the car. But it'll get me through uni.'

'You study?' I was heading out on a date with a uni student. The lectures I had given Steph about dating older boys started to mess with my mind.

'Yeah, I'm doing commerce.'

'How far through are you?' I could have high-fived myself for speaking a whole sentence without getting tongue-tied.

'This is my first year.'

'Oh.' My breathing sounded wrong. Deep breaths. Gasps.

'Let's grab a quick bite to eat. There's a game on TV. I want to get back to watch it.'

'AFL?' I pulled my mobile out and sent mum a quick text to say I wouldn't be home for dinner.

'Of course. Is there any other game worth watching?'

'Well ...' I laughed.

'Did you enjoy the game?'

'Yeah, once I understood a few of the rules.'

'You've never been into AFL?'

'No.'

'You can change.'

I smiled. Did that mean he already had plans to see me again?

He took me to a little café where we sat at a table on the footpath. I was glad to have the distraction of people passing. Aiden smelled good and looked good — all I wanted to do was lean across the table and kiss him. *Gee, I've only just met the guy.* I now understood my best friend's lack of self-control.

'Would you like a wine or beer? Or would you rather a coke?'

'Coke, thanks.' I laughed. 'I'm only sixteen.' I saw the look in his eyes that said every other sixteen-year-old on the planet was drinking, so why wasn't I?

Truth was, the idea of not being in control scared me, especially after watching Jaya and the other kids at parties. Anyway, who would look after everyone else if I got drunk? Not to mention that alcoholic uncle and perhaps an alcoholic gene in my family.

Aiden's hair began to dry and loosen as he spoke. I wanted to reach out and push the loose curl away from his eye. But I didn't. I didn't need to say much. He spoke continuously. I enjoyed his smooth voice. He told me about famous AFL players he knew. I'd never heard of any of them. He told me about the numerous times he'd won the flag. He told me stories of Melbourne, making me want to visit to see all the heritage and culture there.

Our plates were empty and there was a moment of silence where we movie-style gazed into each other's eyes.

'Did you want to come back to mine and watch the game with me?'

'Thanks, but Mum and Dad—'

'We should be off then.'

I nodded.

He went inside to pay for dinner. I took a couple of deep breaths. How long could my heart flap at such a pace? When he returned to the table, I stood. My arm brushed against his. Fire rushed through my body. I looked away to hide my face heating up. He grabbed my hand and led me to his car. As he opened the door, I let his hand go, slipped into the seat and hoped my cheeks would cool in the few seconds it would take him to walk around the car to the driver's side.

He pulled up outside my home and walked me to my front door. He brushed his lips against mine before he said goodbye. I would've loved to have called it a kiss, but his lips had barely touched mine. He returned to his car and left me standing there wanting more.

'Are you doing anything tomorrow night?' He called from the road.

'No,' I said, breathlessly.

'I'll pick you up at around six. We can watch a movie or something.'

'Okay.' I looked at my watch and began to count down the hours.

'So, how was last night?' Priscilla asked.

'Good.' My smile broadened until my cheeks hurt.

'Just good? Nothing else to tell us?'

I pulled the smile down for long enough to say, 'We're going out again tonight.'

'Wow. Go Tabbie. Is he coming today?'

'He didn't say.' We both looked around at the crowd gathering in the church foyer. He'd been once before.

My smile fell when Aiden didn't show. I still had tonight to look forward to. That afternoon, I rested so I'd be fresh when Aiden arrived.

My mobile phone buzzed, startling me with a text message. 'Sorry Tab, can't see u 2night. Same time next week? I'll pick u up at 6. A'

I threw the phone back into my bag and fell face first onto my bed, letting my pillow catch my tears. It was a whole seven nights away. Seriously, I needed to get a grip!

Chapter Twenty-Nine

I GRABBED AN APPLE from the fridge. Mum was in the kitchen, preparing dinner. The week dragged on while I willed it to speed up so I could see Aiden again.

'How are you, love?' Mum stopped chopping veggies for a moment.

'Good.'

'Where's Steph?'

'She hasn't been around for a while, has she?' I took a bite of my apple.

'I haven't seen her all week.'

'Are you worried about her?'

'Aren't you?' Mum began chopping again.

'I've rung both Jason's home number and Steph's mobile, and she's not answering either. And she's not returning my messages.'

'We should go around there.' Mum put the knife down and washed her hands.

'If they're not answering the home number, they must be out.'

'I guess,' Mum said. 'I left a message for her parents, but they haven't returned my call. I'll try them again now.'

'She'll get angry if we interfere. I'll call again.' Maybe I'd get somewhere if I threatened to call her parents if she didn't answer.

I sent a text message, letting her know we were worried and that Mum would contact her parents if we didn't hear from her ASAP. She rang back within five minutes.

'Heya. We haven't seen or heard from you.' I tried to keep my voice calm. I didn't want her to hang up on me.

'It's this new job. Still getting used to the hours.'

'What about school?'

'Please don't tell anyone, but I'm not going back.'

'How can you keep that from your parents?'

'I forged their signature on some papers, so all the letters and phone calls go to Jason's.'

'How is that working for you?'

Stephanie sighed.

'What about school?'

'I forged a letter from Mum and Dad saying I needed some time off and I'd be back next year.'

'The school bought it?'

'I think so. They rang and Jason acted like he was my dad on the phone.'

'Stephanie!'

'Look, I know I'm not Miss Goody-Two-Shoes like you. I'm sorry I'm failing as a friend.'

I had tears in my eyes. She didn't sound herself. The spark was missing from her voice.

'Are you okay?'

'I'm fine.'

'Really?'

'I'm just a little tired. I was about to have a sleep, so I'll talk to you later.'

'Please be careful,' I said, but I think she'd already hung up.

'Is everything okay?' Mum asked.

'She says it is, but her parents don't know the whole story. And as much as I've love you to tell them, she'd be furious with me. They do have her phone number and Jason's address, so they can call her or visit at any time.'

'I don't know. I think we should go and see her. It's a shame her parents don't seem to be interested.'

'They weren't that interested in Toowoomba either.'

'Really? I didn't realise it was that bad. Is that why she wanted to move?'

I nodded.

'If her parents would just allow us to be her guardians ... As it is, our hands are tied. There isn't much we can do except keep in touch with Stephanie and let her parents know what's going on.' Mum scratched her head and gazed out the window. 'I'll give them another call.'

Finally, it was date night. I'd expected to be more excited. As I changed my clothes to get ready to see Aiden, I couldn't help feeling a little dull. Maybe my mind was in overdrive. Was my best friend okay? I prayed for her before heading out.

I wasn't ready for Mum and Dad to meet Aiden just yet, so I waited at the front of the house. It was only minutes until his car rattled to a stop in front of me. I didn't look back, but I was sure they were both standing at the front window, gawking, hoping to check him out. Aiden jumped out and opened the car door before I had time to reach for it. A smile gripped my face.

'Thanks,' I said, as his hand guided the small of my back into the car.

'What kind of girl are you? Do you like action or shoot-em-up or a good old romance?'

'I'm not a fan of guns. Action or romance, I guess.' *Romance.* This guy could romance me anytime.

'Great. Let's see what's showing.'

Aiden rested his arm around my shoulders as we watched the trailers for a couple of minutes then checked the viewing times.

'The only one that I haven't seen is the Tom Cruise movie. Are you okay with that?'

'Sure.'

Obviously I was out of my mind when he asked if I was okay with his movie choice—the only movie I had seen. As the movie began, I realised it was good to sit through it and actually watch it. I was expecting to have the same turmoil that I'd had while sitting beside Danny. But this time I wasn't distracted, maybe because I knew I'd have another chance to feast my eyes on Aiden after the movie. I didn't have to steal glances in the dark.

'I have an early start.' Aiden stood as soon as the credits began to roll. 'So I'd better drop you home.'

'Thanks.' I cringed at how my one-word answers lacked conversation stimulation.

He parked outside my house and leant over before I opened the door to kiss me. Lips, tongue fluttering, more lips. I was out of breath and clutching for the door when we parted.

'See you soon then,' he said.

'Okay,' I whispered, leaving the car feeling dizzy.

'How was your night?' Dad asked, before I stepped inside.

'Nice,' I said, trying to gain control of the spin still going on inside my heart.

'Just nice?'

'Yes, nice.' That was all the information my father needed.

'He'd better make sure he treats you right, or I'll be—'

'Dad, we just went to the movies. Nothing serious.'

Rain pelted our windows as I sat on the couch to see what was on TV. A small knock on our front door made me jump. I flicked the TV off and jumped up to see who it was. 'Hi, stranger!' I swung the door open to let Steph in.

'Hello.' She shivered in saturated clothes. Her eyes swollen. Tears flowed down her cheeks.

I pulled her inside and grabbed a towel to wrap around her, wanting to make everything better but unsure where to start.

'I really miss you,' she whispered.

'Is everything okay?' I rubbed her hair with the towel.

'Yeah. I haven't seen you forever.'

'I know. How's work?'

'I just got promoted.' Steph grinned.

'That sounds great. More money?'

'Yeah, more money.'

'Have you spoken to your family?'

'No.' She looked away. 'They still ring most Sundays. I text them back.'

'How's Jason?' I looked her in the eye, wanting to see the truth behind her words.

'Great.' She blinked, looking away.

'Really?'

'We just had a bit of a disagreement today.'

'You're welcome here anytime, day or night. You know Mum and Dad are—'

'I know, I know, you've told me a million times. Really, I'm okay. We'll be fine, honest. Tell me about you, what's happening in your life?'

'I think I'm falling in love.' I took her upstairs to tell her all about Aiden.

Before I'd finished, she cut me off. 'You'll have to introduce your amazing man to me soon then.'

'Steph, what's it like?' I'd never asked anyone, and I was sure it wasn't like they showed in the movies.

'What?'

'You know, it ... S. E. X.'

'Oh, Tabbie. Is he pressuring you?'

'No, but when we kissed ...' I closed my eyes, remembering our last goodbye kiss. 'It's like ... I don't know how to explain it, but something happens in my body and I just want to, well ... you know.'

'But, Tabbie,' Steph's voice was raspy. 'You said you wanted to wait. Isn't that what they teach you at that youth group?'

'But you wanted to wait and didn't.' Why did I feel like the friendship roles had been reversed?

'I know, but you should wait a while.'

'What's with telling me to wait when you went ahead and did it with Jason?'

She looked into my mirror and bunched her hair up into a knob. 'How long have you known him?'

'A couple of weeks.'

'Just spend some time getting to know the guy. I know it sounds crazy, but—'

'But why should I wait?'

'Because if he really cares about you, he'll wait. Don't be tempted.'

'What if I don't want to wait any longer?'

'Tabbie, this is important to you. If you leave it for a couple more months you'll be glad you did.'

'I don't get you.' I began to question who she had become. She was different again from who I thought she was a couple of months ago.

'You need to talk to one of those church people about this.' Stephanie chewed on the side of her mouth.

'None of them would get it.'

'You're probably right, but you met this guy at your church. He's part of your group.'

He wasn't actually part of our group, just someone we met and watched play football.

'It's really serious.' Steph's eyes welled up. 'You can never go back. It will change who you are. I wish I could have your life.'

Her words sank in. I guess she'd earned her turn to lecture me. What was I thinking? I'd do as Stephanie suggested and take it slow.

Chapter Thirty

Jaya walked through the school gates with puffy eyes.

'What's happened now?'

'I walked in on Dad going for it. Urgh! She was so young, like twenty, if that. I heard him laughing in the bedroom and thought he must have been sorting things out with Mum, so I went in.'

'Oh, how horrible.' My stomach churned.

'And then Mum arrived and saw the floozy, there in her room. Can you imagine?'

'Oh, Jaya.' I went to give her a hug, but she pulled away with clenched fists.

'I hate him. I hate my father.' Her face began to turn red.

I didn't know what to say. I'd hate my dad too, if he did that to our family.

Jaya burst into tears. This time she let me wrap my arms around her. She'd just settled down when the bell rang, ushering us into class.

It had been raining for days—a parallel to Jaya's misery. I was at my wit's end looking for ways to help her.

'Why don't you come to youth group? I could find someone for you to talk to about your parents and stuff.'

'No way! The last thing I want is a bunch of well-wishers telling me everything will be okay.' Jaya stormed off and didn't talk to me for the rest of the week.

On Friday evening, I spent extra time getting my hair to sit just right and double-coated my eyelashes with mascara. I arrived at youth group early and watched the door. Aiden didn't turn up. The only thing that stopped tears from seeping from my eyes was Shelly's invitation.

'We're all going to watch the Aussie Rules game again tomorrow. Would you like to come with us?'

'Aiden's game?'

'That's the one.'

'Yep, I'm in.' My heart quivered.

The next day was wet again so we sat in the car to watch. Aiden hurt his shoulder and needed assistance to leave the field. We didn't see him after the game, and I began to brood. I counted the days since I spoke with him last. *Too long.*

When I'd just about given up hope that Aiden would call again, he rang Friday afternoon and asked me out on a date on Saturday night. I was bummed that I had to decline. I'd already promised to spend Saturday night at Suzie's. After all she'd been through and all the times her parents had said I wasn't welcome, I had to go when I had a window of opportunity. I couldn't let her down.

When Mum dropped me off at Suzie's, I started rambling to keep my mind off Aiden and the date I'd said no to. 'I've hardly seen or heard from Steph. I don't know what's up with her. Something inside tells me not to trust Jason. But what can I do? And I still can't believe the way Jaya's father is carrying on. It's not fair on her, or her mother. My parents are out again tonight—another birthday party. Their social life is better than mine! Anyway, tell me what's been happening with Joey? You've been so quiet about it all at school.'

'I know. Jaya thinks he's a closet gay, so I don't want to talk about him around her.'

'But he's not gay ... is he?'

'No.' Suzie smiled, her cheeks blushing.

'So how's dating with your mum and dad chaperoning?'

'They're actually starting to back off a little.' Suzie looked through the window.

'Everything okay?' I looked over her shoulder.

'Just making sure Mum's still outside at the clothes line. They've even been giving us windows of opportunity to be alone.'

'Ooh.' I leaned closer. 'Do tell.'

'He kissed me last night. Like, just a quick kiss before Mum and Dad came back.' She grabbed my arm. 'Tabbie! So, so, so, awesome!'

Suzie's glow warmed my heart. It was worth missing a date with Aiden to spend time with her. I left the next day feeling refreshed.

The following Friday night, Aiden rang. Before I hit answer, I jumped up and down a few times to calm my excitement. My heart fluttered faster than a butterfly's wings as I said hello.

'I'm off to Melbourne for the weekend.'

'Oh. Are you?' My heart went from flutter to thud.

'Make sure you keep next Sunday afternoon free.'

'Sure,' I said, with a giggle like only a silly twit would do.

What on earth did Aiden see in me? I was just a high school girl. He had a smorgasbord of university girls to choose from.

'Are you still seeing Aiden?' Shelly asked that Friday night at youth group.

Priscilla raised her eyebrows and moved closer to join our conversation.

I nodded, aware of the heat rushing to my cheeks. 'I haven't seen him for a while, but he rang this afternoon. We have plans next Sunday.'

'I guess he's decided church isn't for him,' Priscilla said. 'He hasn't returned since he first visited.'

'And he's away this weekend.'

'I heard he was flying out to Melbourne tomorrow night.'

I opened my mouth to correct her. I was sure he was leaving tonight. But Priscilla continued before I could get the words out.

'But I could be wrong.' Priscilla shrugged. 'I overheard some of the others talking about going to the football tomorrow to see Aiden.'

Maybe Priscilla was right. Maybe Aiden had other uni-style plans he'd rather join in with than spend time with me. He hadn't actually said when he was flying. I'd just assumed it was tonight.

On one hand I held hope that he was interested and wonderful. On the other hand, I remembered all the lectures I'd given my best friend about dating someone in uni. All the questions I'd thrown at Steph came back to haunt me. What are teenage guys really after? Sex. For all I knew, he might hang out at the same hotel Stephanie worked at.

Jaya's parents separated again, and this time it looked like divorce was on the cards. Although she said she didn't care, she was drinking like a fish at parties and seemed to leave behind a trail of boys that she'd kissed. Each Monday she'd brag about who she'd hooked up with.

'So are you just kissing them or —'

'It's none of your business, Tabbie.'

'When you call me to meet you at a party and I come to rescue you, it is my business.'

Jaya turned to walk away then called back over her shoulder. 'I haven't asked you to come for a while now.'

'So?' I followed her.

'So nothing. It's not like I have sex with them or anything.'

'What do you mean "or anything?"' I punched my fingers out to make air quotes.

'It's no big deal.'

Suzie joined us on our walk into school. But I wasn't about to drop the subject.

'Jaya, oral sex is sex. It's one of the most intimate, personal—'

'What would you know anyway?'

I knew in many ways she was right. I was innocent, naïve. But the words I'd just spoken weren't from my own mind. It was like something else spoke through me. And after I spoke, calmness settled on me. I didn't need to answer her question. I'd said enough.

'She's right, Jaya. It's still sex.' Suzie filled the silence.

'What would you know? You spend all your time with a gay guy.'

Suzie shook her head and rolled her eyes.

Both Jaya and Suzie had enough going on in their own worlds. I didn't want to bring up Aiden. Not yet. I kept the excitement to myself and looked forward to Sunday afternoon. I hoped we'd have a relaxing date where I wouldn't have to worry about anything heavy. I'd tell my school friends about him when I had something to tell.

Aiden's shoulder was still playing up by the weekend, so he didn't have the energy to do anything other than watch a movie. This time he agreed to sit through a chick flick. It was funny and romantic. I enjoyed the light-hearted banter of the main characters. It seemed so detached from real life. Imagine if every issue could be solved with a joke and an editing director.

After the movie we had a coffee, and I had an urge to sit on his lap and display way too much public affection. But I restrained myself and sipped my cappuccino. As much as I loved the idea of dating Aiden, conversation tripped like some kind of broken current. I had imagined that when I began dating, we'd talk constantly and always be laughing. I guess it was a bonus that I got to laugh in the cinema.

Aiden walked me to my front door. We stood on the porch pashing. He pulled back. I gasped for a breath and then he kissed me deeply again. His hands rubbed up and down my back. My whole body tingled. There was only a door between us and my parents. Almost dangerous.

'Have you two had a good night?' Dad swung open the door.

I jumped back from Aiden. 'This is Aiden. Aiden, this is my dad, Tom Moray.'

They were pleasant to each other, but I could see Aiden was itching to back away towards his car.

When Dad stopped bombarding him with questions, Aiden faced me. 'Movies again next week?'

'Or maybe something different?' I hated to admit it, but movie dates were a little boring.

Aiden left and Dad ushered me inside. 'I hope you're controlling your feelings.'

'What makes you say that, Dad?' Was he watching us before he opened the door?

'Just remember you shouldn't awaken love until love is ready.'

I nodded and went to my room. The pastor had preached about that and my church friends had mentioned it, but it was the first time I'd heard it from Dad.

Chapter Thirty-One

'Come over,' Suzie begged the following Friday. 'Please. We can have a movie night. Mum and Dad have already said yes.'

Aiden had a night game I planned to watch, but I didn't want to turn Suzie down. I had no idea where I stood with Aiden. We barely talked on our dates, and he hadn't called all week. And Suzie needed me.

Mrs Peters hovered around from the moment I arrived. Soon after the first movie began, she finally left the room for a minute.

'So, are you and Joey still ...?'

Suzie nodded.

'You still only see him when he comes over?'

'That's about it. He's pretty busy with dance rehearsals. When he visits, Mum is always around. We've been out to eat a few times. But Mum and Dad come with.'

'That's stifling.'

'It's good with Joey, though. He's fine, and seems to respect them. You know, they even let him sleep over last weekend.'

'What? That sounds bizarre.'

'I know.' She checked to see if her mother was coming back before she continued. 'He had to sleep in the sewing room downstairs.'

Suzie had a mischievous, almost guilty look on her face.

'But let me guess—he didn't stay there, did he?' I whispered.

'He did.' Suzie lifted her finger to her lips, then leaned closer to my ear. 'But I went downstairs for a while when Mum and Dad were asleep.'

'And?' *Why am I asking?* I wanted to know, but I didn't want to know all the details. I hoped she remembered the recent lecture she'd given Jaya.

'We didn't do it, just fooled around a bit. You know, kissing and stuff. He's amazing and definitely not gay.'

We were still laughing when Suzie's mother returned to the room. It was fun, even being scrutinised under her mother's watchful eye. On my way home, I realised I hadn't given Aiden one thought for twenty-four hours. The moment I did think of him, I realised he hadn't called.

During the next week at school, whispers and conversations about camp grabbed my attention. Even the teachers seemed excited to be planning activities that would have us so exhausted we'd go straight to sleep and not keep them up.

'Have you guys thought of any pranks for camp?' I asked.

'Vegemite on the teachers' glasses. You know, that part that sits on the nose?' Jaya laughed, rubbing her nose.

'Water bombs in their pillowcases?' Suzie giggled.

We laughed together as we threw around new and old prank ideas.

'Do you think Steph will come back for camp?' Jaya asked.

Why was she taking an interest now, when she'd barely mentioned Steph for months?

'As if she'd show her face around here just for camp.' Suzie shook her head.

'Have either of you even tried to contact her?' Oops, that just slipped out.

They shook their heads. Something about their lack of care made me continue. 'Well, why don't you? I don't think things are as great as she'd have us all believe.'

Jaya and Suzie looked at each other.

'She's working long hours, trying to pay bills we don't even have to think about. I don't think her boyfriend is always the Mr Wonderful that she'd like us to think he is. Come on. You're meant to be her friends too.'

'I guess. But it's not like I can go and see her or anything,' Suzie said.

'I wonder if she'd like to come to a party with me.' Jaya pulled out her nail file.

I doubted that Steph would want to go to one of Jaya's parties or take time out to visit Suzie and her parents. It was frustrating how I was the only one of our long-term circle of friends who seemed to care.

'How long is it since you saw Steph anyway?' Jaya asked.

'Last weekend.'

'What's she up to?'

I told them about the promotion and how she seemed happy with her job.

'What about you, Suzie?' Jaya asked.

Maybe I'd hit a nerve.

'What do you mean?' Suzie asked.

'Are you still seeing him?'

'Him? As in Joey? Yep,' she said with a wide grin. 'And he's not gay.'

'Your parents okay with you seeing him?'

'We don't get much time alone. They're always around. But ...' Suzie's eyes widened. 'Once he slept downstairs, and I snuck down after Mum and Dad had gone to bed. I've even left the house a couple of times after they've gone to sleep to hang out with him for a few hours.'

'You didn't tell me the last part!' I glared at her.

'I knew you'd get all funny on me.' Suzie's cheeks glowed with a tinge of pink.

'Does he come to meet you outside your house?' I was sure my jaw gaped. I couldn't believe she'd risked it.

'We mostly meet near the servo.'

'But that's blocks from you.' I reached out and touched her arm. 'It's dangerous, walking around at that time of night by yourself.'

'A couple of times, I swore I heard footsteps behind me.'

'Was anyone there?' Jaya asked.

'No, just me hearing things.'

'Can you ask him to meet you outside your place?' I was still trying to get my head around the fact Suzie hadn't told me this before now.

'It's easier—and safer—to meet at the servo.'

Safer for who? Safer that they wouldn't get caught out. Just the thought of walking around in the vicinity of the servo at night sent a shiver through my spine. I silently prayed. *God, please keep her safe.*

I'd stopped giving Aiden my thought time. We'd only had a couple of dates. Perhaps the relationship had fizzled—if you could even call it a relationship. He caught me off guard when he rang me on Friday afternoon.

'You said you didn't want to see a movie on our next date, so I have something different planned. We've been invited to a party.'

'What kind of party?' A wild uni party wasn't my scene.

'It's not really a party. More like a few friends hanging out. I can pick you up at around seven-thirty.'

'I've got youth group on tonight.' He hadn't bothered to contact me for so long. I should have said no straight away.

'You can miss a night, can't you?'

His voice sent my heart racing. 'Yeah, you're right. I'll be ready.' Why did I give in so easy?

As soon as I hung up, I remembered the last time I'd missed youth group to go on a date. My stomach churned. At seven o'clock I pulled out my phone to cancel, but a knock sounded at the door.

It was Aiden.

Mum and Dad drilled him about Melbourne and how he was coping with being away from home. Mum even offered him some home-cooked meals. It was all sounding a little too cosy. I'd had enough and suggested we should get going.

Aiden started the car then turned to face me. 'I need to swing by mine first and pick up some drinks I left behind.'

I nodded. My thoughts flashed back to Mum and Dad telling me to be careful. Just swing by. That didn't sound dangerous. Surely he'd have flatmates. It wouldn't be like we'd be alone.

Aiden parked on the street, jumped out then came to my side opening my door.

'Come in, come in.'

'I can wait here.'

'I want to show you my pad.'

Against my better judgment, I agreed and followed him inside. He pulled the beer out of the fridge. Three stubbies. He put them in a cooler bag then turned to me. I wanted to ask if we were calling a taxi but our lips connected in a kiss. It was thrilling, passionate, intoxicating. His hands dropped to the hem of my shirt, lifting it as he walked me backwards. My eyes flung open. He was leading me towards a bedroom. His hand had now slipped under my shirt. I pushed it down. He found the button on my jeans and undid it, and I pushed him away with as much force as I could find.

'No!' I spat the word.

'What do you mean?'

'No.'

'You want it, I can tell in your kiss. You want me.'

'No.' I shook my head.

He came towards me again. I pushed him away scratching his neck with my fingernail. A slight trickle of blood oozed out of the scratch. It was an accident. He raised his hand and swept it through the air, slapping my face.

My cheek stung, bringing tears to my eyes. I stepped back, wondering if I could make it out the front door if he came at me again. But he turned away, stormed into the bathroom, and slammed the door. I grabbed my phone when I heard the shower running and ran outside before Mum answered. In less than ten minutes, my family car pulled up to the kerb with both Mum and Dad inside. I scrambled into the backseat, swallowing back tears.

'I'll call the police. We should charge him.' Dad hit his fist on the steering wheel. 'I'll go in there right now and sort him out.'

'Tom ...' Mum cautioned. 'You know that's not the way to solve this.'

'I went inside against my better judgment. He stopped before he really hurt me.' I pulled my knees to my chest.

Once the car had started and we were driving away, my brave face dissolved, and I cried the whole way home.

'I'm so sorry we didn't protect you.' Mum hugged me before I went to the bathroom for a shower. 'This wasn't your fault. He should never have touched you like that.'

My tears turned into sobs in the shower. I could see Mum's shadow beneath the door. I knew Aiden hadn't only hurt me. He'd also hurt my parents with his B-grade act.

Chapter Thirty-Two

WHEN I WOKE UP THE NEXT DAY, more tears seeped from my eyes. I needed to see Steph urgently. I caught the bus, climbed the stairs, and knocked on the door at Jason's place. Steph pulled it open, yawning, rubbing her eyes.

'Did I wake you?'

'Yes, we got home late.'

'Were you working?'

'Yeah, and we went out after work.'

'Where?' I was happy to put off talking about me for a few minutes.

'Doesn't matter, what are you doing here? Why didn't you just ring?'

'You want me to go?'

'No. You know you're always welcome. You are still my best friend.'

'It's horrible!' Tears gushed from my eyes. I wanted to talk to her, but I wasn't expecting to fall apart.

'Come in.' Steph opened the door wider.

'I listened to you. I really did.' I plonked down on the couch.

'Shh.' She sat close to me. 'Jason's sleeping.'

'Aiden was horrible.'

'Oh, no! What did he do to you?'

'He got really pushy and when I said no, he slapped my cheek, saying I'd led him on.'

'Oh, Tabbie.'

'You were right. I'm so glad you gave me that advice to wait. He wasn't that nice, after all. I wish I could find someone as wonderful as Jason.'

'You deserve better than him.' She glanced over my shoulder towards the bedroom.

'Huh?' *Better than the perfect boyfriend?* 'I thought you were happy.'

'I am, but it could be better,' she whispered.

'Why? What's up?'

'Not the right time or place to be talking about that.'

Sorry. I mouthed the word. 'Would you like to come and stay a couple of nights back home?'

'Can't. Work.' Steph shrugged. 'Maybe later this week.'

'I'm at school camp all week.'

'Oh.'

She had an odd look on her face. I couldn't tell what she was thinking.

'I might come and see your parents anyway.'

'Please do.'

'I need some more sleep.' Steph yawned. 'Sorry.'

I left, feeling more concerned for Steph than ever. She seemed almost fearful of Jason. It didn't make sense. She wanted to spend every day with the guy, yet the way she said it wasn't the right time or place to be talking didn't sound like she was talking about a guy she was in love with.

I sat on the cold bench seat in the bus shelter, waiting. Bus fumes irritated my nose as another bus drove away. I wasn't ready to head home. I could walk back to check on Stephanie, but I didn't want to wake her again. Why would she keep staying there if she wasn't happy? My mobile phone buzzed, pulling me out of my confusion.

I checked the time before answering—I'd been sitting at the bus stop for over an hour.

'We're heading down to the beach today. Would you like me to pick you up?' Shelly's cheery voice echoed.

'Bit cold for a swim.' I shivered.

'Sun's shining. It's too cold for a dip, but it's a lovely day to lie on a towel.'

'I'm not at home right now and I don't have a towel.'

'Where are you? Are you okay?'

'Yeah, just ...' It was all too much to explain over the phone. I took a breath wondering whether to go home or hang out with Shelly for the day.

'I can pick you up from where you are. We have a couple of extra towels in the car anyway.'

Why hadn't I called Shelly instead of racing to Steph? I gave Shelly the address of the bus stop and they arrived within ten minutes.

'How was the party?' Priscilla winked as I slid into the backseat.

'Didn't get there.' I shook my head trying to shut down the memory.

'Why not?' Shelly turned towards me, wide-eyed.

'He's a creep! He tried to push himself on me before we even went out.'

'Oh, no. Are you okay?'

'Yeah. I shoved him away. Mum and Dad came pretty fast to pick me up.' I sat in the car, thinking of the irony. These girls never actually talked much about boys, yet they were the ones who seemed to care the most about what was happening in my dating life. When we arrived at the beach, we lay on our towels and let the sun warm our skin.

'Why don't I ever hear either of you talk about boys?'

Priscilla laughed.

Shelly smiled and spoke first. 'I think I tried too hard to find a boyfriend a couple of years ago.'

'Yeah.' Priscilla was still laughing. 'Same here. Still recovering from boy-hunting burn-out.'

I laughed with them, not entirely understanding what they were talking about.

'We aren't making sense, are we?' Shelly said.

'Not exactly.' I rolled onto my side.

Shelly leaned back on her elbows. 'All I thought about was cute boys, then one of my friends fell pregnant. Her family moved away and we've lost touch. But the whole situation kind of freaked me out, and I wish I'd kept in touch to support her. It shocked me. Her boyfriend pressured her to sleep with him. He didn't rape her or anything, but she gave in. I started seeing boys as nothing but crazy, hormonal creatures. I think I'm coming out of that now. For a while there, I was completely rude to any boy who paid me any attention. Now I'm open to meeting someone again. But he'd have to be pretty amazing to distract me from my studies.'

Priscilla nodded. 'There was a time when I would date anyone who asked me out. I got myself into so many compromising positions. I'm still amazed I got through mostly unharmed. I stopped dating boys when I started coming to church. That was the turning point where I no longer looked for a boyfriend. I stopped checking out the hot boys. I heard someone say, never awaken love until it is ready. Then I read the scripture in Song of Solomon. I realised I wasn't ready.'

'You make me feel like a boy-crazed lunatic.'

'Oh, no. No way.' Priscilla shook her head. 'You aren't like that at all. I really chased boys. I mean like all the time. You've just been out on a couple of dates with guys who need to learn some respect.'

While talking about herself, Priscilla had pretty much described Jaya. I lay on my back with my hat sheltering my eyes from the sun. They'd made me think. I'd never stopped to consider my motivation for checking out boys. It seemed selfish.

'I now have complete faith that the right guy for me will come along,' Priscilla interrupted my train of thought. 'When he does, I will know he is the right one. That way. I won't have wasted time on all the guys who aren't perfect for me.'

'Same here,' Shelly said.

The regular crew started gathering at the beach. When Danny caught a wave, my gaze was drawn to him, but I chose to look away.

'I guess those old sayings about window shopping and eye candy are pretty disrespectful.' I sat up, digging my toes into the sand.

'Not always.' Priscilla threw sand over my feet.

'It's more about the attitude and what goes through your mind when you're checking someone out.' Shelly leant forward. 'I check myself when I can't take my eyes off a hot guy—is it lust, or admiration? If it's lust, I take it to God and ask for help.'

I drew a line in the sand with my toe. I would start living more like Priscilla and Shelly. It sure was a different way of life. 'I'm going to make a change. You've both inspired me. But I don't think my high school friends will ever change their lifestyles.'

'Never say never.' Priscilla looked to the sky. 'Pray for them.'

Chapter Thirty-Three

'Jaya's been ringing every half-hour or so.' Mum rushed to greet me when I arrived home.

'Why didn't she ring my mobile?' I pulled it out of my bag to find it was turned off. 'Oh!'

'She said she'd tried it. Said she sent a text message.'

'I'll call her now.'

'Tabbie!' Jaya answered the phone gasping for air. 'The best party is on tonight.'

'Have you just run a marathon? Why are you out of breath? And what makes this party better than all the other parties you go to?'

'I ran to the phone—no marathon. And this is the party of all parties.'

'I'd rather not. I've had a big twenty-four hours.'

'It's going to be awesome. I don't want you to miss out.'

'Don't you mean—you don't want to find your own intoxicated way home across town by yourself?'

'Shut up! I want you to come with me. And you know it's dangerous on the streets at night by yourself. You'd be my safety blanket.'

'As long as we don't stay out late.' I wouldn't have been able to sleep if I'd let her go on her own. I'd had a few weeks off, but now I was jumping back in to be her keeper. She mustn't have been able to find a replacement hair holder for when she puked.

Just after dusk, Jaya and I caught the train across town. She rambled the whole way.

'Have you been drinking already?'

'What's a cooler or two before a party? What time did your mum say she'd pick us up?'

'At ten.' In around four hours. I was already counting down the minutes.

'That's way too early.'

'We leave for camp tomorrow.'

'Whatever.' Jaya rolled her eyes then led the way from the train station.

We walked through two blocks of gigantic homes with manicured gardens surrounded by high fences. I followed Jaya up the sandstone stairs of her friend's home, past the pink flamingo fountain and the huge Victorian stone columns. Waiting at the solid double doors, security ticked us off the guest list, leaving us to push through the heavy doors ourselves.

Vases and ornaments lined the entrance. I reminded my klutzy hands not to break anything. The home opened out to oversized rooms with white shiny furniture. A mirror ball twinkled light around the room from the extra-high ceiling.

The music was so loud I had to shout right into Jaya's ear. 'I can't believe they're letting a bunch of teenagers have a party here.'

'Pretty cool, hey?'

'Or stupid. I don't know anyone here. How do you know these people?'

'Oh, parties. You know.'

I didn't know. I had obviously missed those parties.

Waitresses offered trays of food, while bartenders mixed colourful cocktails and poured beers. I grabbed a spring roll and canapé from a passing tray. Jaya took no food but headed straight for the bar.

She turned and yelled into my ear. 'What would you like?'

'Apple juice, please.' I wasn't game to try the slushies. I was sure they contained an extra punch. I stayed close behind her. This wasn't somewhere I wanted to be left standing alone. Jaya said hello to everyone we passed. Many returned the greeting and knew her by name.

She sculled her first cocktail and went back for another. The glass was empty in no time. 'Just wait here a minute. Super hottie at ten o'clock.' She winked. 'Watch me weave my magic.'

'Hottie?' I repeated as she strutted towards the boy via the bar for another drink.

My cheeks grew warm as she launched herself at him. Her arm reached around his neck as she leaned against his body. I pulled my gaze from her and turned to watch the rest of the room.

'Hey babe, you here on your own?' A greasy-skinned, overly scented boy yelled into my ear.

'I'm here with a friend.'

'You must be a pretty sly thief, because you stole my heart from way over there.' He pointed to the other side of the room.

'That's a really lame pick-up line.' I smiled.

I turned back to Jaya, but she'd disappeared. A shudder rippled down my spine as Mr Pick Up Line moved closer into my personal space bubble.

'I've got to find my friend. Excuse me.'

I wandered around checking every hallway and room until I was sure Jaya wasn't downstairs. I mounted the stairs one at a time. I didn't want to hunt her down or walk in on other couples. But, I also didn't want to leave it too long and walk in on her in a compromising situation again.

Thankfully, Jaya was alone and leaning against the wall in the upstairs hallway.

'Whatsup?' she asked.

I took a quick look at my watch. Nearly three hours 'til Mum would arrive.

'Are you okay? Come back downstairs with me.'

'No's okay. Al's getting s'more drinks.'

'Come on, Jaya. You're drunk. You don't want to stay up here.'

'Yes, I do.'

'My favourite song is on. Come and dance with me.'

'Yeah?' She listened for a moment. 'I like this song too.'

Linking my arm through hers, I led her downstairs to the makeshift dance floor in the lounge room. Soon others joined us. Before the end of the song, the area was so crowded, we were bumping into each other. Another song started.

'I love this song!' I hoped enthusiasm would keep her with me.

'I think I need 'nother drink.' Jaya nodded and kept dancing.

Bottles of water decorated the room, stacked in a pyramid in the corner. I grabbed one and pushed it into her hands. 'Here.'

She drank half the bottle then dropped it, spilling water over the carpet. 'Now where's my drink? And where'd that hot boy go? I need to go pee.'

We stood in the line for so long to use the toilet that we sat, leaning against the wall. Finally, Jaya rushed in to use the facilities. I used the time to send Mum a text message, asking her to come earlier than planned.

'Have you fallen asleep in there?' I knocked on the door.

'Was just fixing up m'hair,' she said as she pushed the door open.

'You need some food.' I led her to a table with a smorgasbord of cold meats, cheese, and crackers.

'Achuwally, I'm thirsty. I'll get y'slushy.'

'No, thanks.'

'Hey, there's Al.' Jaya tripped over her own feet, then steadied herself. 'Come over. I'll introduce you to him.'

'Jaya, no.' Al was about to stick his tongue down the throat of a tall, curvy girl.

Jaya hadn't noticed. 'What? But—'

'Mum will be here in fifteen minutes.' I pulled Jaya outside onto a deck, away from the scene.

Overlooking the harbour, sailboats rocked, and lights twinkled on the water. It was serene, the complete opposite to what was happening behind me.

'Is't already time? Feels like we've only been here'n hour.' Jaya leant against me with all her weight. I had to brace myself to keep upright.

'And a bit.' I straightened her up, so she rested against a wall.

'Really. Amazing.'

When Al and his new girl moved outside to the deck, I ushered Jaya through the house.

'You aren't leaving already, are you?' Mr Pick Up Line stepped in front of us.

'Yes. Our taxi's waiting for us.' I'd rushed my words to get aways as quickly as possible.

'Really?' Jaya asked.

I kept her moving towards the door, stepping around Mr Pick Up Line.

'I thought you said your mum was coming.'

'Yep, my mum the taxi driver.'

'When did she start driving taxis?'

'When you started drinking.' At least this time she was amusing instead of puking.

Chapter Thirty-Four

'Hi, Suzie.' I found her sitting away from the group waiting to get on the bus that would take us to camp.

'Joey stayed over again last night, and Dad walked in on us.' A tear developed and rolled off Suzie's eyelashes.

'Walked in on you?' How could she have been so careless?

'We were just kissing.' Her cheeks glowed red. 'It got ugly. Dad threatened to call the police.'

'What happened?'

'Dad went off at me, then drove Joey home. I snuck out through my window and called him from the public phone at the servo early this morning. He said Dad yelled at him the whole way in the car. I haven't slept.'

'That's horrible. Everything seemed to be going so well.'

'I'm not going to stop seeing him just because of my parents. He's the kind of guy I could marry.'

'Woah, Suzie, you're only sixteen. You can't make that kind of life decision yet.'

'Other people have, and they've survived.'

'But—'

'I'll work it out somehow. I've snuck out to meet him before. I'll do it again when we get back from camp.' Suzie clenched her fists and shook her head. She had a determined look in her eye that spelt danger. There was no use trying to change her mind. I'd rather see her full of life, like this, rather than smothered like she'd been a couple of months ago.

Jaya, on the other hand, rushed towards me with nostrils flared. 'Why did you drag me out of the party?'

'It was getting late, and you were ready to leave.'

'Johnno said you dragged me out before nine o'clock. That's so freaking early.'

'Truth is ...' I checked on Suzie, then faced Jaya again. 'You were drunk.'

'I was fine.' Jaya's hand landed on her hip.

Suzie chewed on her fingernail, watching us.

'But you didn't remember what time we left.' I moved closer to Jaya. This wasn't a conversation Suzie needed to hear. 'You had to find out from Johnno.'

'Time isn't important at a party. I wasn't wearing a watch.'

'If that's what you think, then the fact we left a little early isn't important either.'

'I was having a really good time!' Jaya screwed up her nose.

'If you don't remember leaving ...' Other girls started to look at us so I lowered my voice. 'How would you remember whether you were having a good time or not?'

'Some friend you are!' She took her bag and dumped it beside the bus.

I pressed my lips together. She wasn't about to forgive me or thank me. I looked around for the teachers and waited to board the bus. I wanted to go home. How was it that my ridiculously beautiful and far-from-perfect best friend fobbed me off all the time? How did Suzie find herself living so dangerously? And how did Jaya get so angry with me?

 Spiralling Out of the Shadow

Finally, the teachers called the roll, our bags were stacked in the storage compartments, and we were allowed to file onto the bus.

Jaya and Suzie sat together, and I found myself brooding as my friends' chatter and laughter rose above the drone of the bus. When we arrived at the mountain campsite, they claimed their bags and raced off before mine was unloaded.

I assumed the three of us would be in the same room, but when I found my way to our accommodation, I discovered there were two to a room. Suzie and Jaya had already claimed a room together, so I trudged down the line of doors until I found a spare bed. Unsure who I was about to bunk in with, I heaved my bag onto a small set of drawers. The toilet flushed. Out walked Miss World Candidate, our school's most beautiful girl. Now, more conscious of my pear shape than ever, I slunk my hand over my hip and turned a shade of envious green.

'How lovely,' Anna said in a pleasant tone.

Is she talking to me?

'I was wondering who I'd be sharing with.' She smiled.

'I was expecting more beds in each room.' I thought about walking straight back out the door. But I'd already dumped my bag.

'It's good that there's only two to a room, hey? And the ensuite is a bonus. I was dreading a shower block.'

I had to get out of the cabin, away from way-too-beautiful-to-be-nice Anna.

I pulled on my runners and pounded my feet toward the unknown terrain. While still running on concrete paths, I scolded myself for challenging my friends instead of just being there for them and listening to their problems. The path came to an end, and the mountain earth sank a little with each step. It was like I was on enemy ground. I looked up, wanting to be zapped home by some kind of Fairy Godmother. I wished I was back in my comfortable living room or even at the beach with my friends. But no, I was out in the middle of Woop Woop, sharing a room with Miss World Candidate.

My head throbbed as the past year, played in my mind like a movie. Everything I'd done, everyone I'd kept secrets for. The hair holding, the hand holding, the support. And had anyone returned the favour?

It had been Shelly and Priscilla who'd been there for me. They were always ready to listen and encourage. Pretty much always available to hang out. *Oh, no!* Was I doing exactly the same to them as my friends had done to me? Dumping on them without returning a listening ear?

I ran faster, wanting to push the envy and anger away. The misty mountain air flushed my lungs and helped me think more clearly. Running downhill, I decided it was time to put my best foot forward. After camp I would start to be a friend to Shelly and Priscilla rather than just drain them for my own needs.

The trees seemed taller, the air seemed a little warmer, the atmosphere more peaceful. Small rolling hills one after the other. Up. Then down. A magpie swooped, baring its claws. I swung my arm to shoo it away. It came again. I ducked and lost my footing on some stones, rolling my ankle. I fell hard on my knees, only just getting my elbows out in time to save my face.

Bruised and startled, I stood up, but fell again. I'd stuffed my ankle. *Again.* I couldn't believe it. Tears rolled silently down my cheeks. *How am I going to get back to camp?* No one would know where to find me. The sun had already slunk down, kissing the horizon. If only they'd let us bring our mobile phones to camp.

I looked to the sky. 'Please send someone to rescue me.'

Chapter Thirty-Five

I LAY BACK, CLOSED MY EYES and hoped the pain would subside with time. When I looked up, big puffy clouds floated around the sky. They were pretty enough to distract me from the intense pain. The sinking sun sent dark tree shadows that lengthened across the grass with every minute. Mosquitoes nibbled on my arms and ankles, forcing me to sit up and slap them. My ankle had blown up to three times its normal size.

I tried to walk again, hopping on one leg, but nausea churned my stomach, and the throbbing pain sent my head spinning. I slumped back down onto the stone-infested grass. 'Help!' I called. 'Help me,' I repeated in barely a whisper.

Who on earth would be out here in the middle of nowhere? I had run at least two kilometres away from the camp grounds. Thankfully I wasn't in dense scrub bush. A chopper flying overhead might see me. But who would send for a chopper? Great day to wear earthy green! *Gah.* I fell backwards and punched my fist into the ground. I had no one to blame but myself. I cried. And cried. And cried.

'Hey. Do you need some help?'

Was it an angel? I opened my eyes expecting to see a bright white supernatural being. But standing there in front of me was Miss World Candidate herself.

'Anna! I hope you can.'

'Wow.' She crouched down to inspect my ankle. 'How did you manage to do that?'

To tell her I was running to try and thrash out my envy of her beauty probably wasn't a good idea. I took a deep breath. 'I was running and a magpie swooped me.'

'They can be nasty this time of year.' She stood. 'The air is so fresh out here, isn't it? I saw you take off and tried to follow, but you ran so fast.'

Why would she follow me? The throbbing seemed to get worse as I sat up. 'Do you think you could go for help?'

'I don't want to leave you alone. Here.' She reached out her hand to help me up.

Once standing, I went to swing my arm around her neck for support, but she was so tall I could hardly reach. Instead, we linked arms and she acted like a crutch, supporting me enough to hop.

I groaned in pain. When the campground was in sight, Anna stopped. 'Will you be able to wait here while I get a stretcher or something?'

I nodded clenching my teeth. The pain had increased to the point where I couldn't speak.

She elegantly strode away from me, leaving me wondering what it would be like to be so ridiculously beautiful. I closed my eyes and prayed she'd return soon.

Within ten minutes, a rescue party of teachers and students returned along with the owner of the campground. They loaded me onto a stretcher, and I bounced along in a horizontal position for the next five hundred metres or so.

'We've called an ambulance. It should be here soon.' The campsite owner led us to a smoother path.

   Spiralling Out of the Shadow

Is this my way out? Maybe I could leave and sleep in my own bed tonight.

Anna retreated to our room as soon as Jaya and Suzie arrived at my side.

When the paramedics examined my ankle, they decided it needed to be iced, wrapped, and elevated, but there was no need for further medical attention. 'Get it checked again when you arrive home,' the ambulance officer told me.

I didn't want to stay. I wanted to go home.

'That's good news.' Suzie wrapped her arms around me.

'Maybe I should leave now and get it x-rayed.' I looked to the ambos, hoping they'd agree with me.

'Only if the swelling doesn't go down. I'm sure you'll be fine in a couple of days. Just keep off it.'

'You have to stay. You don't want to miss out on what we have planned tonight.' Jaya raised her eyebrows.

The extra shiny sparkle in her eyes concerned me. *What is she planning?*

There was an old wheelchair at the campsite for accidents like mine, so I was able to roll around rather than hopping. Thankfully the buildings were linked by ramps and paths. Jaya pushed me back to my cabin while Suzie opened the doors.

'We'll come back in half an hour and help you get to dinner,' Suzie said.

'I can help Tabbie.' Anna was lying on her bed. 'We'll meet you there.'

'You don't have to do that.' I looked at her, wondering why she was being helpful.

'Really, it's fine. I'd love to help you.'

Why? I wanted to ask but instead I just said, 'Thanks.'

'Okay.' Jaya was already out the door. 'See you both in the dining room.'

Their giggles echoed through the hallway and under the closed door. Were they laughing at me? No, surely not. They were probably just finalising their planned pranks—something I was no longer able to get involved with. At least they were talking to me again.

'They could have helped me. Really.' I didn't want to put Miss World Candidate out. She'd already done more than I'd expected.

'It's really no problem. I'd love to be useful.'

I looked to the ceiling then the floor.

'You don't understand, do you?' she asked.

'You'd love to be useful? Come on.' I shook my head. She'd been voted the most beautiful in the school every year since year seven.

'Everyone looks at me like I'm a beauty queen.'

'Well, you are. You do the whole pageant thing, and you are beautiful.'

'But what use is that?'

None? I stared at her, dumbfounded. Surely being beautiful would make life easier. Finding a boyfriend, getting jobs, getting noticed, and always being first picked out of a crowd.

'Everyone expects me to always be smiling and always have my hair done just right, always be ready to pose for a photo. I'm sick of it. I just want to do something for someone. That's why I took off into the hills today. I didn't really follow you. I wanted to go for a run too. I was so sick of everything I wanted to scream, "Give me someone to do something for other than myself!" And there you were, like you fell over just so I could help you out.'

I lowered my chin, raising my eyebrows, questioning her wish.

'That sounded selfish.' She grimaced. 'I didn't mean to make your accident all about me. Sorry.'

'It must be nearly time for dinner. Should we go?'

Anna nodded and pushed me along the ramp to the dining hall.

'Do you want to sit here, or with your friends?'

'Here is fine.' Intrigued by what Anna had said in our room, I was interested in seeing how she interacted with her friends, the other beautiful people. It would be better than sitting with Jaya and Suzie and hearing about the pranks I couldn't join in with.

　　　　Spiralling Out of the Shadow

I couldn't help but notice how quiet Anna's table was. The conversation hummed around cosmetics and fashion. *Boring.*

My gaze was drawn to Jaya and Suzie, speaking into each other's ears with giggles and twinkling eyes. I turned back to my plate and pushed the camp slop around until it went cold.

After dinner we played the Hill Top Private version of *Celebrity Head.* It was laughter all around. I waved my hand, trying to get picked but it seemed I was invisible in my wheelchair. I rested my ankle on the bench seat in front of me. The swelling had already gone down quite a bit. The paramedics were right, which meant—*lucky me*—I got to stay for the whole camp. As soon as the night-time activities were over, Anna jumped up and came to my assistance. She pushed the wheelchair in silence.

'Sorry about before,' I said. 'I didn't mean to make you feel bad about wanting to help someone. Truth is, I'd rather go home than stay here.'

'Is that because you're stuck in a cabin with me?'

I shook my head.

'I saw your face when you realised you were rooming with me. You looked disappointed.'

I took a deep breath. *How horrible of me.* I didn't even know this girl, yet I'd made my assumptions.

'I'm sorry. I hope tomorrow will be a better day.'

'Me too.'

We turned the lights out and the dull throb in my ankle kept me from sleeping. Soon I heard giggling and laughter from the other cabins. Tears prickled my eyes, but crying would be pointless. I reached for my bag on the stand beside my bed and grabbed a box of painkillers, thankful I'd remembered to bring them. Once they kicked in, I fell asleep.

The sun streamed through the bare cabin window right onto my pillow, blinding my still-closed eyes. I gave up on sleeping any longer. I hobbled to the bathroom, splashed water on my face, then lay back on my bed with my head up the other end and watched the sky through the window.

'Good morning!' Anna bounced out of bed thirty minutes later and into the bathroom.

'Morning,' I called back to her as I swung my legs around to get up and dress for breakfast.

'Your chair is ready.' Anna held the wheelchair.

'I reckon I could hop up there today.'

Anna tilted her head and placed her hands on her hips. 'The instructions were for you to stay off your ankle and keep it up until you get home.'

Accepting her help, I plonked my butt back into the wheelchair. The dining hall was full by the time we arrived and our supervising teacher, Mrs Ostrich, was addressing the group. Anna wheeled me straight up to the end of a table and slipped into the seat nearest to me.

'It will not be tolerated!' Mrs Ostrich yelled. 'The rules were clearly stated in your permission slips. There is to be no alcohol consumed on school camp.' A vein bulged at the base of her neck. 'It's absolutely appalling that we had to send two girls home last night because they were in possession of alcohol. If you have any hidden in your bags, you too will be going home. There will be a complete room and bag check immediately after breakfast.'

I drew in a quick, gasping breath.

'What's up?' Anna whispered.

'Do you know who she's talking about?'

'No, no idea. Do you?'

I shook my head, craning my neck so I could look around the room, desperate to find Suzie and Jaya.

The gossip whooshed its way around the breakfast table like a bushfire. Confirmation filtered through quickly. My two friends had been sent home, suspended from school, with possible expulsion.

Anna held her breakfast in front of her—an apple. 'I know they're your friends, but what kind of stupid prank were they trying with spiking the teacher's drinks?'

I didn't know. We hadn't discussed bringing alcohol when we were planning the pranks. It would have been Jaya's idea. With what Suzie had just been through with her parents, they made a dangerous duo.

I still hadn't quite worked Anna out, but with my main crew sent home, I had a chance. After a couple of days, she actually seemed like a pretty normal girl. I'd made a new friend and hoped our new friendship would last beyond the camp boundaries.

Chapter Thirty-Six

'JAYA, WHAT WERE YOU THINKING?' I rang her as soon as I got home.

'I grabbed Dad's hip flask on the way out the door. I guess I didn't think. I was planning to drink it myself but the idea of spiking the teachers' drinks kind of dropped into my head.'

'Pretty dumb idea, hey?'

'The good news is, I'm not expelled. Just suspended for a couple of weeks.'

'Yeah, great news.' Only if missing classes leading up to mid-semester exams was good news. 'Have you spoken to Suzie?'

'No. I tried to ring, but her parents won't let me talk to her.'

After I said goodbye, I rang Suzie, hoping to get past her parents.

'Suzie isn't allowed to take phone calls at this point in time,' Mrs Peters said, as though she was a prison warden.

'Could I come round there?'

'No. Goodbye.'

I was left staring at the phone, listening to beep, beep, beep.

I took the next morning off school to see our trusty family doctor for an ankle check-up.

'Hmm.' Dr Frank peered over the top of his bifocals. 'Same ankle again, hey? How about we get an X-ray.'

I wiggled my toes. 'But the swelling has gone down. It'll be okay soon, won't it?'

'Hmm.' He gave me a doctorly look over his glasses. 'Best we check for any fractures.'

There was an X-ray clinic in the same building so I hobbled around there, before heading back to the doctor's. The film showed no fractures, and Dr Frank assured me that if I kept it elevated while I was sitting and used crutches to get around, it should be healed within a week.

I hobbled into school the next day, using crutches as a reluctant necessity, and saw Anna waiting outside her homeroom. Now was as good a time to ask as any. 'Would you like to come to youth group with me tonight?'

'I've been thinking about it a lot since you mentioned it during camp. They won't make me do anything weird, will they?'

'Nothing weirder than *Celebrity Head*.'

Anna laughed. 'I'd love to, but I've already got plans this week.'

'How about next Friday then?'

'It's on again?' Anna pulled out a compact mirror and checked herself.

'Sure is.'

'Alright. Just remind me.'

That Friday, my friends at youth group were refreshing after the week I'd had with my school friends. My sprained ankle kept me seated away from the crowd. Shelly and Priscilla stayed with me while we chatted about how we could change the world.

'You up for the beach tomorrow?' Shelly tapped my crutches.

'Are you serious?' I stood on one leg, rocking backwards and forwards.

'We'll help you. Can't leave you moping around at home. I'll pick you up in the morning, at around ten.'

The next day, Steph flung the door open with a huge grin on her face. 'Tabbie, you aren't going to believe what's happened.'

'You're coming back to school?' I flicked the TV off, wondering what the good news was.

'No, way better than that.'

'You've got an ordinary day job?' I spoke in hope.

'Well, kind of. It's not ordinary but it'll be mostly through the day.'

'What?' I patted the couch, signalling for her to sit.

'A music video producer asked me to work for him.'

'Have you been dancing?'

'Yeah, a little.' Steph took a deep breath.

'When do you start?'

'Monday.' She jumped up and did a happy dance across our lounge room.

'That's great!' I couldn't believe she'd been dancing and hadn't told me.

'Enough about me. What happened with that boy?' She looked at my leg resting on a cushion. 'And what have you done to your ankle?'

She actually sounded interested. I adjusted the bandage and leaned back. 'Well and truly over him. I got a bit intense, didn't I?'

'No, you were just being normal.' Steph sat down again.

We talked like we used to, like we'd gone back in time. I told her Suzie was sneaking around at night, and I was concerned for her safety. I told her how Jaya had been drinking heaps at parties, and throwing herself at boys. While I had her undivided interest, I filled her in on almost everyone and everything.

'You haven't said anything about that church thing you go to.'

'I didn't think you were interested.'

Shelly would be arriving soon. My mind swayed back and forth as to whether I should invite Steph to the beach or stay home with her. If I chose to stay home, I knew I'd miss out and regret not going.

'I'm about to head down to the beach with my church friends. Would you like to join us?'

'Do you mind if I don't? I need to catch up on some sleep. This house is so peaceful.'

'Make yourself at home. I think Mum and Dad are out all day, so the house will be quiet. I'll be back after lunch.'

'Hey, Tabbie.' A familiar male voice caught my attention as I climbed out of the car. 'I'll carry you.'

Danny rushed towards me and a million butterflies flew around my stomach. My jaw wouldn't move to form words. Even my smile fell short of where it should have been. When he touched me, my whole plan to forgo chasing boys fell apart. He whisked me off my feet in one swoop. *Effortless.* Shelly led the way to the beach, carrying my crutches. I knew, from that moment on, I wanted Danny's firm muscles to hold me every day. I wanted his shy smile to shine in my direction.

But it was over too quickly. He gently lowered me down, shook out my towel in line with the other girls and stood back, looking pleased with himself. He went to pick up his surfboard but paused and faced me again.

'Did you want to go for a swim? The water would probably be good for your ankle.'

I smiled. Chivalry was still alive and well and had somehow stolen my voice.

'I'll carry you.' He held his hand out to help me.

'No thanks. Bit cold.' I managed to blurt out. What if I got knocked over in the waves and stuffed my ankle beyond repair? 'I'm happy to just lie here today. But thanks.'

I couldn't take my eyes off him until he reached the water and began to paddle out. Blinking, I turned to catch up on the girls' conversation, which was almost impossible. All that ran through my mind, over and over was, 'I'll carry you.' I could still feel his skin buffing against mine. My cheeks grew warm as I imagined him lifting me up again.

I clenched a fist and reminded myself that I wanted to wait for God to deliver the perfect match for me. I was going to remain single, like Shelly and Priscilla, not waste my time with senseless dating.

I lay back and let the sun blind me until I had to close my eyes. No, I wouldn't let it happen. I could turn off my attraction to him. But, as if to confuse me, when I opened my eyes, Danny was walking towards me. He speared his board into the beach, dripping salty water and kicking up the sand on my towel. Then he spread out his towel beside mine.

My heart raced. He joined in with our conversation about world news—heartbreaking issues of poverty and human trafficking. I saw past his biceps, past his messy hair, past his surfer-cut body and into his heart. My whole body tingled as my neck prickled with heat.

'It's time we stopped talking about all the problems and did something.' Priscilla punched the sand.

'Are you volunteering to head off to the mission field?' Shelly raised an eyebrow.

'Not yet. I'd like to finish uni first.'

'They need money. Missionaries, that is.' Danny brushed sand off his shins. 'The organisations—they all need money to be effective.'

'How about a car wash?' Priscilla suggested.

'When?' I asked, wiggling my ankle, which sent a pain up my shin. I wouldn't be much help at a car wash right now.

'How about next Saturday?' Danny said. 'Instead of hanging out down here, we could hold a car wash and send the money to the ministry in Uganda my parents are off to next year.' He looked down to my ankle. 'Perhaps we could get you a chair to sit on?'

'My ankle might be okay by then.' Wishful thinking was better than being left on the side-lines. It would be a chance to be significant. I looked forward to the car wash with a thrill of hope for the people we could help.

When I arrived home, Steph blinked and yawned like she had just woken up.

'Hey, hi. Looks like you had a good sleep.'

'Yeah.' She stretched. 'I needed it.'

'It'll be getting dark soon. Do you want to stay for dinner?'

'I'd love to.' She smiled but her face was anything but relaxed. 'I'll just text Jason.'

At dinner Mum asked Stephanie about her parents. Stephanie stabbed a piece of food, telling them she'd just spoken to them today.

I didn't buy it. She'd slept the whole time I'd been away, and I doubted whether she'd been in touch with her parents before she'd arrived.

'Steph?' Dad asked.

'I've told them I still live here. And that I stay at Jason's sometimes. What's the difference? I've still got things here.'

'As Francine said, you're always welcome here. Honesty is the best policy and I suggest you tell the truth next time you speak with your parents.' Dad cleared his throat, then took a sip of water. 'Peter is thinking of moving home, so we'll have to move your things into Tabbie's room.'

'That way, if you ever want to come and stay a night, you can bunk in with Tabbie,' Francine said.

'Any time,' I said.

Stephanie opened her eyes wide, gazing from Mum to Dad to me.

'See, we'd all love you to stay a couple of nights,' I added.

'Would you like us to call your parents and tell them about Peter moving back?'

'No!' Steph's eyes were fiery, her hands shaking.

What caused her to look so tense and nervy?

'Thanks, but I'd better get back now.'

When Mum pulled up in front of the three-storey building, Jason's unit looked dark.

Mum wound down the window and called out to Stephanie. 'Do you want me to come up and make sure you get in safely?'

'No, I can see a light on. I'll be fine. Thanks for dinner.' She ran towards the stairs.

I couldn't see anything but darkness in the direction of their unit as Mum indicated to pull out.

'Mum, it's so dark. Should we wait?'

Mum stopped the car.

I turned back. There was a small glow. Maybe I'd missed it before. 'Oh, maybe I'm being crazy. I think there's a light on up there.'

If she needed divine intervention, I hoped it was there, waiting for her.

Chapter Thirty-Seven

THE NEXT FRIDAY NIGHT I introduced Anna to everyone at youth group. Something about her beauty had me playing with my hands. I stood back and chewed on a fingernail as boys from everywhere seemed to swoop in, wanting to meet Miss World Candidate. Anna, obviously used to male attention, didn't flinch with all the interest and invitations to several events over the next few weeks.

Pulling as much air into my lungs as I could possibly fit, I remembered my conversation with Priscilla and Shelly. I reminded myself—*again*—I was going to wait until the right boy came along. In the corner of my eye, my attention was drawn to Danny manning a table where people could sign up for the carwash. I looked away. Volunteering was yet another thing to add to his awesomeness.

'Would you like to help us with the car wash tomorrow?' I asked Anna as we left the crowd to find Mum parked out the front.

'Yeah, sure would. I've had a great night. These people here talk to me like I'm a person, not just a beauty queen.'

'They're different to everyone at school, hey?' Her comment had cut me. *Had I been treating her like a beauty queen too?* I had to work on not judging people.

With an almost-healed ankle, I wasn't completely useless at the car wash.

'Hi, I'm Anna.'

'Yes, I saw you last night.'

That voice.

His voice.

Heat darted up my neck as I pulled my head away from the sudsy bucket.

'I'm Danny.'

Hi, and I'm here too, the one who doesn't want those biceps wrapped around me. Really. I'm fine. Ankle's holding up. Guess I'll just be quiet and let you two get to know each other.

I could see Cupid drawing a heart around them as they conversed. My heart hurt. Begging it to stop, I scrubbed the wheels of the car in front of me until the rubber nearly fell off. I tried to make as much noise as possible, splashing, scratching, scrubbing, to drown out their way-too-smooth chatter.

Back when I met Danny for the first time, at Jaya's party, he couldn't look me in the eye or even string two words together. Now his eyes were not only focused but seemed to feast on the beautiful Anna as he spoke with no hesitation.

As I moved on to the next car, I wanted to tell them to get to work and help. But their conversation continued. I reminded myself my perfect match was waiting for me at the perfect time. The more I reminded myself, the less I wondered what expression Danny's face held. Their voices petered into the hum of the crowd.

'You're trying not to have a thing for Danny, aren't you?' Shelly whispered.

I jumped. *Where did she come from?*

'I know the way you and Priscilla are, and I'm trying to be more like that too. Really.'

'I'm still attracted to guys. I just don't chase them. If someone I was attracted to asked me out, I'd go. I haven't completely shut off.'

I nodded and stood, favouring my good leg. My bucket of water was filthy.

'Let's empty that and get a refill.' Shelly grabbed the bucket.

I limped along beside her without the added hindrance of carrying something.

'But he's not interested in me. Look at them.' I tried not to stare but found it hard to look away from the happy couple.

'You're still so young. And you never know what or who's around the corner.'

I looked away from Danny and watched the water fill the bucket, spiralling, making me dizzy until I glanced up again. Did she mean I might have a chance with Danny, or did she mean I should wait until I'm older, wait for someone else? I shook my head and changed the subject to starving African babies, the reason we were washing cars.

Mid-semester exams were a breeze. I was coping well which I put down to not having a boyfriend, not having parents who were getting a divorce and not frying my brain with drugs or alcohol. My life seemed fairly tame when I stood back and looked at what my school friends were trying to cope with.

'He's so different to other guys,' Anna gushed.

'In what way?'

'He talked to me like I was a person and not an object.'

Hmm, Danny. I smiled. I'd never thought of it that way, but it was true. He did speak to girls like they were normal people, not people he undressed with his eyes. Strange how he only grunted at me the first time I met him.

'Does he go to your church on Sunday as well as youth group?' Anna asked.

'You mean Danny?' *Of course she meant Danny.* He was all she talked to me about.

'Yeah.'

'What did you two chat about at the car wash?' My bag weighed heavy on my shoulder as we left the school grounds. 'I thought he would have mentioned church to you.'

'No, he didn't. I told him all about camp and how you fell over and I was an angel sent to help look after you.'

'Yeah, he goes Sundays.' *How sweet—they were talking about me.* 'He plays bass.'

'Really?' Anna's eyes widened. 'He's a muso?'

Didn't she notice him playing at youth group?

'He hasn't asked me for my number or anything yet, though.'

'You've got it bad, Anna.' I laughed.

'I know. But he is so hot!'

I smiled. She was right. He was hot. I couldn't argue with that.

'Do you know if he's dating anyone?'

'Not that I know of.'

She stopped walking and grabbed my arm. 'Do you mind putting in a good word for me?'

With Anna unable to stop talking about Danny, it was virtually impossible to put him out of my mind.

'Anna, truth is, I don't know him that well. He just hangs out with the same group I hang out with. That's all.'

'Oh, the way he helped you onto the beach and the way he was talking about you made me think you two were good friends.'

How did she know about the beach?

'Look, why don't you come again tonight?'

The added bonus of my new friend, Miss World Candidate, made youth group that night somewhat interesting. Anna made a beeline towards the stage where Danny was setting up to play in the band. I couldn't hear a word the duo exchanged, but her body language? *Flirt city.*

'Are you okay?' Shelly came to my side.

'Yeah, I just don't have what she's got. I wrote her off at school until I got to know her on our school camp. She really is a nice person and she …' I stopped myself before admitting I was bothered by the attention boys paid her. 'She's just so pretty.'

'And you are beautiful.' Shelly put her arm around my shoulders and squeezed me. 'As beautiful as Anna.'

I fought against the tears swelling in my eyes and sucked in several deep breaths until Anna swung her hips and strutted back to us.

'Ready to head off to the beach again tomorrow, girls?' Priscilla said as she walked past.

'Sure are,' replied Shelly.

'Can I come too? I'd love to join you!' Enthusiasm seemed to suit Anna.

Part of me wished I still needed crutches so someone—*ahem, Danny*—would have to carry me. But no, I'd handed the crutches back. I could walk.

Chapter Thirty-Eight

THE UNEVENNESS OF THE SAND made walking awkward and uncomfortable. I'd strapped my ankle and thought I could handle it but cringed with every step.

'Here.' Anna noticed I was finding it difficult. 'Let me help you.'

'Thanks.' It was kind of her, but nothing like the thrill of Danny's biceps picking me up.

We staggered to the group on the beach already in full swing, playing beach volleyball.

'Is Danny here?' Anna asked.

'Haven't seen him yet. He's probably surfing,' Shelly said.

'Great. I might check out the surf then.' Anna dropped her towel in a heap.

Obvious, much?! That's what I wanted to ask but I was impressively self-controlled. The essence of spring warmed my skin. 'How about a swim?'

'Oh, um.' Anna turned back but looked towards the surf again.

'Come on, Anna. You'll see him if he comes out.' I should know—his biceps stood out like beacons. 'I need you to help me get down to the wet sand anyway.'

Thankfully she agreed. In the water she was seriously bad company, bobbing up and down to keep an eye on where the surfer boys were.

Anna managed to keep her hair dry until she got dunked by an unexpected king wave. I could have helped her, but I was too busy laughing. By the time she caught her bearings and collected her matted hair, Danny had caught a wave to the shallow water. In a nasty-Tabbie moment, I chose not to tell her.

She continued bobbing, up and down, trying to find him. When I saw him join in with a game of beach volleyball, my conscience got the better of me. 'Hey, Anna. Danny's over there, playing volleyball.' I tilted my head. There was no way I was about to lift my arm to point at him.

'Wow! He got over there quickly. Let's go and cheer them on.' She all but dragged me out of the water and over the sand until we were standing on the side line.

She was going above and beyond, cheering for her man, who seemed completely embarrassed by all the screaming. Someone needed to give the girl pompoms!

After the game, Danny and his mates wrestled their way to the water.

'Do you think he noticed me?' Anna flicked her hair.

'Um, Anna, I think he was trying not to notice you.'

'Was I over the top?'

'Just a wee bit.' I held my pointer finger and thumb one centimetre apart and then spread them apart as far as I could.

'It must be the cheerleading I did when I was younger. Sometimes I just don't know when to stop.'

She wasn't a bimbo, but sometimes she acted in a way that would be worthy of bimbo status.

'I think he's just shy.' Anna shook out her towel and lay on it. 'I'm going to ask him out.'

Okay, go for it. I wasn't chasing him. She could.

'Hey, Anna.' Priscilla leaned towards us. 'There's no need to rush things.'

'But I really like the guy.' Anna sat up.

Priscilla smiled at Anna and then at me. Obviously, Anna was used to getting her way. I'd probably be the same if I was a Miss World Candidate. But I wasn't. And I had a new plan. The waiting game.

Danny returned to the surf with his board and was still catching waves by the time we left, so Anna didn't get a chance to speak with him. But the next day at church, she hunted him down and asked him out. Much to her surprise, he said no. She didn't understand. I didn't understand. It wasn't even a 'no, I'm busy'. It was simply 'no thanks.' I saw his face flush through shades of pink to red. He rushed away before she could question him.

'Maybe he's never dated before,' Anna said after he'd run off. 'I've got it. A group date.'

'What?' That's what I'd done for Suzie. Did we really need to go there again for Anna?

'Why don't we all go out? He seems fine talking to me when everyone is around, but awkward when we're alone.'

I had to give her props for not giving up. I headed home as the others went out for lunch.

'You're home early,' Mum called through the kitchen doorway.

'Yeah.' I needed to clear my head. 'Thought I'd better get some homework done.'

'Have you spoken to Steph lately?'

'No, not since she was here. Did she call?'

'Her mother rang.' Mum put the jug on, busying herself in the kitchen.

'And—?'

'I think their family have some major issues to work through. Diane seems angry.'

'What did you tell her?'

'Everything I knew. Seems it's not in line with what Stephanie's been telling them. I wish there was something we could do. I think it's time we went over to Jason's and insist on Stephanie staying here.'

'Mum, Steph's pretty headstrong. She assures me everything's fine. I know she wants her independence.' But I was worried about Steph. I had a feeling she wasn't as happy as she wanted me to believe. 'I'd hate for her to run away or do something stupid. I'll call her again.'

'Let me know how it goes.'

'I will. Thanks, Mum.'

Had we failed Steph? Mum and Dad weren't her guardians. Steph's parents were clear they'd only ever wanted a boarding agreement. But what if she needed us and we hadn't responded to her cries?

When I rang, the line went straight through to her voicemail. 'Stephanie. It's me, Tabbie. Remember, your best friend. Give me a call. Hey, your mum's been calling my mum. Just thought you should know they've been talking.'

Jaya clung to her backpack straps as she dawdled into school.

'Welcome back.' I fell in step with her. 'I see they've let you back on school grounds.'

'They were begging me to come back.' Jaya flicked her ponytail.

'Have you spoken to Suzie?'

'Nope. Hopefully her parents don't cut her off from the world forever.'

I nodded. Isolating her would encourage her to sneak out more.

'How's school been?' Jaya asked.

'Yeah, good,' I said, distracted by Anna's wave as she walked towards me.

'Hi.' Anna's voice was smooth and sultry. 'Hey, Jaya, that was a pretty lame stunt you and Suzie pulled at camp.'

Jaya glared from Anna to me.

'Well, I agree with Anna. No sympathy from me.'

'Whatever.' Jaya's hand rested on her hip. 'I'm off to class. Can't push my luck this week. Apparently, I'm still in the bad books.'

Jaya strutted off and Anna turned to face me. 'When can we organise that group date with Danny?'

'Man, you have it bad. Can't you wait until Friday night?'

'Why can't we all go to the movies through the week?'

'It's school holidays next week. Let's wait 'til then. I'll give Shelly and Priscilla a call and see when they're free.' Hanging out with Danny and Anna curdled my stomach.

Suzie also returned to school that morning, just as the first bell rang. She walked briskly past us, with her eyes focused on the path in front of her. I called out hello but she shook her head and didn't look up.

She spent the lunch break in the library and refused to talk to anyone. She looked terrible. How could I help her? She was summoned to the office before the final bell, and I didn't see her again. I tried to call her after school, but her mother told me she wasn't allowed to take calls. I hated that her parents cut her off like that.

The next day, Jaya gave Anna the cold shoulder and turned the other way when she joined us.

'Hi, girls,' Anna said.

'Hey, Anna.' I waved as she continued on to her usual crew.

'I can't believe you're hanging out with her.' Jaya barely waited until Anna was out of earshot. 'I'm away for two weeks and you find someone else to hang out with.'

'Classy, Jaya. You pull a dumb stunt then don't approve of me making new friends.' Sounds around me echoed. I clutched my fist, squeezing it against my thigh. 'You aren't in control of my life.'

'Yes, I was away, but I'm back now.'

Of course she was. I took a deep breath, willing my shoulders to relax. It was pointless saying anything else. Though she irritated the pants off me, most of the time she was a good friend. I took three deep breaths. 'You want to come to the movies with us during the holidays?'

'With us? As in ...?'

'My friends, Shelly and Priscilla, and a couple of others from church.' I missed out Anna. I should have told her Anna was going too.

'Maybe. There's a couple of new movies coming out that look good. But you didn't answer me before. What's it with Anna? Why is she deviating from the beautiful people to talk to you?'

'We are the beautiful people.' I smiled. 'I am. You are.'

Jaya rolled her eyes. Maybe the alcohol was affecting some of her brain cells already.

Suzie was just a couple of metres away, walking towards us with her head down. I couldn't let her walk past without saying hello. I hated how smothered she appeared.

'Hey, Suzie!'

'I can't talk.' She didn't lift her eyes from the path. 'They'll kill me if they see me stop. They've even got the teachers checking up on me. It sucks. I'll try slip out tonight. I'll send you a message.'

She slipped away as quickly as she'd appeared. No one would have guessed she'd even spoken to us unless they were in earshot.

'It worries me the way she sneaks out at night.'

'She's a big girl.' Jaya shrugged. 'She'll be fine.'

'You think so? She meets Joey at the servo. If she goes there regularly, anyone could stalk her.' I couldn't understand why Joey would be okay with her walking around by herself at that time of night.

'Anyway, not much we can do about it. Yes, I'll come to the movies. It's not like Mum and Dad care what I do. Got any cute boys from church who'll be there?'

I raised my eyebrows and shook my head without answering. Didn't she remember Danny from her party? Could he soon have both Anna and Jaya chasing him? That would be horrible.

Chapter Thirty-Nine

JAYA AND ANNA BOTH RANG several times with wardrobe discussions. The quietness of holidays seemed to be overtaken by a frenzy of dressing right. *Seriously?* We were heading to the movies, not a red carpet event.

My palms tingled with sweat as I grabbed my purse and left the house. I still hadn't told Jaya that Anna would be joining us. I hoped she wouldn't lose it at the cinema. Too late to do anything about it now.

The drone of the bus lulled me into dreamland. Knowing Danny had rejected Anna only a few weeks ago gave me a sand-grain-sized hope. Not that I was about to chase him or anything.

While I waited for Jaya outside the cinema, I sent Steph a quick text asking her to join us. More than a month had passed since I'd seen her.

My phone buzzed. 'No. Busy.'

'Everything okay?' Jaya asked as she arrived.

I nodded, and put my phone away. My mind still on the text. *How odd.* Steph would usually sign her name, greet me somehow, or add something friendly, but not this time.

'Let's go meet the others.' I led the way still distracted by Steph's text message.

'Please don't tell me she is with us.' Jaya pointed to Anna at the candy bar.

'Okay, I won't. But please don't make a scene. She's actually nice. Give her a chance. Get to know her.'

Jaya tossed her hair over her shoulder and faced the screens playing trailers as the others in our group joined us. After agreeing to see a comedy, we wandered into the cinema. Jaya walked into a row, then me, then Anna, then Shelly, followed by Priscilla. The others filed into the row behind us, leaving a seat empty beside Priscilla.

Anna stood up, 'Priscilla, can you move over one? Shelly, could you just move next to Priscilla?' She curled her hair between her fingers and plastered a sweet smile on her face before moving into the seat beside Shelly, leaving the seat beside her vacant.

Danny was walking up the other aisle.

'Danny,' she called. 'Danny, over here. There's a spare seat.'

I bit my lip to cover a snicker and stared at the spare seat. Danny shuffled past Jaya and bumped past my knees before landing in the seat between Anna and I. Anna engaged him in conversation and Shelly gave me a knowing look. I sighed. An ache pierced my chest.

'Where have I seen him before?' Jaya slurped on her drink.

'Your party. That infamous one when your parents were away. He's from church, so, you also may have seen him playing bass when you came to youth group.'

'Oh.' She leaned around me to take another peek. 'Are they together?'

I glanced over and my jaw dropped. Anna's hand rested on Danny's knee. 'I didn't think so, but it's looking that way right now,' I whispered to Jaya.

Come on, brain. The right guy will come at the right time. Stop willing it to happen now. Danny offered for me to share his popcorn. After the movie had started, I reached into the box the same time he did. Tingles raced up my arm. I blinked away the spark as Anna whispered to Danny and he whispered back to her. Another pain shot through my heart.

'It's pretty obvious something's going on,' Jaya said quietly. 'Is that why she befriended you all of a sudden?'

I shrugged and shook off Jaya's comment. I was sure Anna and I had a connection that went deeper than Danny. I just happened to be the one to invite her to church where she met him. But only time would tell.

School expected us to put on blinkers for term four. Study had to get most of my focus—that was, if I wanted to pass. I still hadn't spoken to Steph. She replied a couple of times with text messages that lacked friendliness. My intention was to visit her before the end of the school year. But for the next few weeks, I had to keep my head in the books.

When Suzie didn't show up in our maths class, I had a squirming, nauseous pull in my stomach. I waited at her locker at lunch, and she didn't turn up there either. I had a feeling she wasn't okay.

I rang her parents, bracing myself for their abrupt natures. 'Hi, Mrs Peters. Could I speak with Suzie, please?'

'No,' she said with a sniffle.

Mr Peters came on the line. 'No, you can't speak to her. She's ... she's dead.'

All the air inside of me shrunk, my stomach pulled, my head squeezed. Had I heard him wrong? 'I'm sorry, Mr Peters.' I needed to know. 'How—'

'Not as sorry as I am.' *Clunk.* He'd hung up.

The next few days were surreal. I didn't know how she'd died, and I was scared my fears had come to life. If I'd just spoken up earlier. If I'd told her parents she was sneaking around at night. I could never understand why they were so strict on her. They smothered her, trying to keep her out of trouble.

'Mum, I need to know how she died, but Mr and Mrs Peters won't talk to me, and the teachers are saying they don't have any details. Can you find out for me?'

'I'll try, love. I don't understand why they haven't told anyone either.'

Mum rang the Peters straight after I asked her to. I sat in the lounge room hugging my knees listening to Mum's uh-huh's and oh-no's. The clock ticked through the minutes before she hung up.

'It was an overdose. She found her mother's sleeping tablets and antidepressants and took the lot. They went to wake her in the morning. When she didn't wake up, they rang the ambulance. They did all they could ... but it was too late.'

I found myself thanking God that she didn't die while she was sneaking around. But it didn't matter now. She was gone, and I didn't even know if she would end up in heaven.

'Would you like me to take you to the funeral? It's on Friday.'

'I don't know, Mum.' I sobbed. 'It's just too hard.'

'I know it's hard. Think about it. It'll be a chance to celebrate her life.' Mum held me in a tight embrace.

'But her life was too short.' My words choked up my throat until it shut off any more words.

I was sure Steph would make the effort to attend Suzie's funeral, but she hadn't replied to anything since acknowledging Suzie's death. I rang her. As always, it went straight through to her voicemail.

'Hi, Steph. I'm sure you got my messages. Can you make it to the funeral? It's on Friday. Call me soon. I really miss you.'

'No. Working,' she replied via text. 'Miss you too. Don't come round.'

I wondered why she added the last sentence. A chill ran down my spine. I'd told her I was focused on study, so she knew I was flat out and wouldn't be dropping by unannounced. Something in that last sentence made me want to pop in.

Chapter Forty

MUM DROVE JAYA AND ME to the funeral. Because Suzie had been so withdrawn for the last year, not many other students came. The teachers were accommodating, allowing us to take our scheduled test on Monday. They also gave me an extension for my geography assignment.

The seats were set up in a circle around the pulpit. It was agony seeing everyone cry. I couldn't watch any longer and stared at my feet until footsteps grabbed my attention. *Joey.* He stood at the back with blotchy cheeks.

It was horrible. Nobody could see any reason for her to end her life. Everyone spoke from a position of condemnation. I raced out when I saw Joey leaving before the funeral finished. 'Joey!'

'I should have known something was up when she dumped me.'

'When did that happen?'

'Sunday.'

The day before she died. 'Joey, I'm so sorry.'

'I can't believe she's gone.'

I shook my head, trying to blink away the tears.

'Tabbie, you were her best friend. She loved you so much. You were always there for her. Thank you for organising that movie night. The months I've had with Suzie have been the ...' His voice ran out of air. He pushed his fist to his mouth.

I wrapped my arms around him. We embraced, both shaking with tears, until the congregation began to leave the church. Old men rolled the coffin past us and loaded it into the hearse.

'She told me she wanted to be cremated. It should have clicked when she was talking about funerals. But they're taking her to the graveyard to bury her.' Joey swiped the tears off his face. He let go of me and started backing away, with fists clenched. 'They did this to her. Her pathetic, strict, suffocating parents. It's their fault. She was only sneaking out at night to get away from them.'

'She told me. I was worried about her doing that.'

'Me too. She'd ring me from the servo. I'd rush down every time. I hated her being out that late by herself. At least we got to spend ...'

Voices rose as the crowd formed. Joey kicked a rock and took off when Mr and Mrs Peters came into view.

'Joey!' I called after him. 'Call Danny.' *You need a friend right now.*

'How's Joey coping?' Jaya came to my side.

'Not well. He has to go through this alone. I hope he calls Danny or someone. It's like their relationship was invisible. Hardly anyone knew he even had a girlfriend. No one knows what he's going through right now.'

'Did you hear all that crap they said about not knowing where the suicide came from, that she was a happy, well-adjusted child with every opportunity at her feet?' Jaya looked back to the crowd. 'Are we the only ones who know how they treated her?'

'Maybe. But it's pointless saying anything now. It's not going to bring her back. Let's get out of here.' At least now it made sense about her meeting Joey at the servo. I wished she'd talked to me more.

I watched Mum speak with Suzie's parents before she walked over to Jaya and me.

'Can we go?' I asked as I headed towards the car.

'It's been a hard day. Would you like to go straight home or back to school?'

'Home, please.' I looked towards Jaya, and she nodded.

Mum tried to bring some light chatter to the drive home, but Jaya and I sat in silence. We spent the afternoon painting our nails and reminiscing on good times. 'It's just so final.' Jaya broke the heavy silence while our nails dried.

'It doesn't have to be.' I wanted to talk to Jaya about eternity. I hoped the lump in my throat would allow me to continue.

'What do you mean? She's gone.'

'Years ago,' I swallowed. 'God sent His only son, Jesus, so that we could have eternal life.'

'Don't go on with that religious crap now.'

I bit my lip. She was angry. It wasn't the right time to bring up eternity.

The weeks that followed Suzie's funeral had me in a turmoil of study, though I wanted to do anything else. I wanted to knock down her parents' door and scream at them. I wanted to tell them how unhappy she was. Most of all, I wanted to blame them for her death.

I wanted to scream at Suzie. No one forced her to take the tablets. She checked out too early. She had options. She could have run away from home. Moved out. Even if she'd come and lived with us for a while, it would have been better than losing her forever.

It was strange to have a friend one day, then have her gone the next. I didn't get the whole grief thing. The rollercoaster of emotions followed me into exams. I expected Suzie to walk through the classroom door, but she wasn't going to. I knew she was dead, but I couldn't get past the fact she wouldn't be in my life anymore. How could you just drop someone out of your life like that? How did she go through with it? How could she leave us all?

Surely her parents wouldn't have been able to smother her forever. All she had to do was wait a couple more years and she would have been free. Her parents should have been charged for what they did. I could go to the police. But it wouldn't bring her back. She was dead. It was useless.

My days and nights rolled together, lacking lustre, tormented with sadness. I prayed more, hoping to clear my mind. I prayed for Joey. I prayed that Suzie's parents would be comforted. I prayed for God to comfort me. I needed to forgive Suzie's parents.

My grief left me missing Stephanie as well. Her mobile went straight through to voicemail. I tried Jason's landline. It was disconnected. I rang her mobile again and left a message. 'Hi, Steph. I really wish you could have made it to Suzie's farewell. Wish you'd call. I'm about to get into end-of-year exams. Can't wait to hang out with you during the holidays.'

Three days later Stephanie replied via text, 'Ok. Talk then. Not home much, so don't drop in. Pls don't ring.'

It wasn't long now. Now that I'd begun exams, God had answered my prayers. Even after receiving Steph's abrupt text message, a supernatural peacefulness got me through. The whole time, I yearned to see Steph again.

Shelly rang. 'Danny's leaving.'

'Why? Where's he going?' My heart smashed into splinters in my chest.

'His parents are moving to Uganda to be missionaries. He's going with them.'

'Oh.' I sighed. 'What about school?'

'I think he's planning to do senior over two years. Distance Ed. We're giving him a farewell this weekend.'

'Does Anna know?'

'I'm not sure. He only just decided to go.' Shelly paused for a moment before continuing, 'You know he's not into her.'

'I gave up telling myself that a while ago. I think it's just wishful thinking.'

'Let's just say I have inside information, and he's not interested in Anna. Will you come?'

'For sure.' Of course I wanted to go. I had suppressed any feelings I had for the guy with the amazing biceps and incredible good looks, even if I needed an internal brick to keep them suppressed. 'I need to prove to myself that I'm over my silly crush.'

'We'll see.' Shelly laughed.

'I haven't hung out with you guys since …' I couldn't speak the words. *Suzie died.*

'I know.' Shelly had phoned when she found out about my friend's death. 'We miss you, but know you've been busy. Could you let Anna know about the farewell? I'm sure she'd like to say goodbye as well. I'd hate her to find out after the party.'

Chapter Forty-One

I SHOWED ANNA THE WAY to the hall at the back of the church. We walked in to find the full party set-up of streamers and fairy lights. Live band music vibrated off the walls making it seem more like a concert than a farewell. Anna stood beside me, looking in every direction, trying to find Danny.

'Anna, just enjoy the band. Danny will be here somewhere. He's probably up the front. After all, they are playing in his honour.'

'Why can't we push through the crowd?'

'Because that would be rude.'

'You're such a goody-two-shoes.' She rolled her eyes at me but didn't push forward.

Being called a goody-two-shoes remined me of Steph. I wondered again how she was. I must call her tomorrow. The band finished, and the crowd spread out and moved into party mode.

'Do you all party without any alcohol?' Anna asked.

'Anna, we're mostly under age.'

'Danny would be eighteen by now if he's finishing school.'

'He's not finishing yet. He's still only seventeen. Anyway, we're on church grounds.'

'Lame. But I guess this is my last chance to change Danny's mind about me. Nobody has ever rejected me like he has. I'm on a mission.'

Her gung-ho attitude amused me. Even if I said something about her chasing after him, I'm sure she would have had an appropriately inappropriate answer.

'Hey,' a familiar voice came from behind and arms enveloped me. I turned, my heart thumping from being both startled and held.

'Joey.' I twisted so I could see him better.

He smiled. He looked okay. I was glad to see him.

Joey's arms lingered around me for a moment too long. I pulled away. But he left his arm around my shoulder. I figured he was just grabbing a little comfort where he could. But when he spoke the waft of alcohol told me otherwise.

'I called Danny, like you said. He's been great.'

'Have you been drinking?'

'Just a couple.' He shrugged. 'Danny, as I was saying, is the best friend I could have ever asked for.'

I wanted to continue the conversation, but Anna pulled on my arm.

'There's Danny. Are you coming with me?'

'Sure.' I ducked out from under Joey's arm. 'See you later.'

Joey smiled, unfazed, and moved on to another group.

This was the last chance for me to refresh the image of Danny that had been burnt into my memory alongside the image of the original Mr Biceps. I had to admit that it was the image of someone I hoped I would end up dating one day. Right now, even though my eyes lingered, I controlled my feelings to nothing more than friendship. Truth was, he wasn't the dork I first thought he was. He was an amazing, compassionate guy, about to give up life in Australia to serve at an orphanage in Uganda. If I was honest, I would admit that made him even more attractive.

'Tabbie.' Danny broke away from the group he was talking to. 'Thanks for coming.'

'Hi, Danny.' Anna jumped in front of me.

'Hi, Anna. You two came together?' His gaze darted like he wanted to say a million other things.

'We did,' I said, peering around from behind Miss World Candidate herself.

'Before I forget, I'm getting everybody's addresses. I hope to write, but please don't expect anything soon. There's a book over by the door for you to write in your email and home address.'

Anna linked her arm through Danny's and led him off to do the rounds. Stranded, I stood alone. Joey had disappeared as well. I merged into a group talking about the orphanage Danny and his parents were heading to. While I attempted to focus on the conversation in the circle, I kept tipping my gaze towards Anna and Danny. Anna was waving her hands and laughing over the top of the music. I heard her say, 'Yes, Danny is my hero.' And, 'I can't wait for him to return home.' And then the absolute bomb, 'Perhaps I'll pop on over to Africa myself.' My heart sunk a little. She didn't even care enough to know the specifics—he was going to Uganda, not just Africa.

As the party wound down, Anna came back to me for her lift home. Mum was already waiting outside.

'The book!' Anna stopped to add her details as we were leaving.

'I guess I should add mine as well.'

'Never mind.' Anna closed the book when she'd finished. 'I'm sure if he wants to send you a hello, he can do it through me.'

I smiled, opened the book, and wrote my details directly below hers.

'Come on,' Anna called.

'Okay.' I closed the book, only leaving my physical address and not my email.

Anna and Danny had looked so cosy together all night. I wasn't sure what Shelly had been talking about with her so-called inside information. Anna was sure that if Danny was staying in Sydney, they'd have been an item before Christmas. I tended to believe her.

That night clear vivid dreams invaded my sleep. I saw Steph in trouble. I saw her being pushed around. She was hurt. I woke up, dripping with sweat and my heart racing. I was sure I needed to go and see her. Tomorrow. I lay back on my pillow watching the glow of my digital clock. Seconds flicked over into minutes until I fell asleep again. I dreamed about African babies. I saw myself holding a tiny, dark-skinned baby. I woke up with sticky eyes. In the morning I ate breakfast with Mum and asked her if she believed dreams held any weight in life.

'Sometimes I think dreams are just your subconscious working through things. Sometimes they could have a deeper meaning.'

'Do you think God can speak to us through our dreams?'

'Maybe.'

Chapter Forty-Two

I THREW THE LAST OF MY TOAST into the bin and swapped my pyjamas for a T-shirt, shorts, and runners. In the solitude I found nothing but peace as I spent time with God. I asked him if there was any truth in my dreams. If there were signs about real life. I ran and ran and ran until I found myself outside Jason's apartment building. I caught my breath as I mounted the stairs. Jason greeted me at the door.

'She's not here,' he told me.

He looked completely out of it, but not in the same way Jaya looked when she was drinking. Downcast bloodshot eyes warned me he was using something harder than alcohol.

'Can you tell her I dropped by?'

'Sure.' He closed the door in my face.

I took the stairs two at a time and continued running. I prayed for Steph's safety, I prayed she would get out of her relationship with Jason. I didn't trust him. I wished she would call me.

I returned home to have Mum stop me on the way to the shower. 'Hey love, I didn't realise you'd be gone for so long. Danny rang about an hour ago and asked if he could drop by. I figured it would

     Spiralling Out of the Shadow

be alright with you, considering you went to his party last night. Is that okay?'

'That's fine.' My heart tumbled a little. I reminded myself, I was over that crush. I thought last night was the last time I would see him. He was probably just going to ask something about Anna. Taking a couple of deep breaths to calm myself, I ran the shower to cool my burning face and wash my sweaty armpits.

'Tabbie.' Mum's voice was muffled over the streaming water. 'Danny's here.'

Argh. Why did I start washing my hair? He wouldn't hang round 'til I dried it. 'Be out in a minute.'

I turned the water off, jumped out and saw some fluffy bubbles still in my hair. I tried to wipe them away with my towel but I still looked sudsy. I jumped back in the shower to wash away the shampoo, and arrived downstairs two minutes later, still looking a little drippy.

'Sorry.' Danny smiled, looking towards my mother. 'I didn't mean to get you out of the shower.'

'It's okay, I just needed ...' I stopped myself from blabbering. 'What can I do for you?'

'It's just that, um ... you didn't write your email address in my book, and ... well, if you didn't want to, that's fine but I'd like to write to you and email is quicker than snail mail but I understand if you don't want to give me your email address. I have your home address anyway, but just tell me if you don't want me to write.' He shut his mouth and looked like the king of nervousness.

'I can give you my email address.' I looked around to where Mum was standing, but she'd disappeared. I took the book he was holding and wrote in the back. 'Anna's pretty messed up that you're leaving.'

'Yeah.' He scratched his head, sending hair over his left eye. 'Have you got time for a coffee or anything?'

'I'd better get back to studying, after taking last night off. I've still got a couple of exams.'

'Of course you do. And I'd better get back to packing.' He took steps towards the door.

I followed him. Should I hug him goodbye? No. If I did, I just might stay glued there for too long. Awkward. 'Bye, then.'

'See ya.' He lingered for a moment and then ran out to what I guessed was his parents' car. He beeped the horn and waved as he left.

A tear clung to my lashes before it dripped down my cheek. There was no way I was over my Danny crush. How could I be attracted to a friend's possible boyfriend like this? I was glad to see him leave. I needed to focus on school. I needed to get good grades. Maybe the dream about a baby was confirmation I should work toward going to uni and actually being qualified to help communities in need overseas.

'Can you believe he's going and I didn't win him over?' Anna stopped me on the way into school on Monday.

'Well, yes, I can believe it. He's chasing his dream. Something I'm about to do.'

'What do you mean?'

'I'm going to focus on exams ...' I wanted to explain what I meant, but stopped.

Anna didn't seem interested anyway. 'Yeah, exams. He came to see me yesterday.'

'Yeah?' Is this where I tell her he came to see me too?

'Prick.'

Ah ... probably not. 'Why? What happened?'

'He apologised for leading me on and said he probably wouldn't get a chance to write.'

'Oh. I'm sorry.'

'Sure you are. I saw the way you were looking at him. You've got a huge crush, don't you?' She went to say something else but let out a groan and stormed off.

My friendship with Anna was short-lived after all. She didn't give me the time of day after that. I flew through my last few exams and said goodbye to year ten, knowing I needed to see Steph. I continued to pray for her, sensing she wasn't safe. I'd sent text messages every day for the last week, mostly without reply. After dumping my school bag at home, I caught the bus to see her. Traffic was a nightmare. It would have been quicker to walk.

As I approached the staircase, I stumbled at what I saw. Each step I took was suspended in time. There in front of me, lying on the concrete, buckled and bleeding, was my best friend. I urged my legs to run, needing to get to the base of the stairs.

Steph.

Lifeless.

Sticky blood clumped in her hair while a slow trickle oozed out of the wound.

I fumbled to grab my phone and punched in 000. 'I need help!'

The emergency operator took the address and said the ambulance wouldn't be too long. I hoped she was right.

'Steph? Steph! Can you hear me?' There was no response. I lifted her arm and couldn't find a pulse. I leant in close. The faintest whisper of breath swept across my cheek. 'Steph, you'll be okay.' Tears blurred my vision. 'Please, Lord, keep her alive!' I screamed, then sat holding her hand until the siren blared and paramedics took control.

'Would you like to ride with us to the hospital or get your own way there?'

'With you.' I sat in the van, watching the paramedic work to keep Steph alive. It was like time froze as we sped through the city streets to the hospital. *Please don't let another friend die.*

Chapter Forty-Three

'STEPHANIE IS STILL UNCONSCIOUS.' A nurse met me in the waiting room. 'You're welcome to come in and see her for a while.'

I nodded, following the nurse to find Stephanie attached to tubes.

'Hi, Steph.' I tried to keep my voice bright, but I doubted I'd fooled anyone. 'It's me, Tabbie. You're going to be okay.'

She didn't respond. The machines whirred and a digital line pulsed with her heartbeat. I slept in the waiting room for a couple of hours that night, then returned to her side.

Mum was with me, only leaving for a few hours to get some sleep at home. Stephanie showed no change. She was stuck in a coma. But I was thankful she was alive.

When Mum arrived the next morning and saw there was no change, she jingled her car keys, grabbing my attention. 'Tabbie, why don't you come home with me for a while? I'll bring you back after you've had a sleep in your own bed.'

'No, I want to stay here. If she doesn't wake up today, I'll sleep at home tonight. But today I want to stay.'

I walked Mum to her car, then returned to Stephanie's bedside. Her eyes fluttered a little. 'Steph, I'm back. I just had to pop out for a few minutes.'

Stephanie blinked. I pressed her buzzer to call the nurse in. 'Steph, it's me, Tabbie.'

'Tabbie?' She began to cry.

'You must have fallen down the stairs.' I grabbed her hand. 'You've been unconscious for hours. I found you yesterday afternoon.'

She looked frightened. I hated seeing my best friend in such a state. 'It's okay, everything will be okay.'

She fell asleep again. Then continued to drift in and out of consciousness.

'The next few weeks will be hard,' the nurse told me. 'It'll take a while for her body to detox from the drugs and alcohol.'

Over the next few weeks, I spent a lot of time visiting and praying for my best friend. Steph moved into a rehab centre, and I found refuge at church.

'Shelly, please pray for my friend, Steph.'

'I'll do better than just pray for her myself. Let's put in a prayer request. Our intercessors would love to pray for her.'

'Thank you.' If faith the size of a mustard seed can move mountains, I sure hoped God could move for Stephanie.

Priscilla snuck up beside me. 'Are you keen for a day at the beach?'

'I'd love that.'

'Great. We'll pick you up in the morning at nine.'

I wasn't ready when Shelly and Priscilla arrived. I was still in my pyjamas, sitting at the computer, reading the email for the hundredth time.

'Come in.' I heard Mum say. 'She's at the computer. You can go through.'

'Caught!' I laughed looking down. 'In my PJs.'

'No rush.' Shelly smiled. 'But sometime this morning would be good.'

'I'll go and get changed.'

'Hey, how's Stephanie going?' she called after me.

'She's going to be okay now. I just know she will.' I ran upstairs, got changed in a flash and returned, to find Priscilla was now also waiting in my lounge room.

'Everything else okay?' Priscilla asked.

'I got the craziest email this morning. I'll tell you all about it on the way.'

Chapter Forty-Four

WHEN I HAD WOKEN THAT MORNING, the first thing I did was check my email. Not something I usually did, so who knows what I was expecting. But when a message came through from Danny, a smile ignited my face and my eyes were glued to the screen. I hit print as I read the email over and over. I couldn't wait to show Steph tomorrow.

Dear Tabbie,

I hope you did well in your exams. I did way better than I expected in mine. I'm looking forward to stretching year twelve over two years. Now I'm here, it's more incredible than I imagined.

I have a confession. Truth is, I'm in love with you and had to run away from the country to control myself. I wanted so badly to start dating you right now, but I had a feeling it would lead us down a path neither of us are ready for.

I'm sorry I completely lost my voice that first time I met you. All I can say is … it must have been love at first sight. You were amazing, the way you looked after everyone who was drinking and out of control. Anything could have happened to Jaya, but you were there to look after her.

Then when I saw you at the pool … again, I couldn't speak. All I could do was gawk at you like a complete knob. When you fell, I wanted to dive in and save you, but you're so capable and elegant in everything you do, you didn't need me to fish you out.

The way you brought your friends with you to youth group when you started coming, you seemed to really care about them. And the way you took them home when they weren't having fun. I was praying they'd want to come back so you would find it easier to stay, but you kept coming anyway and I wanted to congratulate you for your courage. It's not easy coming into a bunch of high school kids and not knowing anyone. And then when you started coming to the beach, it was almost enough to admire you from a distance until we were both old enough to date without rushing into some crazy teenage romance.

Your beauty far surpasses anyone else I've ever seen. You don't seem to know that you are beautiful, and that makes you even more attractive.

The way you set up the movie date for Suzie and Joey was completely out of this world. I've never known anyone to do so many selfless acts for their friends. At that movie night, I nearly said something, but I was sure you still saw me as that complete knob.

And at the funeral, you took the time to think of Joey and got him to call me. I can't imagine the grief you would have been dealing with yourself.

I thought you had absolutely no interest in me when you went out with Rhett. I'm so sorry you went through with that date. After he told me what happened, I wanted to punch his lights out. I hope you shoved him really hard. I told him to never go near you again.

The day you came to the beach with your sprained ankle gave me a chance to do something for you, just like you are always going out of your way to help others. But when I picked you up, the surge that went through my body was almost too much. It was good the water was cold that day—I sure needed to cool off.

I guess I didn't get it right with Anna. She didn't seem to get the message. I tried to push her away, but the more I said no, the more she seemed to think I'd change my mind. The one thing I didn't mind about Anna hanging around was that I could see more of you.

I know I've got an ocean of courage between us, and I don't know how much longer I would have held out if I was still in the country. I also know you may very well reject me, but I'm hoping you might think about it.

All I am asking is … can we get to know each other a little more over email or maybe even online chats? And we can see where it leads.

Yours

Danny.

— *Epilogue* —

'I don't know, love.'

'Yes, Mum. I know I'd be taking a risk, but Steph is worth it. She's tried so hard the last few months to get her life back in order, but she needs someone to walk with her for a while.'

'Has she asked you to move in?'

'No.'

'What about school?'

'Mum, now you are just repeating yourself. I'm nearly eighteen—'

'Not for another year and a half,' Francine said.

'It's just over a year away now.' I was counting down the days. 'I could move out without your blessing, but I'd rather not.'

'Tom, what do you think?'

I looked from Mum to Dad. Even though the government would support me living away from home, I wanted their approval.

'I know you're always wanting to help your friends, but don't you think this is going to the extreme?' Dad asked.

'No, she needs someone. Her parents seem to be happy to let her drift, but I know she can get past this.'

     Spiralling Out of the Shadow

'It's barely been a month,' Mum said.

'Yeah, two months of grief, rehab, and addiction counselling.' I knew Steph still had a long way to go. 'She needs support.'

'We've asked her to move back here.' Dad scratched his head. 'Why move in with her?'

'She won't move here, especially not with her extra baggage. She feels really bad about how she treated everyone.'

'You really want to move out of home?'

'Yes.'

'Guess we can't really stop you.' Dad wrapped his arms around me. 'You have to remember, while you're such a caring best friend, you mustn't let your friends take over and stop you from living your life.'

'That's right love.' Mum rubbed my back. 'And if you ever need to come and stay a couple of nights to study, please tell us you'll come home.'

'I will. Thanks, Mum.' I hugged them both at the same time. 'Thanks, Dad.'

Keep in Touch...

Visit
MichelleDennisEvans.com
to connect with Michelle on social media

Thank You...

To my daughters, my son and my husband —
you bring joy and laughter into every day. I am so
thankful we are family. I am also thankful to my parents
who first recognised my gift for writing back in my early
primary years when I chose to write dialogue for my
spelling sentences. Thank you to Roald Dahl who ignited
my passion for reading.

A huge thank-you to all of my critique partners and beta readers.
Some stayed with me right through the novel and some helped
with just a few pages. You are all appreciated, and I am scared
if I start naming you, I'll miss someone.
I mustn't forget my local cheer squad and my online friends —
your support is welcomed and appreciated.

And above all I am thankful to my Creator, the giver of life,
the one who showers me with crazy favour and ridiculous grace.

Cause...

I am passionate about seeing girls and women pick up the pieces and move forward in life after major upheaval. One of my favourite local organisations that help to facilitate this is **Yahweh Houses.**

A portion of sales from *Spiralling Out of the Shadow* will go towards supporting organisations that help women and girls.

Spiralling
Out of Control

Book 1 in the Spiralling Trilogy

Print book available at online
bookstores, and
MichelleDennisEvans.com

Spiralling
Solo

Book 3 in the Spiralling Trilogy

Print book available at online
bookstores, and
MichelleDennisEvans.com

Sink, Drift, or Swim

A young adult novel in free verse

Print book available at online bookstores, and MichelleDennisEvans.com

Life Inspired

A beautiful collection of poems

eBook available at MichelleDennisEvans.com or Amazon

You were never designed to slip into depression
or have days of darkness.
Feeling down or depressed is not a weakness,
but a reality in our world.
Beyond Blue and Black Dog Institute
both have an abundance of
information and guidance
on their websites.
I urge you to seek help.
There is a way out of the darkness,
tomorrow is a new day and may just be the day
you turn a corner.

Beyond Blue **beyondblue.org.au**
Black Dog Institute **blackdoginstitute.org.au**